J. MICHAEL STRACZYNSKI

STRACZYNSKI UNPLUGGED

J. Michael Straczynski, 49, is a Hugo Award-winning television writer and producer for such series as *Babylon 5, Murder, She Wrote, The New Twilight Zone, Walker: Texas Ranger,* and *Jeremiah,* currently running on Showtime. His fiction has appeared in *Amazing Science Fiction, Pulphouse,* and an assortment of anthologies, including *Midnight Graffitti, Outside the Box* and his own *Tales from the New Twilight Zone* (Bantam). He is the author of nearly 500 published articles appearing in such publications as *The Los Angeles Times, Penthouse, Writer's Digest, San Diego Magazine, The Los Angeles Herald Examiner,* TIME Inc. and elsewhere. He is also the writer for *The Amazing Spider-Man* and *Supreme Power,* both from Marvel Comics. He is working on a new novel, *The World on Fire,* to be completed sometime next year.

ALSO BY J. MICHAEL STRACZYNSKI
published by ibooks, inc.:

Demon Night

<u>Coming September 2004</u>

Othersyde

ALSO AVAILABLE
J. Michael Straczynski's Rising Stars
novelizations by Arthur Byron Cover

Book 1: *Born in Fire*
Book 2: *Ten Years After*

STRACZYNSKI
UNPLUGGED

J. MICHAEL STRACZYNSKI

ibooks, inc.
new york

www.ibooks.net

CONTENTS

INTRODUCTION

Or:

"YOU GOT A PROBLEM WITH THAT?"

Okay, you want to know the truth? Fine. Here it is.

I've got a lot of problems.

I'm not talking about the fact that I didn't know how to properly knot a tie until this past summer when, at the age of 49, I finally figured it out by watching a clerk knot his tie while I was buying some clothes at a store in Beverly Hills. (It's not normally the kind of place I tend to buy clothes, but there was some stuff I wanted, they had it, so that's where I went, stop looking at me like that, I'm not one of them, I'm among them but not of them, as the Bible says, to the point where a woman outside the store stopped me on my way out and asked me—or at least I thought she asked me—if I was shopping here, and I said yes, then a bunch of other questions about the store followed, at which point I realized that she had asked if I was a *shopper*, as in somebody hired by rich people with no inclination to drag their own sorry asses out of bed to go and pick up clothes for them, and when I explained that no, I wasn't a *shopper*, she shrugged and said, "Oh, sorry, I just looked at you and thought you didn't belong here."

(Like I said... among them but not of them.)

It's not the problem I have with my neighbors, including the one across the street, who recently retrieved her little rat-dog from the curb where it had run away from her house to mine—clearly an escape attempt, the poor bastard—and when she picked it up and trotted back across the street with him said, when she thought I was out of earshot, "I *told* you to stay *out* of the street and *away* from the strange man."

It's not the problem I have with small children, who seem to instantly recognize me for an alien life form and go out of their way to attack me at every occasion. This includes the kid who recently spit at me out of a passing stroller in the Glendale Galleria, another who ran up and kicked me for absolutely no reason on the Third Street Promenade in Santa Monica, and the little girl who, as I was walking to the men's room in the Cheesecake Factory in Van Nuys two weeks ago leapt from her seat and tried to tackle me with a snarl, baring her teeth and shouting *I HATE YOU! I HATE YOU! I HATE YOU!* at the top of her lungs.

It's not even the fact that I can't dance, can't sing, slouch when I shouldn't, talk when I'm not supposed to, and have a penchant for telling network and studio executives where to stuff it when they mess with my words, much to the dismay of my agents, my accountant, and (one assumes) the aforementioned executives who counter that I'll Never Work In Hollywood Again After This, but who call six months later as though nothing had ever happened because they need someone who knows how to connect the right words with the correct emotions.

But on the flip side, at least I can knot a tie now like nobody's business.

No, none of those have anything to do with the problems I've come here to talk to you about today.

My problem is with you.

No, not you *specifically*, as in you the person who had the sobriety of thought, the taste and discretion to pick up this book. I'm not talking about *you* you.

I'm talking about the *other* guy. The one standing beside you in the bookstore, talking on his cell phone in a voice loud enough to be heard by whoever the hell he's talking to without having to use the phone in the first place, informing everyone with earshot—which is, well, pretty much everyone in the store, or the bank, or the concert, or the restaurant—about stuff not *one* of you wants to hear.

I'm talking about the guy who, after you've been waiting patiently at a taxi stand for twenty minutes, suddenly jumps ahead of you when a cab shows up, and when you point out that you were there first, fires back with "Yeah, you were," before jumping in and taking off for whatever dark business he has planned for the evening, which you can only hope will end with a gunshot or a myocardial infarction.

I'm not talking about murder or arson, for which we can one day receive justice or at least validation by the state that crimes have been committed against us. I'm talking about drive-by cruelties and casual unkindnesses, the death of a thousand cuts that slices away a little more of your soul every day, the net result of which is to make us meaner as a people and as a nation.

I have a real problem with this.

I also have a problem with those who use alcohol as a substitute for courage.

I have a problem with the loss of privacy, with the self-professed right of the television media to stick its monocular eye into our most intimate or painful moments in search of an increased ratings share for the eleven o'clock news, sandwiching tears and blood and anguished families in-between the latest from the sports world and the funny clip of the day, which all too often seems to involve a squirrel on a surfboard.

I have a problem with wife-beaters, with a society that puts no value on its citizenry as anything other than consumers or providers of merchandise, with fundamentalist intolerance, censorship, institutionalized hypocrisy, loneliness, cowardice, parking-space wars, little-league manslaughters, unnecessary rudeness and the cancer-like spread of a sense of entitlement, that we deserve what everybody else has, whether or not we've *earned* it, simply because *we want it*, and ought to *have it*, and if we *can't* have it, then by God neither should anybody else.

See, I believe that we *are* our brother's (or sister's) keeper, that we have an obligation to be better than we think we can, that kindness is the greatest human art form, that John Donne was right when he said "every man's death diminishes me," that ambition must be tempered with mercy, that cruelty will inevitably be brought to account, that the role of government should be to elevate and ennoble, that service should be rewarded with loyalty and that despite what everyone tells you, you really *can* fight city hall, and you can *win*.

So: why am I telling you all this?

Because as Stephen King once pointed out, writers write what gets caught in their filters. Which means we spend a lot of time writing about the stuff that pisses us off.

INTRODUCTION

The laundry list noted above, good and bad, proscribes the parameters of the stories that follow. They are about the things that excite me, and the things that annoy the hell out of me; the things that hold promise for us as a species, and the things that give the cockroaches hope that at the end of the evolutionary day, they may be the only ones left standing.

If any of the preceding resonates with you, then I humbly offer the following tales for your consideration.

If not... well, that's fine too. Not everyone feels the way I do about some things.

But if you *ever* jump a cab on me again, I'm taking your head off.

Just so we're clear.

–J. Michael Straczynski
Somewhere in Los Angeles
6 February 2004

SAY HELLO, MISTER QUIGLEY

It was almost noon by the time they got to the house. For the last two miles, Liz hadn't bothered to check the map. The town had changed in fifteen years, but the shape of it, the feel of it remained the same.

"There," she said, and pointed across the street. Already past it when she called out, Jim turned into a driveway further down, did a U-turn, and parked in front of the house.

He shut off the engine. "Nice place."

Liz nodded absently. From here, it still looked reasonably well-kept, but the lack of attention characterized by six months of unoccupancy left it a little ragged around the edges. It had taken Liz that long to decide whether or not to keep the house, or if she was going to personally go and take possession, or if would be better just to sign the papers long-distance.

Fifteen years. Don't be such a baby.

The interior would also need work. After her father died, her mother had tried to keep up appearances, but more often than not things that needed doing just got postponed in anticipation of a vaguely foreseen day when she'd "get around to it all." But that appointment had been missed permanently, and in her mother's absence the list of demands remained: paint and caulking and a dozen small repairs, wiring desperately in need of an overhaul, there was probably asbestos that would have to be removed....

It was a lot of work. But the house could be made clean again.

She would *make* it clean again. And in the process—

She glanced across at Jim, vaguely aware that he was speaking to her. "—do you think? She's all yours now."

"It's smaller than I remembered."

"Liz, that was ages ago. Of course it seemed bigger. And granted,

1

it needs a little TLC—well, make that a lot of TLC—but it'll be fine. Then you can move in, if you still want to."

She nodded. "My mother wanted me to have the house. And I intend to."

"Then let's get started." He climbed out of the pickup and went to the back of the cab. She popped the door and followed him out onto the street, standing back as he unloaded boxes of tools and wires.

She stuffed her hands in the pockets of her sweater, cold despite the sun on her face. Standing outside the house at last, after all this time, she wondered if this was really such a good idea after all. Maybe it *would* have been better if she'd just signed it over to the bank....

Jim turned toward her, hefting the boxes of tools. "Ready to get to work, Madame Assistant Carpenter, First Class?"

"Yeah," she said, and smiled, though it felt false across her lips. "I'm ready."

He crossed the lawn and started up the porch steps to the door. Liz hesitated, then followed.

It was a long time ago, she thought. *Long time gone. Long time dead.*

Time to get to work.

Everywhere was the smell of dust and old furniture and carefully hidden bags of cedar chips to keep away the moths. And here and there, almost a year after her mother had closed up the house to go and stay with her aunt, there was still the fragile scent of her perfume. Jasmine.

Liz moved through the house room by room, opening windows and snapping the sheets off furniture, each step revealing some new artifact of her parents' lives. In the living room she found his favorite chair. She remembered how her mother had been unable to get rid of it even after he passed away. There were too many memories in that chair for her to throw it out, and too many memories filling the house to let her stay.

I'll take care of that soon enough, Liz thought.

She moved to the fireplace, and the mantle covered with a flurry

2

of framed photos, the glass stained by a fine patina of dust. Her graduation pictures from high school and college. Her grandparents. Photographs of the neighborhood, the house—

She stopped. Carefully picking through the frames, she pulled a photo with her face on it out from the back row. She remembered when it was taken. She was twelve. Her father sat next to her in the photo. He was grinning broadly for the camera, holding her in his lap, an arm around her waist. Her own smile was wrong, staring past the camera, looking back at her across the years, trying to sit still, there beside him, and he was holding her—

She threw it across the room. The frame smashed into a wall and rained down in a shower of glass and shredded paper.

Why didn't they see? It was so obvious. It was right there on her face. Why didn't they SEE?

"You okay?"

She turned, and saw Jim standing in the doorway. "Thought I heard something break," he said, and then noticed the glass.

"Just a picture. It fell. Nothing important." She found a broom and stepped toward the debris. "This place is a real hazard. But it'll be okay, once we get rid of—once we clear it out."

She glanced up to meet his gaze. If he doubted her story, he gave no sign of it. "So what's your prognosis?"

"Like I said, it needs a lot of work. You've got some pipes that have to be replaced, with copper if you're smart. The foundation looks pretty solid, but the roof needs some re-shingling, and the wiring is pretty much shot. I wouldn't suggest you run any heavy equipment on the wires until you get someone in to check it out thoroughly. Other than that, there's just a lot of stuff that needs to be sorted, kept or thrown out. Where do you want to start?"

"The attic, I guess. We'll work our way down."

He nodded, and headed back out of the room. She scooped up the broken frame and carried it to the trash box. A fragment of her face stared up at her. *Can't tell, can't tell, no, never tell, there'll be trouble, there'll be—*

She let it fall into the box, shook out the dustpan, and moved on.

The attic was musty and dark, an explosion of boxes and crates and trunks and piles of old clothes. Jim volunteered to start at one end, she'd start at the other, and they'd meet in the middle.

She plowed her way through the first three boxes, making good time. There were stacks of old *LIFE* magazines, broken toys, glassware and crockery, books and clothes, some in need of repair, or too worn to wear and too familiar to throw away, finally just stashed out of sight in lieu of a decision. Most of it could be trashed, but some was in good enough shape to donate.

"Hey, slugger," Jim called. She looked up to see him waving a baseball bat he'd found in one of the boxes.

She smiled at the sight of it. "Thirteenth birthday present," she said, "from my uncle."

"Save it or throw it?"

"Save it," she said, and turned her attention back to the task at hand.

She closed up the third cardboard box and reached for the next, like the rest sealed with clear plastic tape long gone yellow. She tugged at the top. For a moment, it refused to yield. She pulled harder. With a sudden tearing of rotten cardboard it ripped open and down one side, spilling its contents into her lap: musty piles of clothes, and something large and soft that jingled as it fell.

It landed with its face turned up to her own, a grey and white cloth face with oversized stitching, too-large eyes and a grin that ran from ear to ear

(mister quigley)

its limbs long and gangly and dressed in a green-and-black checked motley, stained by food and age, a three-foot-tall jester with bells on his arms and bells on his feet and bells sewn into the cap that was sown onto his head

(Mister Quigley)

and she instinctively tried to shove it away, but it shifted in her grip, soft and resilient, folding back at her, and now she was batting at it, only distantly aware of the noise that came from the back of her throat, guttural and hungry for air

(say hello, Mister Quigley)

as she finally kicked it away, and it jingled as it fell, bells clattering against the hardwood floor of the attic. She scrabbled away from it as she would from a spider.

Jim looked up from his pile of boxes, started toward her. "Liz? Are you—"

She stood hurriedly, brushing off the dust. "I'm fine."

"You sure?" He came up alongside her and looked down at the cloth-and-stuffing jester dumped upside down on the floor. "Who's that?"

Liz glanced down. "Mister Quigley," she said, barely loud enough for him to hear. "Mister—"

She fled from the attic, careening against the doorway but not feeling it, frantic to get to any place that was not this room.

Liz found the coffeepot where it had always been, and pulled out the fresh-ground coffee they'd brought in from town. She would give the pot a thorough cleaning later. Right now, a quick wash would have to do. She needed something to drink, and something to do with her hands that would make them stop shaking, make them feel warm again.

A few minutes later, perhaps sensing that she needed some time to herself, Jim came down from the attic, brushing dust off his workshirt as he entered the kitchen. She sat at the Formica table, facing the wall as he appeared in the doorway. She could feel him looking at her. "You want to talk about it?"

She shook her head. "No."

He waited.

She set down the cup and pressed her hands down flat on the table, letting the coolness seep into her palms. "His name was Mister Quigley," she said. "He belonged to my father when he was a boy. It was one of the few things he still had from that time. He used to keep it propped up in a chair in a corner of the living room. It always made the other kids nervous. I mean, it was nearly as tall as they were, and to see it sitting there, sometimes at night—no, they didn't like Mister Quigley. Not one bit."

"And you?"

"I felt the same way, at first. My father used to tease me about it. In the mornings, I'd come out, and he'd say, 'Well, Liz, say, 'Good morning, Mister Quigley.' And I'd do it. And then he'd look at it and say, 'Now say hello to Liz, Mister Quigley.' It gave me the creeps. But eventually, I guess I got used to him. He was just another part of the family. After a while, we ran out of space in the living room, and my father decided to put Mister Quigley in my room. Since he was good at scaring the other kids, I figured he'd be my guardian. I used to pretend he was there to protect me against monsters. Right before I went to sleep, I'd whisper, 'Watch out for the monsters, Mister Quigley. Keep them far away from my bed.' "

"And did he?"

She opened her mouth to answer, but nothing came out. She stood and carried her cup to the sink. The china rattled in her hands.

"Liz?"

She dropped her cup into the water. "I don't want to talk about it anymore, all right?"

She began washing out the cup, letting the water run until it was so hot it scalded her, even through the gloves. She had to make it clean, wipe it all away. She felt moisture on her cheeks, distantly aware that she was crying. *Can't tell, can't tell, no, never....*

Jim came behind her, put his hands gently on her shoulders. "Liz?"

"I'm sorry." She wiped furiously at the tears. "I always feel so stupid when this happens. I told myself I wasn't going to cry over this anymore. But when I saw him upstairs, I—"

She closed her eyes, squeezing them tight until they hurt, shutting out the tears. She turned away from him and walked back toward the table. She couldn't bear to look at him and tell him.

Make it clean, wash it over and over and over and over.

"You remember I told you how I ran away from home when I was fifteen?"

He nodded. "Some problem with you and your dad. You never said much about it."

She nodded. "Well, see, my mom got sick when I was about twelve, thirteen. She was sick for a long time. And then my dad—my dad would come into my room at night, when she was asleep, and—and he would touch me, and he would—he would do things to me, and there was nothing I could do except lie there...and all

6

the time, there was Mister Quigley in the corner, looking at me, and he saw everything, over and over, and he didn't do anything. He didn't protect me. He just sat there, and watched, and I swear he was laughing, he was looking at me and he was laughing because he didn't belong to me he belonged to my dad and he was supposed to protect me, he was supposed to—"

She slammed a fist into the table, hit it again and again, then Jim was there beside her. He reached for her, but she moved away. "No. Please. Don't."

He stopped. "I'm sorry."

She shrugged, looked away.

"Did you ever tell your mother?"

"No. It would've killed her. But after a while I just couldn't take it anymore. There were times I thought about killing myself, just so I could make it stop. But I couldn't bring myself to do it. So I ran away, and tried as best I could to pretend he didn't exist. It was the only way I could stay sane. My mom and I didn't talk for almost a year after I left. She didn't understand why I did this to them, and I couldn't tell her. Later, when I got my own place, and things calmed down a little, I'd call and talk to her, sometimes, but never to him. Not once. If he answered the phone, I just hung up. Never talked to him. Never came back to visit."

She met his gaze briefly, then looked away. "When he was dying a few years ago, my mom called. She said he wanted to talk to me. I wouldn't do it. She said... she said he couldn't die without just seeing me once more. I told her, 'Yes, he can.' And he did."

The silence hung between them for a moment. "Maybe your father wanted to—"

"I don't *care* what he wanted to do," she said, "or what he wanted to say. My God, hadn't he done enough to me already? I'd killed him in my head a thousand times already, what was one more? Now he's dead, and he's gone, and I'm glad. He can't hurt me anymore, and now this is MY house, my mother's house, and I'll do what I want with it. I'm going to clean it, and erase every trace of him. The best thing I can do to him is make him vanish, to go over this house and get rid of every trace of his existence, to take from him just like he took from me. As far as I'm concerned, he's got nothing to do with me or this house anymore."

She turned away, then felt his hand on her shoulder. This time she permitted the touch. She turned and held him tightly, trying for the warmth that would make her whole again. Clean again.

Somehow, it was never quite enough.

It was getting dark outside when Jim deposited the last of the boxes from the attic on the living room floor. Mister Quigley was in one of them. She tried not to notice.

"Okay, that's the last of it," he said. "These go to the dump tomorrow, those over here you can either sell or keep, and this bunch we can give to charity." He glanced at the box containing Mister Quigley. "I was thinking about it and, well, he's still in pretty good shape. Maybe there's some kid out there who might enjoy him, give him a clean slate. Unless you'd rather—"

"No," she said, too quickly, "that's all right. I agree, it's a good idea."

He stood silently in the hall for a moment. "I can stay a little longer if you like."

"No. It's a three-hour drive back to town, and you've got work tomorrow."

"I could always call in sick. Spend the night here."

She sighed. "Jim, we've discussed this before. I'm just not ready for that yet. Give me a little more time, okay?"

He nodded, forced a smile. "Okay. You're sure you wouldn't prefer staying in a hotel for a while?"

"No. There's a perfectly good bedroom here. My bedroom."

"Sure, I understand, I was just thinking that, with all the bad memories—"

"I'm going to wash them away," she said firmly. "This is my house now, it's the only thing I've ever really owned, and I'm not going to be put out of it."

"All right," he said at last, and headed for the door. "I'll be back first thing tomorrow. Then we'll finish the inside, and start on the wiring and the plumbing. I'll make an engineer out of you yet."

He paused to kiss her, then stepped out onto the porch. "Wait," she said. "I'll walk you to the car."

She followed after him, pausing by the box containing Mister Quigley. Taking a sheet she'd pulled off the sofa, she draped it over the mute jester's form. Satisfied that it could not be seen, she hurried after Jim.

Dinner was quick and simple. Salad, a slice of tenderloin and some vegetables tossed into the wok she'd brought from her apartment. She scraped the plate clean into the sink, and headed back to the living room. She figured she could spend the next half-hour taping up boxes, and the rest of the evening sorting through shelves and closets.

She switched on the living room light. It flickered, then held. She stepped inside, and stopped in the middle of the room. The sheet she'd thrown over the box containing Mister Quigley had shifted, and now lay gathered about him in folds. Its garish painted face was turned up and toward the door, reflecting the overhead light. It seemed almost to be looking at her.

Tentatively, as though touching something unpleasant, she snatched at the sheet and threw it over Mister Quigley. She gave the box a little kick with her toe. This time the sheet stayed put.

And stay there, she thought, and began assembling boxes.

She was standing on a high cliff, overlooking the sea that churned and boiled far below her. Over the roar of the surf she heard something moving behind her, drawing close, swaying as it advanced. She was too frightened to turn, and there was nowhere to run, just the cliff before her and the jagged rocks below, and it was closer now, just behind her, close enough to hear the sound of bells, small and tinny, now a shadow fell across her—

Liz sat up in bed, wet with perspiration, a cry on her lips. She ran a hand across her face, forced herself to breath easier, slow the trip-hammer beating of her heart. *A nightmare, that's all, just a nightmare.*

As the blood roaring in her temples died away, she became aware of a sound. At first she thought it only a carryover from the dream, but as she stared into the night, straining to hear, it came through clearer.

Bells.

Small and tinny.

And a sense of movement outside in the hall, a rustling, like something soft being dragged past her door.

She slid out of bed, and the sound stopped. She sat still for several minutes, trying to decide if it was really gone, and if it had even been there at all. Finally, she nudged on her slippers and stood, slowly opening the bedroom door. She paused again, listening, but heard nothing.

She stepped into the hallway and flicked on the light. It revealed nothing. The hall was deserted, as it had been earlier. She considered going back to bed, then decided to make a fast check of the house, just to be sure. She came to the end of the hallway, and entered the darkened living room. Switched on another light. It flickered, then held.

She turned, and saw the writing scrawled in chalk on the far wall.

Get out of here, Lizzy.

She stepped back as though slapped and fell, her foot tangled in a sheet that hadn't been there earlier, she was sure it hadn't been. Despite herself she cried out at the sight of Mister Quigley in his box, staring vacantly upward. The sheet that had tripped her was the one she'd draped over his box.

The box was at least two feet from where the sheet

(had been thrown)

had fallen.

Say hello, she thought, her gaze drawn against her will back to the garishly painted jester's face. *Say hello, Mr. Quigley.*

She was scrubbing the wall for the third time when Jim came back in the morning. No matter how hard she scraped, enough traces of the chalk remained to make the words visible. *Then I'll wash it a fourth time, and a fifth,* she thought, *and if that doesn't work I'll paint it over or rip out the whole damned wall.*

"I checked all around the house and out back," Jim said. "I found a window unlocked, but it's too small for anybody but a kid to have climbed through. If you like, I can talk to the neighbors, see if any of their kids were out late."

She didn't look up from her work. "It said 'Lizzy,' Jim. No one's called me Lizzy in fifteen years."

"That's because it's a kid's name."

"It's *my* name."

"Yes, and it's also a name that a kid might use to try and annoy an adult," he said. "It must've been one of the neighbor's kids. Look...."

He walked up beside her, and used his palms to measure the distance from the writing to the ground. "About three feet," he said. "If it was an adult, he'd have to lean way down like this to write it. So we're talking a kid, close to the same height."

Mister Quigley is three feet tall, she thought, but cut it off before she said it aloud. *Stop it. You're being foolish.*

"I'm sure you must be right," she said.

"My offer still stands. I can stay over," he said, then added quickly, "on the couch. Just to keep an eye on things. Or we can get you a room somewhere else. If you don't think it's safe—"

She shook her head. "No. If anybody'd meant me harm, they had every chance to do it last night. It's just kids, that's all. I'll make sure everything's locked up this time." She looked up into his eyes. "This is my house now, Jim. I was driven out of it once before, I'm not going to give it up again."

He nodded absently for a moment, then looked away. "You know, I was thinking. Maybe it wasn't such a good idea after all, you coming back here. I think there's still a lot you haven't dealt with, things you need to deal with if you intend to live here."

"I'm doing just fine," she said, firmly.

"Are you?" He pointed at the scrawled writing on the wall. "Then why did this upset you so much? I've seen you deal with kids and petty vandalism before, you've never gotten this angry, this obsessed."

She turned away, didn't answer.

"Is Lizzy what your father called you? Is that it?"

"I don't want to talk about it."

"Well, maybe it's time you did start talking about it. Damn it,

Liz, it's been fifteen years. You can't go around angry for the rest of your life. Maybe... well, maybe it's time you forgave your father."

She wheeled on him, and the rage was there before she could stop herself. "Time I forgave—FORGAVE him? My God. Don't you understand what he did to me?

"Yes, I do, I—"

"No, you don't," she said. "You know it in your head, but you don't know what it feels like. Christ, Jim, it was years before I could let another man even touch me. He did more than use me, he took away everything I had, made me powerless. I couldn't say anything, I couldn't do anything, all I could do was take it, and take it, and take it—"

"I know, Liz, but he's dead now. He's dead, and he's buried, and he can't touch you anymore. It's not him that's messing you up now, it's you. You have to get past all this. You can't hate your father forever. It's not healthy."

"Watch me."

He reached for her. "Liz, please, just listen to me, you've got to—"

She pulled away. "Look, Jim, I know you mean well, but maybe you should just go away for a while," she said. "You've got things to do, and I think I'd just like to deal with this on my own for a while. All right?"

He looked ready to debate the question, then finally shrugged. Looked away. "All right. I guess the wiring can wait another day."

He started across the room, grabbing his jacket off the sofa. "The truck will be by tomorrow morning to pick up the rest of this stuff. I'll be home if you need me."

"Thanks," she said, and went back to scrubbing the wall again. The screen door clattered shut behind her, followed a moment later by the sound of Jim's car starting and driving away. She looked at the barely visible letters. *Almost gone. Just a little more and it'll be clean again.* First, though, she would need more detergent.

She started across the room, and passed the box that contained Mister Quigley. The sheet covering it was exactly where she'd left it the night before. She hesitated, then ripped off the sheet and, in one move, grabbed the stuffed jester by the shoulder and lifted him to eye level. She studied him for a moment with the detached curiosity she might exhibit at some curious insect splattered on her windshield.

"He's right," she said, very softly, very quietly. "You're dead. You're dead, and you're buried, and you can't touch me anymore. I hope you rot in hell for all eternity for what you did to me, 'daddy.'"

With that, she threw him back into the box, bells jingling with the impact. Then she replaced the sheet, and went in search of the detergent.

This time there was no sea, only a black, dreamless sleep suddenly broken by a sound in the darkened bedroom. She sat up on one elbow, listening. The sound had been on the edge of her hearing, gone now, but it had definitely been there.

Liz reached for the flashlight beside her bed and flicked it on. Chalk letters were scrawled on the bedroom wall.

Get out of here, Lizzy.

And NOW, from somewhere down the hall...the sound of tiny bells.

This time, she did not cry out.

She climbed out of bed and pulled on her robe, never letting go of the flashlight. She eased past the writing on the wall, careful not to brush her robe against it, and moved toward the door. She grasped the knob, turned it without pulling, then yanked it suddenly open.

The jingling stopped.

She switched on the hallway light. As before, it flickered, but she could clearly make out the words written in chalk, jagged letters scrawled on both sides of the hall.

Get out of here, Lizzy
Get out of here, Lizzy
Get out of here, Lizzy

From somewhere in the dark, the sound of bells came again, this time coming from the living room.

She started down the hall, switching on lights as she went. Every few feet revealed more of the writing. It covered the walls and doors and sloped down at strange angles. She followed the sound of bells, down to the living room door, and flung it open. The jingling stopped abruptly. She stepped inside.

Mister Quigley was on the floor, slumped against a wall directly beneath more of the scrawled writing. His eyes gazed sightlessly into the light above her.

She crossed the room and picked him up. He was limp in her grip. She looked at him carefully.

There was chalk dust on Mister Quigley's hands.

In an instant, her face twisted into a mask of rage.

Gripping him harder, she stalked through the kitchen and out the side door. She cut around back, heading for the rusted metal trash can. She lifted the lid, crammed Mister Quigley in among the garbage and slammed the lid down again. She banged it flush on all sides, so it would stay on.

"Go to hell," she whispered, and turned back to the house.

She was halfway to the door when there was a sudden clang and a rattle behind her. She spun around to see the lid of the trash can on the ground, still vibrating. She rushed back and peered into the trash can.

Mister Quigley was gone.

Then another sound, a scrape of wood against wood. She turned to see a window open now that had been closed a moment earlier.

Inside. Damn it, he's inside!

She ran back toward the side of the house just in time to see the door starting to close. She rushed the door, sticking her hand through the narrow opening to stop it from closing. She pushed against it, feeling resistance from the other side as something pushed back.

She dug in her heels, put her shoulder to the door, and pushed harder. The door gave way suddenly, as if there were no longer anything on the other side. She grabbed the door to keep from falling forward.

Where? she thought. *Where is it?*

The lights were going on and off again, making it hard to focus. There was the pop of a lamp being knocked over somewhere nearby. She strained to see in the flickering light.

"Come on out," she said, moving into the living room. No sign of him. "Come on!"

She paused long enough to dig through one of the boxes, and pulled out the baseball bat they'd found the first day. She hefted it, and moved slowly toward the hallway.

She stepped past several doors that opened only onto darkness. Continued down the hall as suddenly there was a jingling of bells behind her. She spun around in time to see a door slam shut. She raced to it, then waited. Listened.

The doorknob moved, ever so slightly.

She grabbed it and threw the door open.

Nothing. The room was silent, dark. She ventured a step inside. The window at the far end of the room was open, the cool nightwind blowing the curtains.

She stepped back into the hall. Two more closed doors were ahead of her.

Think, her mind shrieked at her. *Think!*

She lowered herself to the floor until she could see under the doors. She peered beneath the first one, saw nothing but darkness, and moved on to the next.

There was something moving on the other side. She could get just the sense of it, a greyness against the deeper black of the room.

And, ever so faintly, a rustling of motley, and the faint whisper of bells.

Slowly, slowly, she put her hand on the doorknob. Grasped it firmly. Took a deep breath, and threw open the door.

And it was there.

Standing, turned facing toward her.

Just a momentary flash before it hurled itself into the shadows.

She ran after it, swinging the bat, not connecting, flailing madly as suddenly she heard it again, across the room. She spun around, brought the bat down, heard a lamp smash and didn't care, she had to find it, had to—

Another flash of movement.

She swung, and this time connected with a dull thud of wood striking cloth, and a seizure of bells. She slammed the stuffed figure against the wall, heard it bounce, brought the bat down and again found the target.

"Damn you!" she cried, slamming it over and over. "Damn you! Fifteen years!"

Pounding.

"I loved you and you hurt me! I trusted you! And you betrayed me! Damn you!"

The bat arced down in her hands again and again, as if of its own volition, until her arms ached and she fell, sobbing, to her knees, unable to raise it any longer. In the darkness she could just make out the figure, laying slumped against the wall, battered and broken, stuffing ripped out and scattered on the floor, one leg nearly torn off.

"...damn you," she cried, exhausted, and let the bat fall to the floor. She sat heavily, sobbing into her hands.

Then: a jingling of bells.

Startled, she glanced up.

Mister Quigley was gone again.

She stood, and stepped back into the hall. The lights were flickering even more now, but she ignored them, drawn to the sound of bells. This time, however, the sound was different: slower, duller.

She'd hurt it. There was still a chance—

Just as she stepped into the living the lights went out altogether. An instant later, something whirred past her head and smashed into the wall behind her. She cried out, moving just in time to avoid another plate as it sliced through the air and crashed into the wall. More followed, cups and saucers and plates and silverware, a flurry that pushed her back toward the front door, each thrown plate accompanied by the jingling of small bells.

Each volley came closer, driving her further back until she was up against the door. She fumbled for the knob, found it, and lurched outside, slamming the door behind her. She could hear another plate smashing against it on the other side.

Then there was another sound, as the door was locked from the inside.

She rattled the door. It refused to move.

I'm not giving up, she thought, pounding on the door. *He took everything I had, everything I cared about, he took it all away but he's not taking this, too! It's mine and he can't have it!*

She stepped away from the door, staggered backward onto the lawn. "I'll be back!" she cried. "Do you understand me!? I'll be back!"

Silence was her only answer.

She turned, ran away from the house and down the street. A phone. She had to find a phone. She'd go back there with Jim, and they'd find that thing and that would be that.

She was already down the street and out of sight when the first blue-white flash smeared across the front window of the old house.

It was almost dawn when she drove back with Jim. They could smell the smoke even before they turned the corner. The crew of the last remaining fire truck were packing their gear, dragging hoses across the waterlogged and soot-blackened street.

"Oh, Christ," she whispered as he stopped the car. She dove out and raced across the street to what was left of the house.

There was almost nothing left, only the husks of walls surrounding a black pile of debris where the roof had crashed in. The fireplace chimney still stood, precariously balanced on the edge of what had been the basement. The smell of smoke clung to the place, the acrid scent burning her throat.

She felt her knees go weak as she stepped onto the lawn. "Oh, my God, what happened? What—"

One of the firemen dragging a hose stopped. "Are you the owner, miss?"

She nodded numbly.

"I'm sorry. It looks like a total loss. Do you have any insurance? Anyone you can call?"

"I—I think so," she said. "But how—how did it—"

"As far as we can tell, looks like bad wiring." He pointed to the melted wiring, which hung out of the walls and ceiling like thin, blackened tendrils. "The place looked pretty solid from the outside, but it was a real firetrap. We think the blaze started in the bedroom, probably a short circuit. It erupted in the walls and next thing all the wires were burning." He turned to face her. "I know this is a hard time for you right now, but for whatever comfort it might be, you're real lucky."

She focused on him. "Lucky?"

He nodded. "This was the worst kind of flash fire. A thing like this can consume a house in minutes. Just goes up like a match. If you'd been inside when it went up, you wouldn't have had a chance. You were real lucky to be out of there."

With that, he stepped away, joining the others at the fire truck as Jim came up alongside her.

"I was in bed," she said.

"What?"

"The fire started in the bedroom. I would've been asleep." *And I would have died*, she thought.

He kept trying to get me out of there.

He knew. He must have known.

She walked away.

"Liz?"

She didn't answer, heading for the back of the house to examine the damage.

It was even worse back here. The back of the house was made almost entirely of wood paneling.

Nothing left but ashes.

He knew. He must have known.

"Why did you do it?" she asked, looking around. "What do you want from me?"

Then, from somewhere close by: a tiny jingling of bells.

She followed the sound to the low stone wall that separated her property from the house next door. There, at the foot of the wall, was Mister Quigley... or what was left of him. Battered, broken and seared by flame, his legs almost totally burned away. Little remained of his face. He no longer looked frightening, only sad and lost and small.

In his hand was a piece of chalk.

She gently nudged him aside to reveal what was written on the wall behind him.

FORGIVE ME

PLEASE FORGIVE ME

DADDY

She sat back on her heels, and the tears came. Fifteen years' worth of tears. She struggled to speak, but nothing came out but great, gasping sobs.

Finally, when the worst of it had passed, she reached out and touched the cold stone on which the words had been written.

"... I... God, I'll try," she said, then added, "daddy."

Gathering up what was left of Mister Quigley, she walked back to the front lawn, and Jim.

She held him for a very long time.

DREAM ME A LIFE

Roger Simpson Leeds didn't belong here. Everything about the room was wrong. The walls bled out into infinite midnight. Angles refused to meet at conventional places. He blinked, but his eyes were unable to focus on anything, his gaze sliding off walls and chairs and bed as though they were pushing it away, refusing his attempt to bring them into clarity.

And everywhere, for as far as he could see, there were candles, candles on the walls and on the floor and ascending candelabra like glowing steps; candles surrounding framed pictures on the wall, creating brilliant islands amid the overwhelming darkness. And in the middle of those islands, a face, the same face, over and over....

He didn't belong here.

He stumbled as the shadows were split by a sudden shaft of brilliant light from somewhere straight ahead. With it came a wind that chilled him to his marrow. He thrust up one hand, futilely squinting against the brilliance, and in that light he saw her. Again.

I don't belong here.

She spotted him, as she always did, and cried out, a mournful sound born of pain and fear and desperation. "Please," she cried, arms outstretched, "You've got to help me!" She was old, trembling with fear, the lines in her face deepened by the glare from behind, her long grey hair whipped by the furious wind. In her eyes was a fear that seemed almost palpable.

She rushed to his side, clutching at his hands, his arms, trying to draw him toward the source of the terror. "You've got to stop him! If he gets through, I'll die!"

"No," Roger said, and pulled away from her. He didn't want to look, didn't want to know the reason for her terror, but as he lunged away from her, he saw it: a door, the source of the blinding light, held partly closed only by a fragile chain-lock. The door bounced furiously against the chain as someone or something pounded on the other side. Light and wind roared through the narrow gap that

20

had been forced in the doorway. The pounding grew louder, ear-shattering, like invisible cannonballs slamming into the wood, splintering it, a rhythmic sound punctuated by a scrabbling and a scraping and a scratching from the other side.

Somehow the door was holding, but it wouldn't, not for long.

The old woman tugged at him again, frantically trying to draw him toward the door. "You've got to do something!" she screamed over the noise. "Please! Don't you understand? If he gets through, I'll die! *I'll die!*"

"Let me go!" Roger cried. He pulled away, back toward the darkness, back where it was safe. "Get away from me! Leave me alone! I don't want to be here! LEAVE ME ALONE!"

She screamed.

And then the room was silent.

But it wasn't her room any longer.

It was his room. Silent except for his labored breathing as he sat up, forcing his legs out of bed and onto the floor. He stood, unsteadily, and leaned against the nightstand, fighting down the panic and the fear, fighting to slow his heartbeat to less than trip-hammer pace. He staggered to the window and looked out onto the darkened backyard, wiping at his face with the back of his hand.

Again, he thought. *God help me, I don't know how much more of this I can stand.*

"Please, God," he whispered, "make it stop."

"Get anything interesting?"

Roger poked through the mailbox, finding the usual assortment of bills and advertisements and envelopes addressed only to OCCUPANT. He tore them up and walked back toward the front porch of the retirement home. Down the street a bunch of kids were playing touch football. Loudly. Frank Weatherby stayed at his elbow, following him back inside. As always. And just about as loudly.

"Shall I take that as a no?" Frank asked.

"You may." He'd known Frank for twenty years, and now at seventy, two years older than Roger was, Frank seemed to have decided to adopt him. Sometimes he wondered why. And sometimes he wondered if Frank wondered why.

Oblivious to his indifference, Frank paged through the letters in his hand. "Got a postcard from my sister in Detroit. Ruth. You met her, must've been around Christmas, seventy-nine. She says hello, asks if your mood has improved any."

"Hmm."

"Hmm. Good. Eminently quotable. So how's with that son of yours, and the kids?"

"Fine, I suppose."

"You suppose? I thought they were coming up to visit this weekend."

Roger shrugged. Some days he suspected that Frank had a little radar dish in his head, some sort of souped-up range finder that enabled him to know with unfailing accuracy when Roger most wanted to be left alone...and instinctively to do the opposite. "Yeah, well, I told them I just—you know how it is, Frank. I don't have time for a bunch of kids running around all over the place."

"Of course not," Frank said, nodding. "What with the photographers, the mad social whirl, the state dinners—why, it just doesn't leave *time* for anything else. I'm sure they understand. And speaking of which, how *are* Charles and Di these days? They seemed, I don't know, crabby the last time they stopped by."

"You're an evil man," Roger said, moving through the sun-flecked porch and into the cool front room. Someone was watching television, an old sitcom by the sound of it. He supposed eventually he'd have to start learning some names around here. "You're evil from toe to follicle. Have I ever told you that?"

"Frequently, and with great enthusiasm. But then, I'm not the one with the nightmares."

Roger stopped, turned toward him. "You're prying again, Frank. I told you if you did that again, I'd have to hire somebody to hurt you."

"I wasn't prying. I just overheard one of the nurses talking about it a little while ago. They said they heard you again last night. That's three times this week, Roger."

A reply started in Roger's throat, but he bit it off before it hit the air. What could he say? *Sorry I've been waking everybody up lately, but there's this woman who keeps appearing in my dreams, and she's scared, and she says she'll die if I don't help her keep some door shut, and I really don't want to deal with this, or you, or anyone else at the moment?*

He said nothing. Only shook his head and started up the stairs, toward his room.

Frank followed as far as the bottom step. "We're meeting in the rec room at seven for poker."

"Pass."

"I can hold a place for you—"

Roger stopped at the second-floor landing and peered back down at Frank in a way he hoped would be intimidating. Frank looked so small down there, except for the big, hopeful smile he seemed to wear all the time. He hated it when Frank forced him to be harsh. "Frank—the answer is no. You want it any clearer than that, go ask one of the nurses. They seem to know everything around here."

"All right," Frank said, and after a moment, when it seemed safe to assume that the conversation was indeed over, Roger continued on toward his room.

"By the way," Frank called up the stairs, "I hear you're getting a new neighbor. Someone's finally taken that room next to yours."

"As long as he doesn't snore."

Roger wasn't sure—his hearing wasn't what it used to be—but he was reasonably confident he heard Frank mutter, "Who said it was a he?" before heading back into the television room.

Roger hit the top of the stairs and crossed to the closed door to his room, fumbling with his keys as he went. He'd long ago forgotten what most of them were for, but was loathe to throw any of them away, knowing full well that he'd discover he needed them within twenty-four hours.

Someone behind him called, "Good morning, Mr. Leeds."

Roger turned, nodded perfunctorily toward the nurse—and froze at the sight of the elderly woman being wheeled ahead of her down the hall, toward him: grey hair, pulled back so tight he thought it might scream. Eyes vacant, unfocused, fixed on the private domain of her own thoughts. Hands clasped tightly in her lap.

She was silent, seemed not even to note his existence. But in his mind, Roger saw her as he had the night before, in his dream, clutching at him, screaming into his ear....

The nurse smiled at him as she wheeled the chair past him. He crowded back against the door, as though with sufficient effort he could melt into it, away from that chair and its terrible, impossible occupant.

The nurse came to the corner and reached across the chair to open the door to the room next to his. As she maneuvered the chair inside, she glanced back at him. "Well, aren't you going to say hello to our new guest?"

Roger stepped into the television room, knowing even before he arrived that she would be there. But the rec room, and Frank, were on the other side, and there was no other way through. The television was on, as always, and a few others were watching, barely paying attention. The only eyes that never wavered from the screen were *hers*. Her wheelchair had been deposited right in front of the TV, and somehow the effect of canned laughter and those staring, unwavering eyes made his skin go cold.

He walked quickly, glancing down at her as he crossed in front of her chair. Her hands were still clasped tightly together in her lap—so tightly, in fact, that he could see her knuckles whiten from effort. And yet her face remained utterly without expression.

When he reached the rec room, Roger realized he hadn't taken a breath since walking into the other room. Frank was at his usual place at the poker table. He glanced up at Roger and smiled. "Here, pull up a chair," Frank said. "I need another witness—these guys cheat."

The player on his right bristled. "*We* cheat!"

"Good for you," Frank said. "It takes a big man to admit a thing like that." He motioned for another player to continue dealing. "So what do you say, Roger? Sit in on a hand or two?"

"No, I—don't think so."

The other boarder snorted. "Told you," he said.

"So who asked you?" Frank said, and checked the hand he'd been dealt. "Give me two."

"Frank," Roger said, trying to sound casual, "who is that?" He pointed back into the television room. They could just see the wheelchair from where they sat.

Frank glanced up over the rim of his glasses, then went back to his cards. "How should I know? I get my information from nurses." He dropped his cards. "Fold."

"Frank—"

"Okay, okay." He lit a cigarette, sat back in his chair. "Her name's Laurel Kincaid. Word is she hasn't talked to anyone in ten years, ever since her husband died." He shook his head. "She went—*away*. You look in her eyes, all you see is a reflection. Nothing goes in."

"What else?"

"That's it. What do I look like, an encyclopedia? Look, you sure you don't want to sit in on a hand?"

"Positive," Roger said, barely paying attention. "Thanks."

Almost immediately afterward, he wondered if he shouldn't have accepted Frank's offer after all. His business finished, he had no reason now to hang around in the rec room.

But leaving meant walking past Laurel Kincaid again.

What the hell, he thought. *What's she going to do? Bite me?*

Very possibly, he thought, and pushed away the thought as he headed out of the rec room.

"Roger? You okay?"

Roger looked up to see Frank standing in the doorway of the reading room. It was late. He was sitting in his favorite spot, on the winged chair beside the window, trying not to think about sleep. "I'm fine," he said, quietly. The room didn't seem to appreciate noise.

"Surprised you're not asleep," Frank said, glancing at his watch. "You're usually upstairs by ten—"

Roger looked away. "I don't feel much like sleeping."

"You want to talk about it?"

"No, I don't. Look, Frank, why don't you just go away and leave me alone?"

"Because I'm your friend, damn it!" He stepped into the room, came toward him. "We used to *talk*, remember? Twenty *years*, Roger, that should count for something."

Roger said nothing, only stared out the window into the darkness just beyond the frosted glass. He was tired. So completely, bone tired. But he couldn't sleep. Couldn't *let* himself sleep.

Frank sat in the chair next to him, and after a moment he leaned forward, tried to catch Roger's eye. "Nothing's been the same, has it? Not since—" He hesitated, then drew himself up in his chair. "Roger," he said finally, "it's been three years."

"No," Roger said. "It was yesterday." There was no question what Frank was referring to. *Why wouldn't he let it go? Why wouldn't he let him alone?*

It was all so stupid, so—wrong.

"You know," Roger said, and smiled faintly at the memory, "I was thinking the other day about her. We never could get it straight between us, jam or jelly. I'd say, 'Pass me the jam, please,' and she'd say, 'Here's the jelly, dear.' It was a game, I guess. Then one day I was in a bad mood, I guess, and we got into an argument about it. Can you believe it? The stupid, petty little things people argue about—"

He looked away, his eyes burning, moist. *So stupid. So wrong.* "God, Frank, I miss her so much."

"I know. Rachel was a fine woman. But you can't keep pushing everyone away."

Roger turned to gaze back out the window. "I never knew how much I needed her until she was gone. Just—gone. When I had my first heart attack, she held my hand. She said she wouldn't let go, no matter what happened, as long as I held on. She held my hand in the ambulance, and in the emergency room, and she never let go. I think she would've held on till the end of the world if she had to."

He wiped at his face with the back of his hand. "She believed in me, Frank. When I looked in those eyes, all I saw was love. I felt like I could do *anything*. Because she believed in me." He shook his head. "I wonder—I wonder what she would think of me now."

"Why? What's happening now? Come on, Roger—talk to me."

Roger looked at him, but in his thoughts he saw only that closed, dark room, no way in, no way out, heard only that terrible pounding behind the door, that voice, *Help me, please, if he gets through, I'll die!*

"No. You'd think I was crazy. I'm halfway convinced myself."

Frank briefly looked as though he might push the subject. But he didn't. He only clasped his hands and, leaning forward, smiled a little ruefully. "My old father, he never said much of anything useful. But he did tell me two things. First, love never dies. And second, that we're never given anything we can't handle."

"You don't know the situation."

"No, I don't. But I know you. And I knew Rachel. And you don't have anything to be ashamed of."

Roger shrugged, not knowing what else to do, awkward as he always was when he talked to Frank like this. He checked his watch. "It's getting late."

"Roger, I—"

"Look, Frank, I'll be okay," Roger said, cutting him off. "Don't worry, all right? You know how I hate it when you make a fuss."

He walked toward the door, and Frank followed him out. "All right," Frank said. "But if you change your mind, if you need me, you know where to find me."

They stopped beside the stairwell. "You know," Frank said, "this is the longest we've talked in almost a year. I think we should do it more often."

"Good night, Frank," Roger said, hoping it sounded final.

"Good night," Frank said, and headed off toward the TV room.

Roger took a step up the stairs—and hesitated.

She was up there, somewhere, in the room next door to his.

I don't want to sleep, he thought. But the fatigue in his bones told him otherwise. He continued up the stairs, pausing only to glance in the partially open door to her room. Laurel Kincaid slept quietly. Her room was spare, the only obvious decoration a photograph on her bedside table. A man, his hair almost gone, his face weathered by the years. It was, Roger decided, a pleasant enough face. And there was something passingly familiar about it—

Go to bed, he thought, and turned away. Maybe it wouldn't happen this time. Maybe tonight the dream wouldn't come.

He hoped so. He didn't know how much more of this he could take before losing his mind.

"Whoever you are—please—you've got to help me! If he gets through, I'll die! You've *got* to *do* something! *Please!*"

Roger squeezed his eyes shut. It was the same. Starting all over again.

She snatched at his arm, and he pulled back. "I can't help you. Don't you understand? I don't want to be here, I don't even know what I'm *doing* here!"

"Please—"

She reached for him again, more insistently than before, and caught his wrist.

"I said *no*! Leave me *alone*!"

He ripped out of her grip with such force that he fell backwards, toward a table strewn with photos and candles. He twisted around, reaching out, trying to break his fall. Glass scattered and crashed soundlessly to the floor. His hand brushed against a lit candle, and he smelled burnt flesh, felt a searing pain lance up from the palm of his hand. He cried out in agony—

And found the cry still on his lips as he sat up in bed, head throbbing with the sight of that other place.

Then like a sudden tide there came the other pain, spiraling up from his palm, and the smell of singed flesh. Trembling, hardly even aware now of the nurses knocking at the door, drawn by his cry, he switched on the bedside lamp.

A black smear, like soot, marked the burn that was already blistering in his palm.

"Dear God," Roger whispered, "dear sweet God."

Bright sunlight flooded the dining room, accompanied by the clatter of dishes and the chatter of voices, and Roger wondered why, why on *earth* they all seemed incapable of eating their breakfasts quietly. Couldn't they see he hadn't slept? Couldn't they see he was dying inside?

No, he thought. They couldn't. Which, on balance, was probably all for the best.

He shifted the fork to his left hand, the one that wasn't bandaged.

He was right-handed, but could only bear the discomfort of holding the fork for a few minutes in that hand before turning it over.

He looked up as a nurse stepped up to his table. "How's the hand?"

"Better."

She nodded. "Good. And I'm sure we won't have a problem like that in the future, but I did want to remind you again that we have very strict policies concerning smoking in bed."

Roger put down his fork, letting it clatter loudly on his plate. "If you'll read your chart you'll see I don't smoke. It just—it was an accident, all right? Now, is there some other rule I should be aware of?"

Her expression didn't so much as flicker. "No, Mr. Leeds, that will be quite sufficient. As long as you *are* aware of our policies. I'll check on the dressing later."

She walked away. Roger watched her as she stepped out of the dining room just as another nurse wheeled in Laurel.

He went back to his eggs, hoping the nurse would continue to wheel her through the dining room and out onto the patio behind the house, hoping that perhaps she had already been fed, hoping not to have to look into those vacant eyes one more time.

The patio door rattled shut behind him. She was gone. He let out a long, slow breath, and realized that his hands were trembling.

"Roger! Have you been outside yet?" Frank came over to his table, rubbing his hands and looking flushed. "It's glorious. After breakfast, what do you say we go for a walk, get a little sun, hmm? You know you're awfully pale these days, you could use some sun."

Roger tried to wave him away. "No, I—"

"Say, what happened to your hand?"

Roger tried to tuck it away, under the table. "Nothing."

"Oh, no. Nothing I can't see. *This* I can see. Therefore this is something. I've been reading Socrates again. You can tell, can't you?"

Roger slammed his fist into the table, bolted up out of his chair. "Jesus, Frank—can't you ever *shut up*?"

He charged past Frank, not knowing, not caring where he was going until he realized he was outside.

Where she was. Sitting in her chair in the shade of a eucalyptus tree, next to the shuffleboard court. Not moving. Staring, but not seeing.

He started to turn away, to go back inside, but stopped at the memory of his outburst. Frank would be hurt. He'd find a way to make it up, later, but now was not the right time. He looked back at Laurel, and hesitated.

I've got to do something, he thought, *anything, or I'm going to go mad.*

Pulling his feet as though they were held in concrete, he forced himself to walk across the patio and sit in the chair facing her. He looked into her vacant eyes, and for a moment said nothing, not knowing how to begin.

How else? he thought.

"Hello. My name—my name's Roger. I think we've met."

Nothing.

"I don't mean to bother you, but it's just that—I'd like some answers. I need to know... am I losing my mind? That *is* you, isn't it? In my dreams. Even before you got here, even before I saw you—you were there, weren't you?"

Nothing.

"Look, you must be able to hear me. You picked me—called me—somehow. What I can't figure is, why me? They tell me you haven't talked to anyone since your husband died. So what do you want from *me*? You want me to protect you from that—thing behind the door, whatever it is? Is that it? Because if it is, then you'll have to find someone else. There's nothing I can do for you, Mrs. Kincaid. I can't protect you. Hell, I couldn't even protect my own wife, when she—"

Oh God, he thought, and stopped. The familiar pain lanced through his heart. He stood, walked around the chair, trying to throw it off, trying not to deal with it. He couldn't deal with it, not yet. Better to remember the other moments.

"She was a good woman. Kind, decent—she took in every stray cat on the block. You would've liked her. Hell, everyone did. And Sundays, when the kids would come over—"

The kids.

How long had it been?

His mind turned away again, but this time there was nothing else to focus on, nothing but the one thing he wanted most to avoid. He sat back in the chair, suddenly feeling old, so very old. It still hurt. God, how it hurt.

He began slowly.

"Toward the end, she started to—we were in the hospital, and she could barely see, and oh God, she was in such pain, and she kept calling out for me, and I was right there but she couldn't *see* me and she kept pleading with me, please, God, stop the pain, help me, calling my name over and over, and *I couldn't do anything*! I just—held her hand and I said I wouldn't let go. Just like she did. But then I felt her hand tighten once, on mine—and that was all.

"God help me, I'm still not sure she even knew I was there."

He reached for a handkerchief to wipe at his face. The woman opposite him was unmoved. She stared ahead as though he weren't even there.

Just like Rachel, he thought, and his cheeks flushed hotly. This wasn't fair. This wasn't right. Why was she *doing* this to him?

To hell with her, he thought, with a flash of anger. To hell with her for making him feel that pain all over again, feel this useless and old and impotent.

"Mrs. Kincaid, that thing, behind the door, whoever, whatever it is—it's going to come through soon, isn't it? Look, I don't know what you're afraid of, but it's not my problem. I just want everyone to leave me alone. Get out of my head! *Leave me alone!*"

He stood, knocking the chair backward, and fled from the patio, away from those terrible, vacant eyes, not looking back, but knowing she was still staring, staring, staring....

Leave me alone!

The television was no help.

Roger stared at the screen through slitted lids. He'd found the old black-and-white in his closet and had propped it up on the dresser, where he could watch it from his bed. Carson had come and gone, as had the repeat broadcast of the local news. He'd switched around until finally finding an old Rock Hudson movie whose name he couldn't remember, and he felt too tired to get up and check the *TV Guide*.

He rubbed at his face, trying to keep alert. Somehow watching the flickering grey and white and black images seemed to make his eyes even more tired. Since it was so late, he had to keep the volume down, reducing the dialogue to a soft murmur that soothed more than awakened.

I won't go to sleep, he thought, *I won't*. Everything inside him said that tonight was the night when all hell was going to break out with Laurel, and he was determined not to be a part of it.

He palmed his eyes. They were dry and sore. Just a little longer. Just until daylight. Then he'd be safe. The nurses would come to wake her, and he'd get his sleep then, pleading a cold or bug of some sort or other. The television murmured somewhere far away, outside his closed eyes. Just a little longer—

—and it was cold, and dark, and she was there, screaming at him, "Help me! You've got to help me! If he gets through I'll die! You've got to—"

Roger jerked upright in bed, heart slamming against his ribcage. He'd dropped off. Just for a moment, but it had been enough for her to drag him into her dream. He sat up, letting his feet find the floor. He couldn't risk it happening again.

He found his slippers and robe and stepped out into the hall. The place was quiet. Hoping not to be discovered by the nurses, he made his way downstairs to the kitchen. He chose a clean pan instead of the tea kettle. Less noise.

While the water heated, he spooned out a double dose of instant coffee into a big mug. Warmed his hands over the heating coils. Rubbing his arms to spread the warmth, he wandered into the sitting room. There, across the room, was his favorite chair, and beside it, Frank's chair.

I never knew how much I needed her until she was gone.

The words seemed to linger in the cool night air. He could almost see Frank in his usual place, looking at Roger as he had earlier, full of sadness.

And it was nothing compared to his own.

She kept calling my name over and over, and I couldn't do anything!

There are times I'm afraid, Frank. And I think of her, and I'm ashamed. Ashamed of what she'd think of me.

What indeed? he thought. *What indeed?*

Behind him, from the kitchen, he could hear the water coming to a boil. He padded back to the stove and stared into the churning water for a moment before turning off the heat.

I couldn't do anything!

Not then. No, not then.

He picked up the pan and emptied the water into the sink, returning it to its usual place before switching off the light and heading back up the stairs.

Rachel would want him to do it, he thought, as he closed the door to his room. To try, at least, as he hadn't been able to try for her.

God help me, he thought, then lay down and closed his eyes.

The wind screamed all around him. It clawed at him like a living thing, and she was there, in the middle of it all, clutching at his sleeve, her face desperate, frightened.

"Help me—please—you've got to *do* something!"

Then the light.

And the door.

And the pounding.

Wood splintered, the door bounced frenziedly back and forth on the chain-lock, and over it all, over the noise and the wind, there was her terrified voice.

"Please!"

And the photographs. Everywhere. He could see them in more detail now than before. Some were of Laurel with another man, and some of the man alone. A familiar face.

"You've got to stop him! Please! If he gets through, I'll die! Don't you understand? I'll *die!*"

He charged the door and slammed into it, bracing it with his shoulder. He pushed, pushed for all he was worth, pushed for Rachel and the memory of his helplessness. He shoved with everything he had, and the door went back only the barest fraction of an inch. The pounding now was so loud he thought it would deafen him. He could feel it, feel him, on the other side, pounding the door with cannonball force.

He looked back over his shoulder at Laurel, who hung back, watching through wide eyes. "Help me! Give me a hand!"

Laurel shook her head, stepped back a pace. "I—I can't! Please, you've got to hurry! He's getting through!"

He pushed.

The door pushed back.

The photographs on the wall bounced and swayed with each impact.

Whatever it was, it was powerful. And determined.

"What is it?" he cried back to her. "What's behind here?"

She said nothing. Only watched, as silent as if she were in her wheelchair.

She hasn't talked to anyone since her husband died, Frank had said.

The words reverberated outside his head as well as within. She glanced around furtively, frightened. Could she hear them as well?

The pounding grew louder.

Then his own words, caught in the wind and whirled around him. *You haven't talked to anyone since your husband died.*

She clamped her hands to her ears, closed her eyes. "Shut up!" she cried. "Shut up! SHUT UP!"

He looked back at her, and his grip on the door loosened.

The candles.

The photographs.

The door.

Dear Lord, he thought.

"My God," he said. "You're not keeping someone out, are you? You're—you're *keeping someone in!*"

The wind and sound reached deafening proportions. The pounding at the door became one prolonged hammering.

She looked at him, and Roger thought that he had never seen anything, or anyone, more pitiable. "Please," she said, her voice small and frightened, "if he gets through...I'll die!"

"Then pray I'm doing the right thing," Roger said—and let go of the door. He staggered back, seized one of the brass candlesticks, and brought it crashing down on the chain-lock.

"No!" she cried out. "*Nooooooo!*"

It was suddenly the only sound in the room.

The door stood open. For a moment, there was only a brilliant light, then a form appeared in the doorway, silhouetted against the light.

The man in the photographs.

Without looking at Roger, he stepped across to where Laurel turned away and sat on the bed, not meeting his gaze. He sat beside her. "Laurel—"

"No," she said, her voice tight with pain.

"It's time for me to go."

"No, you can't go. Please—"

"It's been long enough. Too long. You have to let me go. This isn't even me anymore—it's just a shadow, a memory."

"I can't live without you. If you go, I'll die."

"No, Laurel, listen to me. I love you. I want you to go on, I *need* you to go on, so that my life will have meant something. Live, Laurel, for me, for the kids, for what we had, forty beautiful years."

"No," she moaned, but the protest was gone from her voice, leaving only resignation and weariness. She leaned forward, laying her head on his shoulder.

He brushed her hair away from her face. "You were always so strong, you were always there for me. Now I need for you to be strong for me one last time."

She sobbed something into his shoulder, and Roger could see her pain reflected in his eyes. "It's all right," he said, holding her. "It'll be all right. But I need—I need you to let me go, Laurel. Live. Please."

She said nothing for a moment, then sat back a little, still refusing to look into his eyes. "How can I let you go," she said, her lips trembling, "when you never even said good-bye?" She tried to smile, just a little, for him—but it faded as she finally met his gaze.

He ran the back of his fingers along her cheek. "Good-bye, Laurel, my true, my greatest love."

Then he stood, touched her hair, and started to walk away, toward the darkness just beyond her room. Roger took a step toward him, but stopped. Where he was going, Roger couldn't follow.

"It was you who called me here," Roger said, "not her, wasn't it?" The figure nodded without looking back at him. "Why? Why me?"

He looked back, just once. "I think you know."

Then he continued on toward the darkness, which seemed to stretch out before him, the room becoming elastic, as though it were leaving him more than he was leaving it. Then, gradually, the candles went out, one by one. The last thing Roger saw was Laurel sitting alone on the bed, face turned to catch one final glimpse of the figure before it vanished at last.

Alone, so terribly alone.

And then nothing...only the faint traces of predawn glow that seeped into his room.

It took Roger a moment to realize that he was crying.

The dining room was its usual flurry of noise, the smell of eggs and bacon filtering out into the hall. Roger searched for Frank in the line of others waiting at the buffet. He straightened his collar. It had been a long time since he'd last worn a suit.

"Frank," he said, spotting his quarry at the bacon bin, "have you seen Laurel?"

"Hey, look at you!" Frank said. "Nice suit, Roger."

"Frank—"

Frank gestured with a slice of burnt bacon. "She's out back, I think."

"Thanks." He headed for the patio door.

"No problem," Frank called after him. "By the way, we're having a poker game tonight at seven, I'll hold a place for you!"

Roger didn't answer. Later, there would be time. Just before he stepped out the door, he heard one of the boarders turn to Frank. "Why bother? You know he never comes."

"Ah, eat your corn flakes," Frank said.

Roger smiled, and let the door clatter shut behind him, searching for the familiar wheelchair.

He found it, and for a moment, his heart sank within him. She sat in her usual place, staring without seeing toward the shuffleboard courts, hands folded together in her lap.

He crossed the patio, and sat down in the chair opposite her, searching her face for some clue that what he'd seen and heard the night before had been more than just a dream. But he saw nothing in her eyes but his own reflection.

"Hello," he said at last.

No response.

"I know you're there. I know you can hear me. And I can wait." He folded his arms and sat back in the chair. "I can wait as long as I have to."

For a moment, there was nothing. Then, slowly, her gaze tracked up from the ground, pausing just a moment at his bandaged hand, then slowly fixing on him, as though it took an effort to focus on anything outside her own thoughts. She licked her lips, and when she spoke, it was little more than a whisper.

"You've burned your hand."

Roger sat forward, glanced at the bandage. "Yes."

"On a—candle."

"Yes."

She met his gaze. "I'm sorry."

He was about to respond when the breakfast bell chimed from inside the kitchen. He smiled across at her. "Last call for breakfast. Would you like something to eat?"

She hesitated a moment and then smiled. It was faint, and small, but Roger thought he had never seen anything more glorious. "Breakfast—would be very nice, I think."

Rubbing his hands, Roger stood up and went behind the wheelchair, pushing it toward the patio door. "An excellent decision. Now let's see—we've got bacon, we've got eggs, and toast, and marmalade—I mean, *jam* and *jelly*—and we've got hash browns, but I wouldn't go near them if I were you—and I hear there's a poker game every day at seven...."

He opened the door and helped maneuver her through. It was going to be a good day, he decided, a very good day indeed.

RENDEZVOUS IN A DARK PLACE

The chapel was small and simple, but filled with flowers and people and the subdued sound of an organ playing somewhere discreetly out of sight. Daylight filtered in through the stained glass windows, throwing patterns of shifting color on the polished surface of the coffin.

The service concluded, they filed past the coffin one at a time, making their silent farewells and then moving on. Some ran their hands along the sleek wood, as though trying to reach through the cool surface for one last embrace. Some could not bring themselves to touch the coffin, but their desperate and solemn love was no less apparent.

Barbara LeMay, at the end of the line, lingered beside the coffin when her time came at last. She ran her gloved hand just over the surface of the coffin, barely an inch from the dark and polished oak. She closed her eyes, and when she opened them again she gazed down at the face that reposed within, her own calm reflecting the quiet tranquility she saw there.

A voice came from beside her. "A great loss."

She turned to find the reverend standing at her elbow, then let her gaze return to the coffin. "Yes, it is."

"Were you a relative?"

"Hmm?" she answered distractedly. "Oh. No, not at all."

"A friend of the family, then?"

She turned to him again, her hand leaving the coffin only reluctantly, as she might release the hand of a lover. "No, I'm afraid not. Actually, I don't know anyone here. They're all strangers to me."

She smiled at him, and rested a gloved hand on his arm. "But it was still a lovely service, Reverend. A very lovely service."

She squeezed his arm gently, then moved past him, to where the others were gathering for the reception. She glanced back just once, burning the scene into her memory.

It was perfect. So terribly, terribly perfect.

Jason LeMay pulled the three heavy grocery sacks out of his rented car and duck walked up the sidewalk, trying desperately not to break anything else. He fumbled with the key to his mother's house only to find it unlocked, as usual, and despite his repeated warnings.

He pushed through, kicking the door closed before slumping against it. Why was food so heavy? Why was the kitchen always twice as far from the front door whenever he was carrying something heavy? Why was it always so dark in here? And where was his mother?

"Mom?"

From somewhere upstairs she called back. "I'm changing. I'll be right down. Put them in the kitchen."

"Right." His left hand was getting numb where it clutched the third sack, which supported the second sack, which was balanced up against the first sack, which he now noticed was torn along one side. *I'll never make it*, he thought, but charged ahead toward the kitchen anyway.

To his surprise, he made it with the bags intact.

Mostly.

When he stepped back into the living room, his arms numb, she was coming down the stairs. As usual, she was dressed in a black dress and black shoes. The light in the room was subdued, contained safely behind thick curtains hung at the front window.

"I fear I must report your dozen eggs have just turned magically into ten." He flexed his arms, feeling the blood gradually starting to return. "I think gravity had something to do with it."

"You look exhausted, Jason," she said. "Go and sit down. I'll unpack."

"An excellent idea," he said, and walked across the room, toward the overstuffed sofa that was the room's centerpiece.

"Thank you for going for me," she called back. "It's been such a busy day."

"No problem." Before collapsing on the couch, he glanced again at the curtained windows. It was dark as a cave in here. A brief search revealed the drawcord. He opened it, letting in the daylight. It filled the room, warming him immediately.

"Would you like something to eat, Jason? You must be starved."

"I'd love something," he called, and sat heavily on the couch. It was remarkable how different the place looked when fully lit. Sunlight glinted off tiny porcelain figures and plates behind glass cabinets, and chased shadows out of the corners where they had claimed homesteaders' rights.

Barbara emerged from the kitchen carrying a tray loaded with a glass of milk and a plate covered with finger sandwiches. "Here you go, dear."

"Thanks."

She circled around the couch, heading back the way she came. As he leaned forward to take one of the sandwiches, the sunlight went away. Darkness descended on the room, and the eager shadows rushed back to reclaim their territory. He glanced back over his shoulder. She had closed the curtains again on her way out.

He briefly considered getting up and opening them again, but he was too tired, she was too determined, and he was hungry. He took a bite, then another. "These are good, Mom."

"Thank you," she called from the kitchen.

"So what did you do today? You said you were busy."

He could catch an occasional glimpse of her in the kitchen, putting away the groceries as she spoke. "Well, first I went by to pay my respects to your father. We have to talk to the grounds keeper again. I found some paper wrappers in the grass. People should be more careful of these things."

"I'll talk to him," he said, then added, more quietly, "again."

She swept back into the room, carrying a carefully folded napkin. "Then on the way in, I stopped off at Forestview. They were having a lovely service."

Not again, Jason thought, and swallowed the last of the sandwich. "Mom, Forestview is at the other end of town. You'd have to go clear around the world for Forestview to be on the way in."

She looked at him in that way of hers that said she wasn't

listening. "You're spilling crumbs," she said, and handed him the napkin before heading back into the kitchen.

"As I was saying," she continued, "it was a lovely service. I suppose there must have been a hundred, maybe a hundred and fifty people there. There was a reception afterward. They served the most wonderful finger sandwiches."

Jason stopped in midbite. Looked at the finger sandwich in his hand. *Couldn't be*, he thought. But he put the sandwich down anyway, glancing up as she came back into the room and sat in the chair opposite him. "So who was the service for? I hadn't heard of anyone we know dying."

"I don't know," she said. "Well, I mean, I heard his name a few times, but you know how I am on names."

"You don't—" He took a moment to compose himself. "Mom, I thought we'd settled this a long time ago. You've got to stop going to funerals for people you don't even know."

"Why?"

"Well, it's—*wrong*, that's all."

"They had white roses," she said. "You should have seen them. White roses, tied with tiny red ribbons. Silk, I think they were. One for each year. They had them arranged in this tall vase—I believe it was carnival glass—so that they were lit from behind by the sun. I don't think I've ever seen anything so beautiful. And there was music, and there were such words spoken, such love, such peace in that place."

Her eyes were distant, her thoughts inward. There was a slight, wistful smile on her face as she thought about it. "When I go, I think I would very much like something like that. Would you see to it, dear?"

"Mom—"

"I believe there's a vase in the attic that would be just perfect."

"Mom, will you stop it? You know I don't like to hear you talk like that."

"I know you don't. But we have to be prepared for these things."

"Prepared? Mom, they didn't prepare as much as this for the Allied invasion of Normandy Beach. Besides, I talked to your doctor last week. He says you're healthy as an ox."

She nodded absently. "Did I tell you about Mrs. Rosenbloom? They told her the same thing. Last week, she went to bed and didn't wake up. I think they said it was an aneurysm. These things happen, Jason. We hate to think about them, but—"

"No. That's where we part company, Mom. You *don't* hate to think about them. You *love* to think about them." He stood up, pacing behind the sofa. "Why is it every time I see you, every other word is death? When I invited you out to the Coast to see Margie and the kids, you couldn't. Because you said you couldn't make any long-term plans. How the hell am I supposed to explain that to the kids? 'I'm sorry, Gramma can't come for Thanksgiving because she can't make reservations because she doesn't know if she'll be alive or not?' You hurt them."

She looked down at her hands. They were so white, almost translucent. "I'm sorry. Really, I am."

"I know. I just wish you'd stop all this. Wear something other than black. Get outside once in a while for something other than somebody's funeral. Let some light in here."

He threw open the curtain again. She winced at the sudden flash of daylight, but didn't move to stop him. "This *obsession* of yours, it's not good. It's not healthy. It's morbid. I love you. And I want you to see your grandkids grow up."

"I'll try. Really I will."

"What's to *try*, Mom? You just—" He stopped as his watch beeped at him. He switched it off and looked across at her as she stood up and approached him. "Damn. I have to go, Mom. Plane to catch."

"Then go," she said, and touched his face. "And give my best to Margie and to Ben and Susan. I'll be fine. Really."

"All right. I just hate the idea of you living out here in the boondocks. I want you to promise you'll keep the doors locked around here, okay? It makes me feel a little better."

"I will."

"I didn't mean to yell," he said, and studied her face for a moment, then kissed her cheek. "I'll give you a call as soon as I get in. See you in a few weeks, Mom."

"Good-bye, Jason."

She always said good-bye, he thought as he stepped out into the cool afternoon air. Never *see you*, or *until later*. Only *good-bye*.

Let it go, he thought, and climbed into the rented car to begin the long drive back to the airport.

Halfway there, he thought back, and couldn't remember if he'd heard her lock the front door or not.

Barbara awoke suddenly to the sound of thunder though she knew it was not the thunder that had awakened her. She sat up on one elbow, peering into the night that filled her bedroom, listening for the other sound that still echoed in her ears. After a moment, it came again—a creak of floorboards, and a muffled drag *thump* from downstairs.

She slid out of bed, finding her slippers and robe on the dresser nearby, and felt her way out of the room to the hall. It was dark downstairs, and she could feel draft even through her heavy robe.

"Hello?" she said. Silence. She flicked on the light switch at the top of the stairs. Down below, the door was open, a brisk, wet wind ruffling the curtains beside it. Water was pooling on the floor. She edged down the stairs, eyes watchful, until she reached the door and closed it. She reached for the living room lights—

"Don't—don't try it."

She turned, slowly, to the source of the voice. A young man stood in the middle of the room. He braced himself against the sofa, one arm hanging limp at his side. Even from here, in the dim light from the stain well, she could see a dark smear of blood on his shirt. There was a gun in his other hand. He was drenched from the storm, shivering, and in pain.

"All right, lady, don't—don't move, don't call the cops, or," he squinted against the pain, which shivered through his body, "or I swear, I'll kill you, I swear, I'll—

He never finished the sentence. He swayed, then fell, unconscious, to the floor.

Barbara went to him and gently put a hand on his chest. His breath was ragged, shallow, and when she pulled back her hand it came away covered with blood.

He's dying, she thought, and with that thought came another: *He'll come. He'll come here, tonight.*

In spite of herself, she tried to call an ambulance but when she picked up the receiver she got only static. The storm had knocked out the lines, as they sometimes did. But at least the radio worked, and she turned it to local news station.

Not wanting to risk moving him up onto the couch, she found a blanket and covered him where he lay on the floor, hoping it would keep the cold away. She grabbed one of the pillows from the couch and set it under his head as gently as she could. A first-aid kit in the closet let her bandage up as much of the wound as she could, but it was bad, and deep, and without doubt fatal. This done, she moved around the room, turning on only a few lights here and there, just enough to see by, never taking her eyes off the young man on the floor. She didn't dare look away. In that moment, she might miss it. Miss him.

She started back when she heard the young man stir. She went to him, knelt down beside him as his eyes fluttered open. For a moment they seemed unable to focus on anything, then they finally found her. He licked his lips, managed, "Who—"

"Shhh," she said. "Don't try to talk. I did what I could, but it's—bad, I think. Very bad. I tried to call the hospital, but the lines are down. It happens sometimes in a big storm. I could try again."

He shook his head. "No. Don't want t'die—in no hospital."

"I didn't say you were dying."

His eyes met hers. "Yes, you did," he said, and glanced away. "Knew it soon's they shot me. Funny, ain't it, how you just—know—"

He stopped as a spasm of pain shot through him. He bit his lip, barely holding on to consciousness. When he opened his eyes again, it took him longer to focus on her. "I *am* dying, ain't I? Just—tell me straight, okay? Nobody—ever tells you nothing straight."

She hesitated just a moment, then nodded. "I'm—I'm not an expert, but—yes, I think you're dying."

He let his gaze linger on her, and she thought she saw a light go out behind them with her statement, as though in spite of everything he had been holding out some small hope that she would say otherwise. With the pronouncement, he let his head loll to one side, away from her.

"While you were unconscious," she said, "I turned on the radio. It mentioned a robbery. Some all-night liquor store."

"Twenty-seven dollars and change," he said. "Ain't that something." He licked his lips again. They were dry, parched.

"I'll get you some water," she said, and started to rise.

But he grabbed for her, getting only air. "Wait—don't go."

She sat back down, resting a hand on his chest. He was cool to her touch, and seemed to take some comfort from the warmth of contact. "Don't worry. I won't leave you alone. I understand. Perhaps better than you know. I'll wait with you. We'll both wait together."

He nodded, his eyes closed, and then went away again.

Barbara did not move.

She would wait with him, as she had promised.

It was half an hour later when she felt the room suddenly go cold around her. At the same moment, the young man's breathing became shallower and less frequent. A breeze brushed the back of her neck, and she turned to see the curtains rustling even though the windows were closed.

She sat up, straining to see in the half light, listening for the slightest sound. A curious hush descended on the room. The sound of the clock ticking on the wall grew muffled, as though wrapped in cloth.

Something had changed in the room.

She was sure of it.

"It's you, isn't it?" she said to the night, her voice low and carefully calm. "You're here, aren't you?"

At first, there was no response. Then something separated from the shadows, a lightless shape deeper than the surrounding night. Its face was obscured eclipsed by darkness.

"I...am here," he said.

She stood, moving slowly, not wanting to startle him, if that were possible. "Are you surprised?" she asked. "That I can see you?"

"No."

"No, I guess you wouldn't be. We've spent so much time together, you and I. I guess it makes one a little more sensitive than most."

"Yes."

"I was in the hospital once, and the woman in the room next to me died in the night. When it happened, I–*felt* you nearby. I thought, at the time, that it was a dream. But it wasn't."

A sound from the floor distracted her. The young man forced open his eyes, and tried to focus on her, this time failing in the attempt. "Who–who you talkin' to?"

She knelt down beside him. "No one. No one at all. It's all right."

He nodded distantly. "...'s cold in here."

She pulled the blanket tighter around him, then stood. "He can't see you."

The darkness before her seemed momentarily to shiver, then reappeared across the room, nearer to the young man. "For him–I will not exist–until his time."

"Where do you take them? To a better place?"

"Sometimes."

"It must be beautiful."

"It is a place, like any other." With that he knelt down–no, she corrected herself, seemed to flow downward–toward the young man.

"Wait," she said.

He did.

"Why don't you take me–instead of him?"

"What is he to you?"

"No one," she said. "Nothing. But he does not see the beauty in you. I do. I've seen it in a million ways. Peace. Freedom. Tranquility. The poignant, fragile beauty of that one final exhalation, the gathering of the soul, the ceremony, and so much more."

"It is his time."

"But he can't appreciate you, as I can. I have no one here, not really. Not since–"

The shimmer again, and now he appeared at the other end of the room. When he spoke, it was in a voice colder than she had ever heard. "No," he said.

"But why? I thought such things were possible."

46

"I cannot take life—where there is none to take."

He moved slowly, flowing through the room, and though she could not see his eyes, she could feel them on her nonetheless. "I have seen you in so many places," he said, calling to her from the shadows. "You have called my name so many times. You have worshipped at my altar, walked in my shadow, seen my reflection in the faces of others, and still it is not enough. You do not run from my touch, you seek to embrace it—and yet I cannot take you more than I can take this table...for neither of you lives."

"I—don't understand."

He flowed toward the young man, and paused, letting the shadow of his hand fall across the face below. For a moment, the shadow seemed to oppress the young man, but then he fought back, struggling against the touch that had not yet come.

The darkness flowed back a little, but only a little. "You see how he resists me, even in sleep? He cherishes life, even in pain. He clings to each second for in each second is the possibility of joy, however often defeated. Even now, this close to me, he is more alive than you."

"I have become the totality of your existence. Your days and nights are full of the thought of me and nothing else. You have made death a lifestyle—and I only come for the living."

And then he did.

He knelt beside the young man and suspended his hand an inch above the sweating, frightened face. "I bring you peace and sleep," he said. "Do not be afraid, for I alone of all will never leave you."

For just the barest moment, the young man's eyes met his, and in that flicker of recognition Barbara saw no fear. There was only peace and resolution, and then the eyes closed one last time, never again to open.

She went to the young man and touched his wrist. No pulse beat beneath the skin.

When she glanced up again, *he* was gone.

"You can't do this," she said, distantly aware that she was crying. "Please, you can't just leave me. We've spent so much time together—it would be rude."

Silence.

"*What do you want me to do?* Go feed the pigeons in the park? Is that living? I don't have anyone else, don't you understand? My son doesn't need me anymore. Everyone I knew is gone. They're with you. *You took them away from me and now you won't even take me!* What, am I not good enough? Not pretty enough? Is that it?"

The cold in the room began to fade. She grew aware of sounds returning, the night wind outside beating against the house. Her hands flew to her face, and she glanced around frantically, vainly searching the shadows for the darkness that was no longer there. "I'm—I'm sorry I yelled. Please, just stay with me a moment, that's all. Just—a moment."

But the night did not respond, and she was alone.

Barbara watched impassively as the two uniformed officers rolled the stretcher out the front door, only marginally listening to the sergeant sitting beside her on the couch.

He touched the young man. But not me. He would not touch me. He would not touch me.

She looked over at the officer, wondering vaguely what he was talking about, why he was still here. "I have to give you credit for a lot of courage, Mrs. LeMay," he was saying. "Dead phone or not, I think most folks would've been out the door in a second as soon as he fell."

She shrugged. "He was harmless. And he was in pain."

"No, not anymore. That's what they say, isn't it—the only two constants being death and taxes."

She smiled, and in smiling thought her face might crack in two. "Not always," she said. "He didn't touch me. Not once."

The officer studied her for a long moment before closing his report book and standing up. "You sure you'll be all right, ma'am? Maybe you should have a friend come over—"

"I'll be fine, officer. Thank you."

Though he looked unsure (*he doesn't understand, no, but then none of them would, not in a million years*), he nodded and headed for the door, reminding her to call if she had any further questions or recollections.

Then she closed the door, and the silence that had been waiting eagerly in the shadows crept out to reclaim its dominion.

Jason was carefully solicitous on the phone. She put his fears to rest, she was perfectly all right, no, nothing was stolen, and she didn't want to bother him with it, knowing how busy he was. And of course there was no need for him to fly out again, plane fare was so expensive these days. Yes, she would be more careful about locking the door. She would talk to him tomorrow.

"Good-b—" she started, and then caught herself. "Good night, Jason," she said, and set the receiver back in its cradle.

She would be fine. Just...fine, she thought.

And continued crying.

She emerged from the bedroom, wearing a lie. She went to the mirror to inspect it. The dress was green, and there were flecks of silver sown through the fabric, and it seemed so loud, so out of place. Walking stiffly, as though in costume, she went to the closet and found the box of makeup. The tints and powders were dry from lack of use. She had to moisten them with water from the sink to use them.

She tried the mascara and the rouge and the powder, and now the lie was on her face, and the more she applied the greater the lie became, and it was laughable, and it was pathetic, and she looked like some dime-store mannequin, and her mascara was streaking with tears, the tears she vowed would not come again, and she picked up the box and threw it on the floor, scattering colors and pigments into their component untruths.

She sat on the floor for a long time, crying, before she remembered the medicine cabinet.

The pills were easy enough to find. The date on the prescription wrapper had expired, but that hardly mattered, did it?

Not in the least, she decided, and shut the door.

Barbara sat alone in the living room, watching television with the sound down. Somehow it was better that way. The bottle of pills, still unopened, sat on the table in front of her.

She was sitting in just that same position when—was it hours or only minutes later? she wondered idly—the room grew chill around her, and the image flickering across the television seemed to recede into darkness.

And his voice came to her from the shadows. "I have hurt you."

"No." A lie. "Yes."

From another corner of the room. "It was not—my intention."

"No, it never is."

"How have I hurt you?"

"I've been asking myself the same question a lot, these last few days," she said. "It just seems as though, one by one, everyone I knew went...away. They went with you. I suppose, in my way, I got jealous. You took them away, and if I couldn't have them, then I wanted you too. So I started finding out everything I could. About you." She searched the shadows, and for a moment thought she glimpsed movement. "And I began to see why they went with you."

"It was their time."

"Was it?" she asked, and then nodded. "Yes, perhaps it was. But there was more to it than that. I saw it in their faces, after they had seen you. No more pain, no more weariness, no sadness or loss. Only peace. I saw a gift beyond any I could ever hope to offer. I went to hospitals, and I heard the cries of people in pain, people who were crying out for help, crying out—for you. In the end, you're all we have, aren't you?"

He did not answer, and she felt him now in the darkness behind her, moving slowly, so slowly. "My husband always did everything he could to make me happy," she said. "I loved him for that, but I suppose I would have loved him regardless. Then, at the end, he was in such pain, and I could not do the same for him, couldn't make the pain go away. You did that. For him. And for me."

A whisper of movement, a nod in the shadows. "I remember."

"I was so glad for him, so glad that it was finally over, that I—I believe it was then that I began to fall in love with you."

"It is not permitted."

"No, I suspected as much." She glanced at the bottle on the coffee table. "After you left, I—well, there were quite a lot of pain pills in the cabinet, left over from some back problems a while ago. I thought about taking all of them. Whatever you say, even you can't stop me from making it my time, can you?"

Silence.

"I thought as much. But I just couldn't do it. I tell myself that perhaps it would be too—forward. But the truth is that I'm too much of a coward, even for that. It would seem I'm not even very good at dying, am I?"

She looked down at her hands, and the wetness on her cheeks told her that she had again broken her promise to herself. She rubbed it off with the back of her hand, noting as she looked up again that the darkness had drawn closer, and was in front of her now, near enough almost to touch.

His voice was soft and low. "There is a thing I have heard said among the living. There are always—possibilities."

She gazed up at him, trying to see a face through the shadows. "What kind of—possibilities?"

He moved slowly around her, circling her. "Do you love me?"

"Yes. I wasn't sure before, but—yes. To the heights and depths my soul can reach."

"Then there is—a way."

The darkness shifted and he held out a hand to her. She reached for it, but hesitated before touching his hand.

"Now, at the last, are you afraid of me?" he said.

"No," she said, and took his hand. It was warm to the touch. "I'm not afraid."

Then she looked up, and for the first time saw his face. He was beautiful.

He stepped away, holding her hand.

"Where are we going?" she said.

"Where we are most needed."

And then the world melted away from her.

There was light, all around her, and she was dimly aware of standing, though she could not feel the floor beneath her feet. The first thing she became aware of were the voices.

I'm afraid he doesn't have much time left. Cancer's eaten away virtually everything. Have you checked back with the front desk?

Yes, Doctor.

And there's still no next of kin?

They're still checking. Though it doesn't look like we'll find anyone before it's too late.

Gradually, the bone-bright white gave way to forms and movement. The doctor, shaking his head, moved away from the nurse, who stepped across the room to a bed covered with an oxygen tent Inside lay a man. She would have guessed he was in his sixties, but somehow she knew he was fifty-two. The cancer had gnawed away at him with terrible efficiency.

The nurse dabbed at his forehead. He was pale, frightened.

He licked his lips. "Is it—is it cold in here?"

"Yes, it is. It's colder in here than it should be. I'll have it checked." She started away from the bed.

He reached for her hand. "No—please, don't—don't leave me. It's all right."

The nurse smiled sadly and looked as though about to reply when the speaker in the ceiling buzzed sharply through the room. *Code Blue, Oncology Ward, Code Blue.*

Her face tightened, and she started to pull away. "I have to go."

"No, please—"

"I'll be right back, I promise."

She touched his hand briefly, then rushed across the room, reaching for her beeper.

"Wait," he called, almost inaudibly, but she was already gone. He closed his eyes, and his breath came in a long, low, ragged sigh. "I want—a drink of water," he said, softly. "Just a drink of water. Please, someone."

He looked up at a warm touch on his arm. "Here you are."

He took the offered paper cup, letting her steady his hand as he drank in small, careful sips.

"Better now?" Barbara said.

He nodded, and then his lower lip started to tremble. He turned his face away from her, so she would not see him cry. "I'm sorry," he said.

"Don't be."

"It's just—I'm afraid. And it hurts—oh, God, it just hurts too much."

"I know. It's all right. I'm here. I won't leave you."

He turned a little, and the tears on his face reflected the harsh light of the overhead fluorescents. She stroked his pale face, gently, soothingly. "I bring you peace and sleep. Do not be afraid, for I alone of all will never leave you."

He looked up into her eyes, and in that instant she knew that he believed.

Then she passed her hand over his face, and Barbara felt him leave, felt his presence pass through her on its way—elsewhere.

What had he said? *A place, like any other.* Perhaps, in time, when she had proven herself further, he would show her.

That would be nice, she thought.

She stepped away from the bed as the nearby monitors and screens started beeping and flashing and buzzing. Doctors and nurses came from down the hall, rushing past her without seeing her, their image in return already growing faint to her eyes, swallowed up into the light that seemed to come from every direction, caressing her, holding her, lifting her away from this place.

Then at last there was only the light, and him.

"Did I do well?" she asked.

He smiled and softly stroked her hair. "You did—fine."

Then he took her hand, and together they moved on through the white, to where they would again be most needed.

THE CALL

Norman Blair unlocked the front door of his apartment and shouldered past the door, careful not to drop the shopping bags or step on the cat or trip over something the cat might have left there as a greeting for him when he came back from the office.

He made it to the kitchen safely, and Catt blinked down at him from his perch atop the refrigerator. "Hi," Norman said. The cat looked at him as cats sometimes will when they're momentarily unsure who this person in their kitchen is, what he's doing here, and if there's food involved. Doubtful that it was worth the effort to find out, Catt yawned and closed his eyes.

Must've had a hard day, Norman decided, and began unpacking the groceries.

Norman jerked awake to the sound of applause. He rubbed sleepily at his eyes, squinting at the television, where the end credits of some sitcom or other were rolling past. The aluminum tray from his TV dinner was still on the coffee table, and he had forgotten to change out of his good shirt.

He glanced at the clock. A little past midnight. *Got to get to sleep*, he thought, and forced himself to stand and put away the debris from dinner. Letting the television drone on in the background, he cleared the sofa and pulled out the hidden bed, getting the pillows from their usual shelf in the linen closet.

He perked up a little at the sound of big band music coming from the television. Norman recognized it instantly as Glenn Miller's 'Sliphorn Jive'. A moment later, the music gave way to an announcer's voice. "Tommy Dorsey! Glenn Miller! Artie Shaw and Benny Goodman! Finally a collection of their biggest hits. Songs from the big band era, from 'Moonlight Serenade' to 'Pennsylvania 6-5000,' a gathering of the finest of swing by the finest performers. Only a limited number of these special-edition sets will be made available to the public, so call 727-4221 and order while supplies last. Operators are standing by twenty-four hours a day."

Norman scrambled frantically for a pencil and something to write on. He'd been a fan of big band music for years, ever since high school, when it was so far from fashionable that he had gotten strange looks even from the class nerds. The collection sounded perfect—just the sort of thing he could turn on and leave going in the background while he ate or read.

He found a pencil and quickly scribbled the number on the back of an envelope before dialing. He waited as the line connected, and he heard a ringing from the other end. It rang for a long time. *Must be getting a lot of orders*, he thought, and turned his attention back to the television, and the announcer.

"A special set for those who still remember," the announcer was saying, "or who want to discover for themselves some of the very best. Includes Harry James, Woody Herman, and Kay Kyser, and such classic hits as 'Begin the Beguine,' 'String of Pearls,' and 'I'm Getting Sentimental Over You.' For immediate service call 727-4221."

As the phone at the other end rang for the tenth time, Norman glanced down at the number he had scribbled down.

727-4212.

Oh, jeez, he thought, and pulled the phone away, about to hang up when there was a *click* on the other end of the line.

"Hello?" It was a woman's voice, small, tentative. *Must've been sleeping*, Norman thought.

"Uh, yeah, hi," Norman said. "I—um—I'm sorry, I think I dialed the wrong number."

"Excuse me?"

"I—listen, I'm really sorry, it's just a wrong number, and I probably woke you up—"

"No, it's—okay." She paused for just a moment, then continued, her voice a little firmer. "I was just sitting here and I heard the phone ring. For a minute I was afraid whoever was calling would hang up before I got here."

"Yeah, I know what you mean. I hate it when that happens. Really, um, annoying."

What a charming conversationalist you are, Norman, he thought. He always seemed to run out of steam two minutes into a conversation with a woman.

He was still trying to think of what to say next when her voice drifted across the line to him again. "What's your name?"

"Norman. Norman Blair."

"You have a—very nice voice."

She said it softly, sounding almost as shy as he felt. He lowered his eyes instinctively, even though there was no one's gaze to avoid. "Thank you. So do you. What's your name? I mean, if you don't mind my asking."

"Mary Ann."

"Mary Ann. It's a good name."*Just be casual*, he thought, *she doesn't seem in any hurry to get off thephone.*"Listen, would you like to talk a bit? If you're not busy or something."

"No," she said, "that would be nice."

For the first time that night, Norman smiled.

Norman's office was fifteen feet long by twelve feet wide, with one window at the far end (looking out onto another building across the breezeway), two identical desks, two identical lamps, two identical computers, running two identical accounts payable programs, and two identical filing cabinets. The only thing that was not identical to anything else was Norman's office mate, Richard Leeks.

"So where was I?" Norman said.

"Talking to some strange woman for an hour." When Richard spoke to him at all it was reluctantly, and almost always without looking at him. There were times Norman wondered if Richard was entirely aware of his existence. Today, though, Norman hardly noticed.

"An hour and a half," Norman corrected him. "That's the amazing thing about it. It wasn't like she was a stranger at all. It was—I don't know—*special*, somehow. I mean, she was a little nervous at first, but after a while she started talking, and I started talking, like we were old friends, and next thing I knew—"

"It was an hour and a half later."

"Exactly. She was friendly, and funny—God, I haven't had that much fun in ages. Now I can't decide what to do next. I mean, she said I could call her back tonight, after seven. I guess she works late. But I'd really like to meet her, I just don't know how."

With a look of long-suffering patience, Richard put down his pencil and turned in his swivel chair. "Norman, a year and two months we've been sharing this office. For a year and two months I've been able to come in here, and sit at my desk, and pretend that I was all by myself, because from *that* side of the room came only a blissful silence. I like silence. I have five kids. I'm sitting here with this terrific urge to give you five dollars and send you to the movies. Alone.

"Look," he said, and sighed, "you want my advice? Ask her out. Suggest lunch, dinner, ice cream, and a trip to the zoo, go crazy. Fact is, she wouldn't be spending that much time talking to somebody she didn't want to meet. Simple problem, simple solution. Yes?"

Norman considered it, nodded.

Richard smiled. "Good. Now, you're a nice man, Norman, but for the next hour, I would very much like to have no noise. It would make me a very happy man."

With that, Richard picked up his pencil and turned back to his figures. Norman swiveled around in his chair, once again facing the wall.

"Thank you," Norman said.

"That was a noise."

Norman checked his watch. Again. 6:59 P.M. He wasn't supposed to call until seven. He paced the room slowly, having worked out that each circuit, properly paced, was equal to one minute. It made the time go faster, and let him check the room for dust bunnies at the same time.

As he finished his circuit, he noticed Catt standing in the doorway to the kitchen looking at him in *that* way again. But now it was 7:01 P.M., and Catt could look at him as though he had three heads and feathers, for all he cared.

He picked up the phone, dialed. It rang five times, then six, before there was a *click* at the other end.

"Hello," she said.

Norman smiled. "Hi. It's me."

"I know."

When Norman looked up again, it was 10:30 P.M. He was sitting on the couch at one end, his arm running along the back of the sofa. Embarrassed, he realized that he was sitting as he would to make room for somebody else. He changed position and shifted the phone to his right ear; the left one was getting uncomfortably warm against the hard plastic.

"That's when I left Fayetteville for Los Angeles," he was saying, in answer to her question about his background. She'd recognized the faint Southern accent in his voice. Most folks didn't notice it. She did. "That was about a year after my brother died. Things just weren't the same anymore. I don't think my mother ever got over it. So I figured I'd come out here and try to find a job."

"You never did tell me exactly what you do."

"Nothing that would interest you. Just—work, you know how it is."

"No, really," she said, her voice sincere. "I'd love to hear. I have time."

Time, he thought, and glanced again at his watch. It had been over three hours. "Well, it's late, though, and I probably should let you go."

"All right," she said, and Norman thought her voice sounded genuinely regretful. "Just one more thing. I just want you to know, Norman—I really enjoyed our talk last night. And tonight. I wanted to thank you."

"Well, same here," Norman said. He took a deep breath. "In fact, I was thinking, and I was wondering if maybe you'd like to get together some time, maybe lunch or dinner, a movie—anything you want."

"Oh, Norman," she said, and he could hear rejection imminent in her voice.

"No rush," he said, talking quickly. "I mean anytime you want, it's okay."

"You're sweet, but...no, I really can't. We have so much fun just *talking*, why do we have to change it? I've been disappointed by people so often—can't we just leave it at this?"

Norman closed his eyes. *Damn.* It always happened like this. "Sure," he said, "I guess so."

"I've hurt you, haven't I?"

"No," he said, again too quickly. "Really, it's okay. Like I said, I just enjoy talking to you. If you want to leave it at that, it's all right with me. Honest."

There was a long pause from the other end. "Promise you'll call me tomorrow?"

"I promise."

Norman reached forward, picking up another folder from the pile on his desk. The chair squeaked. He sat back again to read it. The chair squeaked. He shook his foot as he read. The chair emitted a series of short, mouse-soft squeaks. He realized he didn't have the right file. The one he wanted was on the far end of the desk. He reached as far across as he could.

His chair SQUEAKED.

"All right, Norman," Richard said, exasperation in his voice. "Give."

"What?"

"Five days now, and you've been absolutely quiet. Not a word."

"I thought you liked it quiet."

"It's the *way* you're being quiet. It's a very *loud* kind of quiet, Norman, like sitting next to a tuning fork vibrating just on the edge of what you can hear. Makes my ears itch." He sighed, and it suddenly occurred to Norman that Richard talked to him in about the same way that Catt looked at him. "It's that woman on the telephone. She turned you down, right?"

Norman nodded.

"So big deal. It's just one person. So what?"

Norman struggled to find a reply, then finally opted for the truth. "Do you think it's possible to fall in love with someone over the telephone?"

Richard considered it. "No," he said, and returned to his computer.

Norman waited to see if anything else was forth-coming, then turned back to his work. His chair *squeaked.*

Twice.

"Okay," Richard said, "you win. I can see right now I'm not going to get any peace, so can I give you a piece of advice? You say you want to meet this woman, but you don't know who she is or where she lives. All you have is a phone number. Have I got it surrounded?"

"Yes."

"All right. You ever heard of reverse listings? You call the operator, you say you've got this number, you think it's the one you have to call, say it's an emergency or something, and you ask the operator to tell you who belongs to that number. Say anything you have to. Once you get the address, you cruise by her place and just sort of run into her by accident. After that, you're on your own. Okay? Can we have some quiet now?"

Norman nodded and turned back to his work, careful not to let the chair squeak beneath him. Then, remembering his manners, he started to swivel back—

"Don't say *thank you*, Norman," Richard said without looking up. "I don't think I could stand it."

It had taken him most of his lunch hour to find the address, and now that he had arrived, Norman still wasn't sure this was the right place. He looked at the address on the side of the building, at the address on the paper in his hand, and back at the wall again. They matched—but it was not what he had expected.

The white-on-black sign at the front door announced this as the William L. Feist Museum of Contemporary Art. Not at all what he had anticipated. He had imagined a small white house, with plants hung from the porch and ivy growing on a window terrace.

Not that it mattered, he supposed, and pushed through the heavy glass door. The operator had promised him that 727-4212 was inside here somewhere, and that meant Mary Ann would be here too.

Inside the lobby, he looked around. Halls crowded with paintings of oil and acrylic, statues, and kinetic art in an explosion of colors and shapes spilled out away from him in every direction. Only a few couples and what looked like art students punctuated the carefully arranged displays.

"May I help you?" came a woman's voice at his elbow.

He turned, half expecting to find Mary Ann, but the voice was different, and the name tag the clerk wore read SHARON. "Yes," he said, "do you know if a Mary Ann works here?"

She said the name aloud a few times, then shook her head. "I don't think so—but it could be one of our student interns. We bring in a lot of them from the junior college."

"Do they work late?"

"Sometimes. I'm not sure who you would check with, though. The assistant director should be back from lunch soon. He might be able to help you."

"I'll wait, then," Norman said. "Thank you."

He stepped down the hall nearest him and wandered among the artwork. Most of it was a puzzle to him; Norman found modern art as generally incomprehensible as cuneiform, but as he passed others examining the displays he tried to look dutifully impressed.

It was as he passed an extension phone in one of the adjoining rooms that the idea occurred to him.

He went over to the phone, checked to make sure the room was empty, then lifted the receiver. The number on the extension was 4209. He reasoned that if he dialed 4212, then the correct extension should ring. Then it was just a matter of following the sound back to the correct department. Surely they would know something about Mary Ann.

He punched in the numbers, and almost instantly he could hear the ringing in the receiver. He pulled the phone away, and listened. He could just make out the sound of another phone ringing in rhythm down the hall.

Leaving the phone off its cradle, he followed the ringing back to a room at the far end of the building, just off the main hall. He went to the phone, picked it up, and pressed the plunger to cut off the ring. The number of the extension was 4212.

He hung up, and looked around the room. It was one of the least crowded with displays. A few paintings lined the walls on either side of a neon-and-glass-and-stone thing that crouched in the corner like a brooding galaxy. A handful of masks that looked distantly African were tastefully arranged in the far corner. The closest display was a statue that sat less than a foot from him.

There was no one about. Which didn't much matter. He'd wait. He'd never been late coming back from lunch before, not in five years. Surely he was due at least one. Eventually someone would show up. Maybe even Mary Ann herself.

His attention turned again to the statue. It was a full-size sculpture (bronze, from the look of it) of a young woman, attractive, sitting forward with eyes downcast, as though in deep thought or prayer. One of her hands was outstretched in supplication, and it had been shunted up against the wall so that its hand was barely inches away. He felt his gaze drawn to it almost in spite of himself. There was a compelling sadness about her features.

"I see you're admiring the sculpture," someone said.

He looked up to see a woman standing beside him, clutching a museum pamphlet. He nodded, then noticed that she wasn't looking at him, only at the statue. "It's very nice."

"Yes," she said, her voice tinged with regret. "Terrible story, that one. Last thing she ever did. A self-portrait. I never met her myself, but if this is any indication, she must really have been something."

She shook her head, frowning. "Why on earth a woman as talented as that would kill herself I don't know. Oh, there were the usual rumors, of course, lover's quarrel and all that. Damn shame. To think that we'll never see anything else from Mary Ann Lindeby."

She sighed, then moved on to the next room. She might have said something more, but Norman didn't hear it. There was a curious rushing in his ears that he distantly recognized as his own heartbeat.

He bent down to examine the brass plaque screwed into the base of the sculpture. It read *MARY ANN LINDEBY—SELF-PORTRAIT IN BRONZE*.

He followed the subtle lines up to her face, and then away to her hand. The hand that was outstretched so that it nearly touched the wall.

The hand that was barely inches from the telephone.

He had been late getting back to the office. Late arriving home from work, most of which was now a blur to him. Late getting Catt's dinner out of the can.

And now it was 8:30 P.M., and he was late in calling her. He paced the room nervously. He didn't have to call at all. He could just forget the whole thing. But then he would never know for sure. Could he live with that?

No, he decided, and reached for the phone.

It rang for a long time before she answered.

"Hello, Norman."

"Hello, Mary Ann."

"I—didn't think you were going to call," she said, more hesitant than he had ever heard her before. Almost afraid. She was quiet for a long moment before continuing.

"I saw you today, Norman," she said. "You came by." And now, suddenly, as though her resolve had finally failed, she was crying on the phone. "Oh, why did you have to do that? You've ruined everything."

"Then—it was you? That—"

Quietly: "Yes, Norman, it was."

Norman felt as though he had been kicked in the stomach. The floor seemed to tilt beneath him. He was aware of a sound from the receiver, but he couldn't make any sense of it. Nothing made sense.

"No," he said, somehow finding his voice. "I can't deal with this. I can't. This isn't happening!"

He slammed down the receiver. Got up. Paced the room.

It was crazy.

But he knew in his heart that he couldn't leave it at this.

Couldn't leave *her* like this.

It would be rude.

Steeling himself, he went back to the phone and dialed.

This time it rang only once before her voice came on the other end. She was still crying, great, gasping sobs that tore him apart to hear.

"I'm sorry, Mary Ann," he said.

"No, it's me," she said, and there was such pain in her voice, such hurt. "I'm the one who should be sorry. For putting you in this position. I never should have answered the phone. But—it's been so *long*, Norman, so long since I've talked to anyone. It was dark, and I was alone, and I was so lonely."

"I know," Norman said, his voice small in the receiver. "So was I."

Silence hung between them for a moment. "I should go now," she said.

"No—wait, I mean...you can't just go away like that."

"It's for your own good, Norman. Forget about me. It never happened." He could hear her control breaking over the phone, and in a voice thin with effort and strained with tears, he could barely hear her say, "I'm sorry, Norman. Good-bye."

Then before he could say anything, there was the *click* of a disconnect at the other end of the line.

He dialed again.

It rang without answer.

He let it ring anyway.

Finally, after he had lost count of the rings, he set the receiver back in its cradle and sat back on the couch, peering into the dark.

She was gone.

At 5:01 P.M., Richard switched off his computer, grabbed his jacket, and with a nod in Norman's direction, headed out into the cool evening. He was smiling.

The office had been blissfully quiet for three whole days.

Norman came home with the usual two bags of groceries and set them on the counter. He opened a can of cat food and set it out on the floor. Catt rushed by him and began lapping it up. Norman watched the cat for a while—it hardly ever seemed to mind if he watched—then went into the other room.

He sat down on the couch and switched on the television, leaving the sound off. Somehow, the voices on the TV bothered him; the tiny speaker filtered the voices, reminding him of things he didn't want to think about.

Besides, Catt seemed to like the quiet.

Norman lay without sleeping. The digital clock beside the bed glowed 2:37 A.M. The thin light reflected off the pamphlet that had arrived in the mail that day, the one he had requested over the phone two days earlier. It was a guide to the current exhibits on display at the museum.

The green glow from the clock shone off the picture of a sculpture. A self-portrait by Mary Ann Lindeby. Somehow the light made it look gloomy, not at all as real or as warm or as vibrant as he remembered it.

Photographs don't do her justice, he thought.

Before he realized he was doing it, he reached for the phone, and dialed 727-4212.

After the twenty-fifth ring, he let the phone settle back in its cradle, then reached over to slide the pamphlet out of the light of the digital clock.

"...damn," he whispered, and the night swallowed his words.

Richard stood up from his desk and stretched. "I'm going to lunch. Be back in an hour."

Norman nodded, momentarily startled out of his reverie. When he turned back to his papers, he glanced at the figure that he had been unconsciously doodling on the page. It was a woman posed sitting forward, hand outstretched, eyes downcast.

I can't take this any longer, he thought, and got up from his desk, careful to lock the door to their cubicle on his way out.

Half an hour later he was standing in the museum again, in the same room with her. He waited until one of the interns had finished exchanging one painting for another, then sat on the cushioned seat in front of the sculpture.

Well, now what? he wondered. *What are you going to do, talk to her or something?*

Why not? he decided.

"I miss you," he said, tentative at first, his whispered voice sounding harsh and loud in the room. "I miss talking to you. It was the only thing I had to look forward to when I came home. After a while, it was the only reason for *going* home."

He studied the bronze face, but there was no reaction.

Don't be stupid, he thought. *What did you expect?*

He forced himself to continue. "You were the only one who ever made me feel I was wanted. That I wasn't just some jerk. And now—"

He stopped abruptly as two other patrons browsed through the room. When they left after only a cursory inspection, he wondered if they had heard him, and decided that he didn't care.

"Don't you *understand*?" he said. "I used to feel I was nothing. That I had nothing. And then—then there was you. And everything changed. And I thought: my God, I'm in love. For the first time in my life I am honestly and truly in love. And then it all just...went away."

He looked away from her. "Without you, there's nothing left for me. It's not worth it. I'm sorry, Mary Ann, but I just—can't go on like this."

He looked up again.

The sculpture was crying.

A thin line of moisture flowed down her cheek from the corner of one eye. Stunned, he got to his feet and walked closer. It was there, he wasn't imagining it. He reached out to touch the tear-streaked bronze face—

"Excuse me."

Norman turned to see the museum guard standing behind him.

"I'll have to ask you not to touch the exhibits, sir," he said.

"Of course," Norman said, "of course."

The guard lingered a moment longer, perhaps making sure that Norman had understood him before stepping out of the room.

As soon as he was gone, Norman looked back at the statue. The tear streak was gone, if it had even been there at all.

You're losing your mind, he thought, and headed out of the museum.

Norman awoke to the shrill sound of the phone ringing in his ear. He pulled himself to the edge of the bed, fumbling for the receiver. The clock read 3:45 A.M. He found the phone and snatched it up on the third ring, and managed to figure out which end went to his ear. "Hello?"

"...Norman?" Her voice was distant, as though she were calling from a tremendous distance. "Oh, Norman, it was so hard to call you—it took—almost everything I had. It's dark here, so *dark*—I don't know how much longer I can talk."

The line blurred with a rush of static for a moment, then cleared. "I heard what you said—about not going on. It scares me. It's what I said when—" And now she was crying, her voice heavy with hurt. "He left me, Norman. He left me and my life fell apart. There was nothing left, nothing else—mattered. I was so lonely and hurt and I couldn't make the pain go away, it just stayed with me so long and so hard and I couldn't take it anymore and I had to do something I—oh, please, Norman, please say you didn't mean it, please."

He struggled with his words, wanting to say the right thing, not knowing what it was. Then, finally, "I love you, Mary Ann."

"No, please—"

"I do, and I'm sorry, I didn't think it would happen, I didn't expect it, ever, but—I can't help it. I love you."

The static returned again, like the sound of a wave crashing on a distant shore, and then he heard her, so soft he could barely make out the words. "Come to me, Norman. Come to me now, tonight."

"But the museum—it'll be closed."

"Don't worry. I'll take care of it. But come, now, before I change my mind. Hurry!"

The line cut off, leaving only a dial tone in its wake. Norman racked the phone and threw off the sheets, stepping out into the chill night that filled the room.

Norman walked up the sidewalk in front of the museum, looking nervously over his shoulder. In three hours it would be light, and crowded with people. But now there was only the night, and the cold, and the museum. Lit by floodlamps on all sides, it was the brightest thing on the street.

He made his way around back, searching until he found a metal fire door. He pulled at the handle, but it refused to budge, locked from inside. Spotting another door down the length of the building, he started toward it—

—when there was a *click* at the door he had just tried.

He walked back to the door and tried the handle. It swung freely open. With a final glance around, he stepped inside.

He felt his way through the rooms, trying to get his bearings in the dark. Some part of his mind realized that the door would be discovered unlocked sooner or later, that museums had security guards just like banks did, but for the moment none of that mattered. He had to find her. That was what was important.

He managed to work his way up into the main hall. From there it was a matter of going straight down to the end, trying not to knock anything over, then left—

And he was inside the room. The dim light from the hall stopped at the door. The room was pitch-black inside, and *different*, somehow. He felt it instantly, the way it felt when he stepped out of an airplane; a difference in pressure. And something else. A sense of movement in the darkness.

"Mary Ann?"

The darkness answered. "I'm here."

And a hand touched his face.

Somewhere, down the hall, he heard a door open and close, a transistor radio briefly audible, then silenced. The guard would be making his patrols. Surely he would find them here, together. But it didn't matter. Nothing mattered.

"Tell me you love me, Norman," she said. "Oh, God, it's been so long since anyone's told me they loved me."

"I love you."

"Then stay with me. Please. I don't want to be alone anymore."

Footsteps down the hall, coming closer. The distant glare of a flashlight, reflected off portraits, growing near.

Norman hesitated. "I—"

"*Please.*"

He nodded, quickly, furtively, in the darkness. Then he felt her holding him, cold, but tightly, as though she would never let go....

The guard came to the end of the hall and swept the adjacent room with the flashlight beam. There had been a noise, of that he was certain. And the rear door had been unlocked.

But so far, there was nothing out of the ordinary.

He let the glow from the flashlight linger just a moment on the sculpture at the end of the room. It was an impressive piece of work, even in the semidark. A man and a woman, locked in an embrace, faces inches apart, gazing into one another's eyes. His hand was on her face, as though lovingly, delicately touching her cheek.

He would have to come back and look at it again, the guard decided, and moved away down the hall.

THE SALVATION OF LYMAN TERRELL

"**A**nd in conclusion, ladies and gentlemen of the jury, I believe we have shown, clearly and conclusively, that there would not have been time for the defendant, Mr. Price, to leave his home, reach the home of the victim, commit the heinous crime that was committed that night, and return to his home, where he was seen less than twenty minutes after the murder."

Lyman Terrell surveyed the twelve men and women seated in the three ascending rows of seats. They were quiet, contemplative, some looking down, others glancing with some nervousness at his client. *Nervous because they're going to convict, or nervous because they're going to have to stand up for his innocence?* He couldn't tell. He could only continue.

"There is no question that what happened to Claris Montagne was a terrible injustice," he said, forcing himself to avoid thinking about the appointment that would be waiting for him when he finished today. He couldn't allow himself to be distracted. Not now.

"Her murder was a crime whose depravity and cruelty will stay in the minds of every man and woman who has sat in this courtroom over the last two months. We have seen the agony of her sister, Elizabeth, during her testimony. She is deserving of our sympathy and our outrage at this crime. But it would be an even greater injustice if an innocent man were convicted of a crime he did not commit. The law states that you must be certain beyond a reasonable doubt. I believe we have shown that there is far more than just a reasonable doubt. Thank you."

Lyman edged back around the table to his seat. Beside him, his client, Bill Price, sat with his hands folded in his lap, looking uncomfortable in the five hundred dollar suit they had been able to find for him. He was scared. Lyman couldn't blame him. As defense attorney, it was Lyman's job to project confidence at every step. There was no question in his mind that Price was innocent, and despite the sweat running down his back, which was sticking to the folds of his jacket, he had to make sure that confidence was communicated. The question was, would the jurors come to the same conclusion?

"Thank you for your closing statement, Mr. Terrell," Judge Farrell said, then nodded to the door beside him. "Ladies and gentlemen of the jury, if you will proceed through that door, you will be shown to the jury room where you may begin your deliberations. This court will remain in recess until the jury has reached its decision."

With that, Judge Ginsburg stood, and the courtroom stood with him. Lyman watched as Ginsburg left first, followed by the jury. They filed out one by one, holding their notepads, eyes downcast, their thoughts a mystery to everyone, even each other, until they would reach the jury room, where for the first time they would be able to discuss their feelings about the case.

And then...?

"Mr. Terrell?"

Lyman turned to face his client, whose pale blue eyes seemed even paler. His dark hair was close cropped, neatly combed, quite different from the long, stringy hair he'd had when Lyman had first taken on the case. Appearance was everything in court.

"What do you think?" Price asked. "I mean, is there a chance—"

"I don't know. I've been an attorney for twenty years, and I've never yet been able to tell with any degree of certainty what they were thinking. All we can do is hope for the best."

He looked up to see the bailiff approaching. "Mr. Price, if you will come with me I'll see you back to the holding cell."

"Right," Price said, visibly shaking. Lyman wished there was something he could say to make the waiting easier, but there had never been anything before that worked. That didn't leave much chance of coming up with the magical words this time.

Price started away with the bailiff, then turned at the door that very soon might close on him forever. "Mr. Terrell... you gonna wait around while they decide?"

Lyman shook his head. "It can take hours, days, even a week or longer for a jury to reach a decision. Far too long to wait around.

And I've... got a doctor's appointment in a couple of hours. But the office knows where to find me. When they reach a decision, they'll call."

Price nodded absently and allowed himself to be led out of the courtroom. Once the door had closed, Lyman picked up his briefcase and forced himself to straighten despite the sharp, sudden pain that shot from his neck up into the back of his head. He had worked hard to ignore it during his closing arguments, but now he could think of nothing else. Most of the time it was a dull ache, but when the pain came in earnest, it was so sudden and intense that it made him flinch, as though he'd been slapped in the back of the head.

Guess it's time to find out what the jury has in store for both *of us*, he decided, and headed slowly out of the courtroom.

Doctor Pete Evans worked out of a medical building across from New York University, where he taught at the school of medicine. Despite being a patient for ten years and a friend for eight of them, whenever Lyman stepped into the office he felt like a not-terribly-bright student called before the professor for a private lecture. Pete liked to talk, to lecture, to sermonize. So Lyman took the doctor's silence as he entered the examining room as a bad sign.

Don't get crazy, start reading into things. He's probably just having a busy day.

Maybe so, he decided as Pete opened up the folder in his hands and studied it for a long moment. *But he's taking an awfully long time to find something to say.*

"So how's it going?" Lyman asked.

"It's been a day." Pete rubbed tiredly at his eyes.

"Should I get up on the table, or—"

"No... no, that won't be necessary," Pete said, and closed the folder. He folded his arms and leaned against the wall. "Lyman, I've been a doctor ever since the early Mesozoic period, give or take a geological epoch, and there are some things you never get used to, some things you never quite figure out how to tell someone. Except... the only right, the only fair thing to do, is come right down to it."

Lyman felt his gut clench. *Oh, God*, he thought. *Oh, God... here it comes.* Two weeks ago, he'd come in with a persistent sore throat and difficulty swallowing. A laryngoscopy had found a lump in the back of his throat. *I'm sure it's nothing serious,* Pete had said. *But better to run some tests, just to be sure.*

"The tests came back from the lab today. You have a tumor located behind the mouth, just under the brain stem. It's about the size of a lemon. It's malignant, and it's metastasized throughout the area."

Lyman nodded, numb. The room seemed suddenly cold, terribly cold. He focused on not trembling. It didn't work.

"I'm sorry," Pete said. "I'm just... I'm sorry."

Lyman nodded again. It was the only thing his body seemed able to do in response. After a moment, he found his voice again.

"It's okay, Pete," he said. "I was afraid it'd be something like this, couldn't sleep at night thinking about it... but we all do that, you know? You always think the worst, but when it comes down to the wire you always find out it's not the worst, it's just something that—"

He looked away, his voice failing. He couldn't seem to get enough air. "I'm sorry—"

"Do you want to lie down or—"

"No... I just need a moment, that's all," Lyman said. "Isn't there anything we can do? Radiation, surgery, chemo?"

"If we'd known about it twelve, even six months ago, yes, a combination of radiation and chemotherapy might have had some impact. But it's far too advanced now; the only dosage that would do any good in attacking the cancer would pretty much kill you. Same thing for surgery. There's a mass of brain tissue between us and the tumor, and—"

He stopped, looked away for a moment. *This has got to be hard for him,* Lyman thought absently. *Almost as hard on him as it is on me. Almost.*

"Obviously you can get a second opinion, but I've already taken the liberty of talking to about half a dozen of our best people in this area, both here and at the university. They all agree with the diagnosis. There's nothing we can do in the amount of time we have."

"How much... God, I can't believe I'm asking this, it's so soap opera... how much time do I have?

"As I said, it's extremely advanced, it's—"

"How long?"

"A few weeks. Maybe a month at the outside."

Lyman's arms were shaking. That fast? That soon? He couldn't seem to wrap his brain around the notion.

Of course not, that's because there's a tumor in there, idiot, he thought bitterly.

"I'm sorry, Lyman," Pete said. "I'm so sorry."

"Mr. Terrell?"

Lyman looked up from behind his desk to where Robbie Chase stood in the doorway. Robbie was one of the newer clerks at the law office of Gelman, Ferrar, Bryce and Terrell. He was in his early twenties, full of energy and eager to please.

I want to be twenty again, I want to do it all over, it's not fair, I don't want this, I don't want this, I don't want to die, I don't want to die, I don't want to—

"Mr. Terrell?" Robbie repeated.

Lyman forced the panic down, straightened in his chair. "Yes, Robbie, what is it?"

"I've got those papers you asked for. On the Price case, so we can file an appeal in case—"

"Right... right. Just leave them on the chair, Robbie, thanks."

Robbie did as asked, then paused to glance back at him. "You okay, Mr. Terrell?"

Lyman nodded. "Yeah... yeah, Robbie, I'm fine, just... thinking, that's all. If I need anything else, I'll call."

"Right."

Robbie was halfway out of the door when Lyman stirred. "One thing."

"Sir?"

"Can I ask you a question?"

Robbie grinned. "I thought law clerks weren't supposed to have any answers until they got their name on the front door of a place like this."

"Well, I guess we can let it slide this time."

"Thanks. So what's the question?"

"If you found out... let's say you found out, today, that you had...oh, about a week to live, maybe three. What would you do?"

"You mean after I finished throwing up?"

Lyman smiled ruefully, remembering what had transpired in the men's room moments after leaving Pete's office. *The kid's smarter than I thought.* "Yes. After that part."

"I'd get ten thousand second opinions. Then I guess I'd take every penny I had and party until I dropped. Or... no, you know what? I've never seen the pyramids. Always wanted to, ever since I was a kid. Even used to dream about them. Always figured I had time, that I'd get around to it one of these days. If I knew I had a week to go... I'd get my ass on a plane, and go see the pyramids.

"*Then* I'd party until I dropped. Why? You doing some kind of survey?"

"Yes. Some kind. Thank you, Robbie."

Robbie grinned. "Sure thing, Mr. Terrell."

Once he was gone, Lyman touched the intercom. "Carol?"

His assistant's voice came through the speaker. "Yes?"

"Get me..." He allowed a tired smile. "...get me ten thousand second opinions."

"Sir? I—"

"Private joke. Check with Dave in medical law, have him pull together a list of the top hundred specialists in brain surgery and cancer research."

"Yes, sir. Are we taking on a new case?"

"I hope so, Carol. I truly do."

Stepping out of his bathroom, Lyman washed down another pair of painkillers and picked up the phone on the fourth ring. The pain was constant now. He'd gone from Vicodin to Demerol immediately after the diagnosis, and within just a few days had gone from Demerol to Pamidronate. *Next stop, morphine,* he thought as he brought the phone to his ear. "Yes?"

"Mr. Terrell? Dr. Timmerman. I'm sorry to call you at home so late—"

"It's all right. Time is at kind of a premium right now."

"I wanted to let you know that I've gone over the records you faxed over this afternoon and consulted with several others here at the office, and... well, I'm sorry, Mr. Terrell, but I'd have to concur with the initial diagnosis. There's not much that the medical profession can do at this point that wouldn't kill you just as fast as it killed the cancer."

Lyman nodded silently for a moment. This was the seventh call tonight. "I see," he said at last, realizing that he should probably say something.

"Have you been speaking to many other doctors?"

"All of them. I've gotten about twenty calls since the faxes went out. All the same as yours."

"I'm sorry."

"Yeah... me, too," Lyman said. "Thanks for looking it over."

"Sure thing. I just wish I could've had a better answer. Take care of yourself, Mr. Terrell."

He cradled the phone and sat heavily for a moment before rising to fix a drink. He knew that he shouldn't mix alcohol and painkillers, but he wasn't planning to operate any heavy farm equipment, and at this point, what difference did it make?

What difference did anything make anymore?

He studied his reflection in the mirror above the oak bar in the house he had shared with his wife before the divorce five years earlier. He'd always imagined finding someone else to fill in the silence once he had the time to do some serious dating—and after all, at forty-nine he was only graying a little around the temples, his face reasonably unlined, though much more tired looking lately—he'd assumed that there was always time, he'd get around to it eventually.

Who knew he'd suddenly run out of eventuallys?

"And I've never been to the pyramids either," he said quietly, to the room.

Tomorrow I'm going to have to start telling people, he decided. He'd held off telling anyone until now in anticipation of some measure of hope being introduced into the equation, but he could no longer conceal the effect the painkillers were having on him. If the Price adjudication dragged on for much longer, he'd have to get one of the other attorneys to take over the case.

Telling Cindy would be hardest. When she'd left him, she did so without anger or recrimination. She'd just fallen out of love with him and in love with someone else. He knew she still cared for him, in her way. But he couldn't wait any longer, it wouldn't be right and—

He started as the ringing telephone shattered the silence of the house for the eighth time that night. He finished his drink and reached for the phone. *May as well get this out of the way.*

"Hello?" he said.

A thin voice at the other end of the phone said, "Lyman Terrell, please."

"Speaking."

"Mr. Terrell, this is Dr. Mulfi Ibalis. You sent over a fax to my office this afternoon." There was a trace of accent in the voice. Lyman guessed Indian, possibly Pakistani. "I spent quite a long time this afternoon going over it and talking to my associates—"

"Right, well, I can probably save you some time and—"

"I believe there may be something we can do for you."

It took him a moment to process what Ibalis had said, and even then it didn't line up. He couldn't allow himself to hear what he had just heard, couldn't allow his hopes to be rekindled only to be dashed again.

And yet....

"I'm sorry, could you repeat that?"

"I think we may be able to help you. You must understand that there are no guarantees. Yours is a very advanced case, a very serious case, but—"

"But you're saying there's a chance."

"Yes, Mr. Terrell. I think there may be a chance. The treatment is radical, difficult, and very expensive."

"I can cover it. Whatever it is, if this is for real, I can cover it."

"Good. Can you come by my office first thing tomorrow morning? Say about eight?"

"I'd be there at dawn if I thought it would do any good."

Ibalis laughed quietly. "I'm sure that will not be necessary, Mr. Terrell."

Just one chance, God, that's all I ask, just give me one chance to fight this thing.

That's not so much to ask, is it?

Is it?

"And you think this Ibalis can help?"

Lyman shrugged. Telling Charlie Gelman, the senior and founding partner in the firm, had been the hardest, and the most necessary. Charlie had believed in him when Lyman was just a first-year law graduate looking for a berth. Whatever happened, Charlie had to know the truth.

"I don't know," Lyman said. "I went to his office this morning, and he ran some tests. I checked him out with Stan in medical law, and he's had a pretty good success rate with cancer patients. A surprisingly good success rate, actually. He hasn't published a lot, but not everyone does. Looks like he was trained in New Delhi, then came out here about ten years ago. So at least he checks out, so that's a start. I'm supposed to come by again during lunch for the results and a patient conference."

Charlie nodded soberly. He had taken the news quietly, as he did everything else, but there was real concern in his eyes. "You know you have the support of myself and everyone else in the firm, right? No matter what comes, the firm will stand with you. You are not only one of the finest attorneys I've ever worked with, you're a good and decent man, and I hate to lose a combination like that. If there's anything we can do... anything at all... just ask."

"I appreciate that, Charlie, but for now I'd prefer to keep this between just the two of us." He glanced at his watch, stood. "I'd better get going. Takes a while to get across town at lunch."

"I understand. Oh, before I forget... any word yet on the Price murder case?"

"The jury's still out. The judge called them in yesterday to ask if they were deadlocked, but they said they were still working, just needed some more time. A clerk over at the courthouse tells me they've asked to have testimony read back to them, go over all the evidence... but I can't imagine it'll be much longer."

"Lyman... if you want off this, to put some time into putting your affairs in order, seeing other specialists—"

Lyman shook his head. "I want to see this through. Besides, it's better if I don't have too much free time. Keeps me from thinking about things."

"I understand," Charlie said as Lyman stepped out into the hall. "Take care of yourself," he called across the room. "And remember what I said. Anything at all, just let me know."

"I will, Charlie. Thanks."

"Mr. Terrell, good to see you again. Please, sit down."

Charlie did as asked. Doctor Ibalis was a small, thin man, with an almost disproportionately thick mane of hair that was graying at the temples, with another shock of gray hair going from the part at the front of his head in a nearly straight line to the back. His face was lined by sun and weather, but there was a gentleness to it that helped put Lyman at his ease. "Can I get you anything?"

Lyman shook his head. His throat was now in so much pain that swallowing anything was almost more than he could bear. He'd lost ten pounds in just the last few days. And the less he thought about the headaches, the better. "I'm fine," he said. "With all due respect, I just want to get to the point. So what's the prognosis?"

"Well, the lab work confirms what everyone else has told you. It's an inoperable tumor, extremely fast-moving, quite vicious by any standards."

"So that's it, then?"

"Not entirely."

Ibalis sat on the chair opposite Lyman in the small, white examining room. His dark brown eyes locked onto Lyman's eyes and held them. "Mr. Terrell, for the last five years, we have been working on a new kind of treatment for this sort of situation. We've only used it in a handful of cases, on a purely experimental basis... but in each case so far, it has worked."

"Even in cases like this?"

"Yes. Before I can even discuss it, however, you'll need to sign this non-disclosure agreement." He reached into a drawer and pulled out a printed signature form. "The treatment uses a proprietary technology we've developed, and we don't want any information concerning that technology to get out until we've finished our tests and can patent the process. It is not always successful, hence the release form, but I think we have a very good chance with this one."

Lyman studied the form. It was a fairly straightforward release form, absolving Ibalis from liability if the treatment didn't work. He took out his pen and signed at the bottom. "There you go."

"Thank you," Ibalis said, as he took the form and returned it to the drawer.

"So how does this treatment work?"

"A cancer cell is, essentially, an invasion of the body by cells that have mutated into something the immune system cannot handle, against which the body's basic defense mechanisms are useless. Rather than try and fight it, we have tried a different approach. If you cannot fight what it *is*, why not make it into something you *can* fight?"

"I'm not sure I'm following you."

"Using a highly intense burst of radiation and a chemical cocktail we've developed, we go in at the cellular level, the genetic level, and by manipulating the DNA code we can change the nature of the tumor itself. We destabilize it and reconstitute it as something similar but manageable, something we can deal with. But there are limits to what we can do, we cannot totally reconstitute it. It remains as an invasion of the body, but we can transform it into another *kind* of invasive force, like an infectious disease."

"You can change it from a tumor into, what, a virus, like the flu?"

"Something like that. It's far more complex, but that's the sense of it, yes."

"And then I can get rid of it?"

"Yes, should the procedure prove successful. But there are no guarantees, Mr. Terrell, and the procedure is very expensive. Since this is an experimental treatment it's not covered by any medical programs, which is why we only offer it to select clients, those we feel can afford it."

"I can handle the payment. Even if I have to mortgage the house, it's worth it if I'm alive. I can always buy another house. I can't buy another life."

"Just so, Mr. Terrell."

"So when would we have to do this?"

"Right now."

"Now?" Lyman hesitated. He hadn't expected this. He'd thought there would be time to prepare, to look at other options.

"With every moment that passes, the tumor grows," Ibalis said. "The larger the tumor, the more difficult the transformational process becomes. It's no different than checking into a hospital with a major heart attack, and going in for bypass surgery right away. It's truly a matter of life and death, Mr. Terrell. We can't afford to waste time, and there are others waiting in line for appointments. But if you really need the time—"

"No... no, I don't," Lyman said. "After all... it's not like I have anything to lose."

"Very true, Mr. Terrell. Very true indeed."

When Lyman Terrell opened his eyes, his first thought was, *Did it work?*

He was lying in a white hospital bed, in a private recovery room in the Ibalis medical suite. He was wearing latex gloves, presumably to support the bandages where they'd pumped the anesthetic and IV into the back of his hands. His muscles hurt, and his limbs felt as heavy as lead, but he'd been told to expect that. He was also thirsty, the back of his throat sore from the oxygen tube.

But as he moved his tongue around to check out the soreness at the back of his throat, he noted that it did not feel the same as the original pain. And though his brain was still a bit muddy from the general anesthetic, the headache seemed to be gone.

Don't get overconfident, wait for the doc to tell you whether or not the treatment worked. Don't go looking for signs to reinforce what you want to believe. It's a long fall if you get your hopes up without cause.

Even so, his throat did seem to feel better.

He closed his eyes, and he seemed to remember bits and pieces of the procedure, vague memories that slid further away from his grasp with each passing moment. Voices, *blood pressure normal, heartbeat and respiration nominal—that's got it—give me twenty cc's—stand by to initiate radiation—watch your focus—all right, clear—clear—clear—*

He looked up as the door to the room opened and Dr. Ibalis stepped inside.

"Good, I thought you might be awake," Ibalis said. "How are you feeling, Mr. Terrell?"

"Tired. I feel like I've been run over by a truck."

"To be expected. As I said, the procedure is very physically demanding. But you should be able to leave fairly soon."

Lyman hesitated, almost afraid to ask the question that was demanding to be asked. "Did it... I mean, was the—"

"The procedure was a complete success."

Lyman's mouth moved for a moment, not sure he'd heard right. Could it be that easy? Was it possible? Though he could feel hope stirring inside, a flutter of excitement, he remained cautious. But he wanted it to be true, God help him, he wanted it to be true.

"So... what, you're saying it's gone? That I'm cured?"

"Almost. There's one remaining step."

See? Told you not to get your hopes up.

"So it didn't work?"

"Not at all. The first stage worked perfectly. Now comes stage two. By now you have noticed that you are wearing latex gloves, yes?"

"Yeah, kinda hard to miss that. I woke up and there they were... I seem to remember the nurse telling me not to touch them. Is there more chemo coming, or—"

"No, not at all. As I explained to you earlier, the treatment destabilizes the tumor and changes its nature. In this case, the tumor has been dissolved and reconstituted in your system as a kind of virus."

"Okay, I think I get that, but—"

"The destabilization lasts only twenty-four hours. During that time you may pass it on to someone else, just as you might pass on the flu to someone else, sometimes without even knowing it."

"Wait a minute—"

"The difference, of course, is that you will know that it has taken place, because you must do so deliberately, by hand. Because viruses can be most easily transmitted through the sweat glands in your hands, we set the genetic markers in the transformed cancer to seek out those specific areas, thus preventing accidental transmission through other parts of the skin. This is why we've given you the latex gloves. Now, obviously you cannot go walking around outside wearing latex gloves without attracting attention, so when you're ready to go we'll give you a pair of leather gloves with a latex lining. This will help minimize the risk of accidental infection."

"Wait, this can't... you can't seriously expect me to give this to somebody else."

"It's the only way to get it out of your system, the same way a carrier of a disease may pass it on to others without getting it himself. In time, with more funding from individuals such as yourself, we hope to find alternate means of removing the transmuted cancer cells, something less radical, but for now—"

"No, I can't accept this, it's—"

"You came to me in a desperate situation, Mr. Terrell. Desperate situations sometimes require desperate means. You are not the first, you will not be the last."

"I don't believe you. Nobody would willingly do this to someone else, sentence them to a—"

"There you are mistaken. One of our clients gave his tumor to a relative who was already dying of AIDS and offered freely to help him. Another gave his tumor to a man who had tried three times before to kill himself, a man who had no interest in living. And there was one case in which the donor enlisted the support of a healthy man in exchange for a million dollars, to be given to his family after his death, in order to get them out of the debt he had inflicted upon them through a gambling habit. Needless to say, we don't approve of that particular approach. Generally it's better to find someone who is going to die anyway in the same amount of time. That way it doesn't make a difference. You'd be surprised how many people are willing to —"

"But it *does* make a difference! I mean, what if you infect somebody with this thing and they find a cure to the disease he's already got?"

"Such things never happen in a matter of days, Mr. Terrell."

"There's spontaneous remission—"

"Rare and overrated. Look around, Mr. Terrell. How many young men are sent off to fight and die every day, to save the lives of others? How many people, dying of old age, suffering without relief, would gladly accept a quick way out in return for helping out someone else, or in exchange for security for his family? People live and die every day for far less noble reasons than what I have just described to you. I assure you that as much as this is not an easy thing for you, it is no easier for me or anyone here. But it is, quite literally, your only hope for survival."

"And if I *don't* infect somebody in the next twenty-four hours? What happens then?"

"The tumor will re-stabilize, and there will be nothing we or anyone else can do to save you. And, to be honest with you, that has happened from time to time; a very few people find they cannot, or will not, complete stage two of the procedure. We regret it greatly when that happens, but it's not our choice. It's *your* choice, Mr. Terrell. We've done all we can.

"The rest... is up to you."

"Mr. Terrell?"

Lyman looked across to Robbie as he stepped back inside the office. It was almost five o'clock. "Yes, Robbie, what is it?"

"We were looking everywhere for you, but nobody knew where you'd gone. Is everything okay?"

"Yes, I'm... it's fine. What's up?"

"We had another request from the jury on the Price murder case. They want another look at our evidence files, but Mr. Gelman didn't want anything to go over without your say-so—"

"Not a problem. Give them whatever they need."

"Will do."

"Robbie? One other thing."

"Yes sir?"

"I'm done with the files I'd asked Carol to get me from medical, so you can pick them up on your way and drop them off with Matt in claims."

"Sure thing."

"And while you're there..."

Lyman hesitated. *I'm not saying I'm going to do this, I'm just checking into it, just looking around. Window shopping.*

He looked away, past Robbie to a far away point in his own mind. "I seem to recall that we're handling the insurance claims for about half a dozen terminal patients, some of whom have nearly exhausted their financial resources. Could you bring me their files?"

"Sure thing, Mr. Terrell," Robbie said. "By the way, love the gloves. Very stylish."

Lyman nodded but said nothing. He continued toward his office, where Carol looked up at him with relief in her face. "I've got Mr. Price on the phone again, calling from detention. He hadn't heard anything and he's been frantic with worry."

"I'll take it in my office."

He stepped into the paneled office and picked up the phone as he sat. "Hi, Bill. What's up?"

"Just checking in, Mr. Terrell. Have you heard anything?"

"No, nothing new, I'm afraid. The jury is still reviewing the material."

"Should it be taking this long?"

"The longer they deliberate, the better the chances of acquittal."

"I hope so, Mr. Terrell. I surely do hope so. Anyway, I just wanted to say that I appreciate everything you've done for me... whatever happens."

"Well, we're not done fighting yet, Bill, so hang in there."

"I will. Thanks. I gotta go now, there's a real big guy behind me wants to use the phone."

"Understood. I'll call you as soon as we know anything."

Lyman racked the phone and looked at his hands. The gloves were hot on the inside, body heat retained by the latex, but the leather was cool to the touch. He glanced at his watch. *A little over twenty hours left. What the hell am I going to do?*

Can I really do this? To anyone?

Can I?

The hospice at St. John's Hospital downtown was a place of green gardens and soft pastel walls. The nurse who had met Lyman at the entrance preceded him down one of the many hallways that were lined with photos of donors and smelled of antiseptic. Though he had never seen it, he knew that his ex-wife's face was on one of those photos. She had donated considerable time and effort to fundraising for the hospice, on the principle of *There but for the grace of God goes you or me.*

If you only knew, kiddo, if you only knew.

Then he remembered that the nurse was talking, and he pulled himself back to the present, and the guided tour. She was attractive, but her eyes were tired. How else could anyone be who dealt with this much death every day?

"All the non-infectious patients are kept here and given as much care and help as we can, for as long as we can," she said. "Most of them are AIDS patients and cancer patients, but we have a few from the other divisions of the hospital as well, deep-coma patients on food tubes and respirators, that sort of thing."

"It's... very nice."

"Thank you, it's nice to get the feedback," she said, flashing a tired smile. "It's also very rare. Though we get a great deal of support from the families of our hospice patients, and donations from people like yourself and your wife, very few actually come by to inspect the facilities. I suppose they feel more comfortable supporting the idea than seeing the reality."

"I suppose so."

She let the smile disappear and glanced out the window. "Is it cold outside today?"

"Pardon?"

"I noticed you were wearing gloves."

"Oh, no, it's just... I've got a cold, and don't want to spread it to anyone else. Accidentally."

"Very thoughtful of you. I wish more people felt the same way. It seems like no one is ever willing to take responsibility for their lives if it involves even the slightest inconvenience."

They stepped into a room where an elderly patient was in bed, watching television with the sound off. His face was deeply lined, his eyes sunken, the skin tinged with a yellow pallor. IV tubes and sensors snaked through the aluminum bed rails to an assortment of machines on either side of the narrow mattress.

"This is one of my charges, Frank Neilson," she said. "How're you feeling today, Frank?"

"A little better than yesterday," he said, his voice whisper-thin. "Thanks."

"That's good. This is Mr. Terrell, I'm taking him on a tour of the facility. He and his wife have made quite a few donations to the hospital."

"That's very good of you," Frank said. "But I could tell you were a good person by looking at you."

Lyman fidgeted uncomfortably under Frank's gaze, not sure at all if any part of him could be called a good person right now. "No, really, it's... thank you, I—"

Frank reached out a trembling hand and placed it on Lyman's gloved hand. "It's okay, you know."

Lyman stiffened. "What is?"

"Being nervous around somebody who's dying. Everybody is. Cigarettes got to me. Left lung's collapsed, right one's full of cancer and just about ready to go. They figure I've got maybe a few days left."

"I'm sorry."

"Don't be," Frank said, and managed a wink. "See... I don't believe 'em. I think there's always hope. Maybe on the last day I've got, they'll find something... so I've at least got a chance. As long as I'm breathing, there's hope, right?"

"Yes... yes, I suppose there is."

"Funny thing," Frank said. "You look more worried than I do."

"I've... got some decisions to make."

"Must be pretty tough."

"Yeah," Lyman said, his voice quiet. "Yeah, they are."

"Well, y'know, it's a funny thing, but the one thing I've learned is that in the long run, whatever decisions we make are the right ones. They put us where we're supposed to be, you know what I mean?"

Lyman nodded, but didn't reply.

Frank patted the gloved hand. "So don't worry. Like I said, you look like a good man. I know you'll make the right call."

"I'll certainly try. Thank you for your time, Frank."

"Not a problem. I wasn't doing much anyway. Come on back anytime. Maybe I'll be here. Maybe I won't. But either way, Death's gonna know he was in one hell of a fight."

As usual, the alarm beside Lyman's bed went off at 7:30 A.M. But he was already up and dressed. He switched off the alarm and moved into the kitchen. Pouring a cup of coffee from the automatic brewer he'd set the night before, he sat in the breakfast nook, and looked out at the street.

It's so strange to think I won't be here to see this very soon. I'll be gone, but this will still be here.

How very strange indeed.

When the clock showed eight A.M., he picked up the phone and dialed the private number he'd been given the night before. It picked up at the other end, and a familiar voice came on the line.

"Yes?"

"Dr. Ibalis? Lyman Terrell."

"Ah, good morning, Mr. Terrell. How are you?" he asked, then paused before asking, "Are you... better?"

"No. I haven't been able to—"

"Yes?"

"I can't do it. I've spent all of yesterday wandering around hospitals and hospices, looking at dying people, sick people... I've been down every back street in this town, looking at homeless people, lost people, drug addicts and hooker and pushers, people who are probably never going to be anything in this world, and I just... I can't do it. I can't give this... *thing*... to someone else.

"Dr. Ibalis, I'm an attorney, a *defense* attorney. My job is to save lives. To help people. I can't... I just can't do this."

"Not even if it means saving your own life?"

"Not even if it means saving my own life."

There was a long sigh at the other end of the phone. "I see. Well, you are not the first to say this, and you will probably not be the last. But at least you had the option. Still have it, in fact, until this afternoon."

"Doesn't matter. I've made my decision. I'll spend what time I have doing what I've always done, until... well, until I can't do it anymore. I just... well, I just wanted you to know."

"I understand, and though I am disappointed, for what it's worth, I respect your decision."

"Thanks."

"You're welcome. Goodbye, Mr. Terrell."

"Goodbye."

He racked the phone and leaned back in his chair. It was a hard decision, but it was the only one he felt clean making. Once the tumor returned, he would again have only about a week, maybe two. Time enough to put his affairs in order, do what needed to be done.

He looked back across the street. Kids were starting to come out of their homes, shouldering backpacks on their way to school.

So strange, to think that I won't see this anymore, he thought. *So strange.*

He stood and pulled on his coat, heading for the door as the phone rang in the foyer. He picked it up to find Carol's voice at the other end.

"We just got a call from the Court Clerk. The jury foreman says they're ready to render a verdict in the Price case. The judge is going to reconvene in one hour."

"I'm on my way," he said, and hung up the phone.

It would be nice to go out with a victory, he decided as he looked out at the morning sky. *Real nice.*

Lyman was seated at the defense table as the door to the holding pen opened and Bill Price was ushered inside by the bailiff. Instead of the expensive suit he'd worn earlier, he was wearing the orange prison jumpsuit. Now that the verdict was in, there was nothing to be gained or lost by his appearance. He smiled for Bill's sake, but the smile wasn't returned. As Price sat beside him, the jury was brought in through the other door.

"Look at the way they're looking at me," Price said. "They found me guilty, I just know it."

"Try not to get excited, Bill, we still don't know—"

He broke off as the judge was announced by the bailiff. A moment later, the judge entered and took his place behind the bench.

Lyman felt his stomach tighten with nervousness, awaiting the decision. *Let me go out with just one victory, God, is that really so much to ask for?*

The judge turned to the jury box. "Mr. Foreman, has the jury reached a verdict?"

"Yes, we have, your honor."

"Very well," the judge said. "Will the defendant, William Edward Price, please rise."

Price stood, and Lyman stood with him. Lyman could see that he was shaking.

"The foreman will now read the verdict," the judge said.

The foreman unfolded a sheet of paper in his hands, and read what was written there. "Your honor, on the charge of murder in the first degree, we the jury, in the above entitled action, find the defendant, William Edward Price, not guilty."

Yes! Lyman thought as the courtroom exploded all around them. *Thank you, thank you—*

"I don't believe it," Price whispered, wavering on his feet. "I don't—"

"Congratulations," Lyman said. "You're a free man."

"I am?"

"You are."

Eyes brimming with tears, Price embraced him. Lyman looked past him, to where the victim's family was devastated, embracing each other in agony and betrayal. The victim's sister, Elizabeth, covered her face with her hands, weeping openly.

You arrested the wrong man, Lyman thought but didn't say, because this was neither the time nor the place. *It happens. Keep after it, keep after the police, and sooner or later you'll find the right man. And I hope you do, I truly do.*

"So how does it feel to be a free man, Bill?" They were in a private room in the courthouse set aside for lawyer/client conversations.

"I feel good," Price said, changing into the clothes he'd been wearing when arrested. "But I'll feel a lot better once I get my street clothes."

"What, you don't think prison orange looks good on you?"

"I don't think it looks good on *anybody*," Price said, then grinned. "You did it. You did it, Mr. Terrell. I owe you so much."

"It's all right, Bill. I needed something like this almost as much as you did."

"I doubt it. I mean, I was facing the death penalty. I'm telling you, Mr. Terrell, you don't know what it's like, thinking you're gonna die like that."

"I... think I may have some idea," Lyman said quietly. "So what are your plans now?" Better to get the subject off death. He'd had more than enough talk of death lately. He wanted to talk about life instead for a while. *It'd be nice for a change of pace.*

"For starters, I'm gonna go out and get completely stinking drunk for three days."

Lyman laughed. He realized he hadn't laughed in over a week. "Excellent choice," he said. "And after that?"

"After that... I got some business to attend to."

"Oh?"

"Well, you heard what some of those people said about me during the trial—"

"You have to let that go, Bill. It's over."

"No, it's *not* over. It'll never *be* over. Every time I walk out on a street in the old neighborhood, they'll be there, staring at me, like they know something. Like that lousy sister, Liz, sticking her nose in where it didn't belong—"

"Bill, c'mon—"

"She was always doing that, just sticking her nose in, again and again." He was prowling the room now, getting more and more agitated. "I tell you one thing, though, if she'd stuck that damned nose in five minutes earlier there'd be nobody to—"

Lyman felt his blood go cold in his veins. "Nobody to what?"

Price stopped, realizing where he was and who he was talking to. "Nothing, I—"

"You said if she'd been there five minutes earlier—"

"Look, I... you said they can't try me twice for the same thing, right? Once I'm clear, I'm clear, right?"

"Double jeopardy, that's correct. But what—"

"Okay, okay, just so's I'm clear on that. See, thing is, you've been real good to me, Mr. Terrell. Real good. You believed in me when nobody else would. So you should know... I was there that night Claris died.

"You gotta understand, the two of 'em, Claris and Liz, they were always watching me, sneaking around and badmouthing me to everybody, talking about how I got sent up once for drugs, well big freakin' deal, everybody has something in their past, but they wouldn't let go, they just kept at me and at me until one day I just couldn't take it anymore, and I went there, and I did it, I took care of one of 'em but the sister was out shopping, out *shopping* can you believe it, and I didn't finish the job."

"God," Lyman whispered.

"But I'm going to now. By God, you can bet on that, Mr. Terrell. I'm gonna finish the job right this time, send her to hell right alongside her sister, where they both belong. And this time I know all the stuff I did wrong last time, I know all the ways to make sure they don't get me again. You know those people, Mr. Terrell, you know what they are... they got it coming, you know? Yeah... three days drinking and I'm gonna go back there and finish what I started."

Oh God, oh God, oh God—

"So how do I look?"

Lyman forced himself back into the room, back into the horror he had created. "What?"

"I said, 'how do I look?' "

"I can't... I can't think right now...."

"Then I guess I must look pretty cool, huh? Knocked your brain right outta the box." He glanced at his watch. "Two o'clock. I'll be outta here in time for happy hour, get an early start on my drinking, y'know?"

Three o'clock?

Price went to the door and knocked hard. "Yo, buddy, you can let me out now. Hey!"

Three o'clock.

Twenty-three hours since—

He looked up at the sound of keys jingling in the door lock. It opened to reveal the guards waiting outside to escort him past the onlookers outside to where a cab would be waiting.

If he goes on a bender for three days, it'll be too late for him to do anything except—

"Anyway, thanks for everything you did for me, Mr. Terrell," Price said. "I owe you one. You ever need anything, and I mean anydamnthing... you call me. Okay?"

He started out the door.

"Mr. Price? Bill...?"

Price stopped in the doorway. "Yeah?"

Lyman pulled the glove off his right hand and extended it. "It's... considered somewhat traditional... to shake the hand of the man who just saved your life."

"Oh, yeah, yeah it is, isn't it?"

He stepped over and shook Lyman's hand.

Lyman returned the favor, and with his revealed hand shook Price's hand vigorously.

"Whoa," Price said with a grin, "you must've been more nervous up there than I was. Your hand's all hot and sweaty."

"Is it? Must've been the gloves."

"Well, doesn't matter," Price said. "I'm always glad to shake the hand of justice."

"So am I, Mr. Price," Lyman said. "So am I."

ACTS OF TERROR

Saturday

Louise Simonton stepped down off the porch, heading to where the mailman was coming up the sidewalk. He noted her with a nod and a smile as he slipped envelopes into the mailbox. "Morning, Mrs. Simonton," he said.

She returned the smile, quickly, furtively. "Good morning."

He riffled through the rest of the mail, putting it in her hand. "You can always tell when it's Saturday. Supermarket sales, fliers, bills, all the junk mail seems to pile up."

"I'm sure it must be very heavy."

"You get used to it after a while," he said. "That should do it. Oh, yeah, I almost forgot. There's this." He reached into his bag and pulled out a cardboard box with her name printed on it in familiar script. "Here you go."

Mail in one hand, she reached for the package, and as she did, the shoulder of her dress slipped just enough to reveal the bruise it had been concealing. Dark and flecked with red, it stood out starkly against her pale skin.

The postman frowned as he handed her the package, and his eyes met hers. "Looks painful."

She glanced at the bruise, and hurriedly slipped the strap back into place. "It's nothing, really. I was cleaning out the upper cabinets in the kitchen and I stood up—rammed right into an open door. Silly of me, I guess."

She risked a glance back at him, saw the doubt in his face, and looked away again.

"Happens to us all, Mrs. Simonton. But—" Again the frown, an expression of things better left unsaid. "Do try to be a little more careful."

"I will. Thank you."

As the postman crossed the street, Louise turned her attention to the package in her hands. She started back up the sidewalk toward the house, a tentative smile appearing as she gently shook the package, wondering what could be inside.

"Jack?" she called as she stepped up onto the porch and into the house.

The living room was surprisingly dark coming in from the brightness outside. She found Jack bathed in the flickering light from the television. He was watching football, his expression distracted.

"Jack?" she said again, setting the mail down on the sofa beside her as she sat. "Got something from my sister." She began to unwrap the package. It was bound tightly with the kind of clear tape that was almost impossible to rip. "I wonder what it—"

Then from the chair: "No."

She flinched instinctively, even though he'd said it quietly. He had spoken without looking at her, as though trying to avoid being distracted from his game. "But I wasn't going to—I just wanted to see what it was, that's all. It's just that it's my sister and it's been so long."

His eyes never wandering from the television, he spoke to her as to a child. "It's one-oh-five. One o'clock is lunch, Louise. Lunch. One o'clock. Go in and fix lunch. Now."

Biting her lip, she set the unopened package down on the sofa with the rest of the mail and started for the kitchen.

"Any *decent* mail?" he called back to her.

"Just a bill from the electric company. They say they'll turn off the power if we don't take care of it. If we could just send them a little—"

He turned, and for the first time, looked at her. Fixed on her. There was something darkly feral in those eyes, something that seemed to relish the imminence of possible violence.

She had intruded on his consciousness. It was the last thing she had wanted to do.

"Are you saying I'm not doing my job, Louise? You saying I'm not a good husband? I don't take care of you the way you'd like?"

"No, Jack, no, I'm not. I didn't mean that. No, I didn't."

"I mean, it's easy to complain when I'm out there working all day and you just sit around here and do nothing."

She stiffened, just a little. "I do—"

But the sentence died at a look from him. *That* look, the one she had come to know so well. The look she'd seen just before...

Just before.

"You do what, Louise?"

She lowered her eyes. "Nothing, Jack."

At the sound of crowds roaring from the television, he turned away. "Now you see? You've made me miss something."

"I'm sorry."

If he heard her, he gave no sign, his attention back on the tube. It was as though she was barely in the room. "Go on. It's one-ten, Louise. Ten minutes past one o'clock. You know what one o'clock is, don't you?"

"One o'clock is lunch," she said, and wiping her hands on her apron, she stepped into the kitchen.

They ate in silence. Soup, sandwich—a BLT, the bacon crisp the way he liked it—a beer for him and an orange juice for her. As she ate, she glanced furtively past Jack to the living room, to the package that sat, unopened, on the sofa.

He looked up, catching her before she could turn away. "What are you looking at?"

"Hmm?" She tried to appear interested in her food.

"You keep glancing up every five minutes, so I figured there must be something real interesting."

"No, it's—I was just wondering if I could open the package now. It might be—I don't know—perishable or something. You know how Lynn is, always sending cookies and things."

Her words trailed off into silence.

She cleared her throat. "Can I open the package now?"

He grunted an affirmative and returned to his lunch.

Leaving the unfinished sandwich, she crossed to the living room, expectation once again bringing a smile to her face. She sat down and unwrapped the package with careful, precise movements, prolonging the pleasure of anticipation.

"Cookies," he called to her as she unwrapped. "Like she thinks we need cookies. If they *are* cookies, you're sending them right back, you hear me? We can feed ourselves just fine."

She dug through Styrofoam peanuts and felt something cool and hard. She pulled it out, brushing aside pieces of packing to reveal the tiny figurine. It was a porcelain dog, a slender Doberman with wide eyes, exquisitely detailed and painted and gleaming with the late afternoon light. She turned it in her hands, a tiny sigh of delight escaping from her lips. "Oh, Lynn—you remembered!"

"Remembered what?"

She turned to see Jack standing in the doorway. Instinctively, she clutched the dog closer. "It was—well, it was my birthday Friday."

"Ummm." He stepped closer, reached for the figurine. "Let me see it."

She hesitated. "It's nothing, really, just a little dog, she sent it to me, please—"

"Did I say I was gonna do anything to it?" he snapped at her. "Now let me see it or I'll give you something to be afraid of."

She handed him the figurine. He turned it casually in his hand, looked at its face. "Woof-woof," he said, and laughed, as though expecting it to bark back. "Woof!"

She wanted to take it back, but she knew if she did she would startle him, and if she startled him he'd break it, and it would be her fault.

It was always her fault.

So she sat and waited and did nothing until, finally, he handed the figurine carelessly back to her and returned to the kitchen to finish his lunch.

She cradled the figurine against her cheek, its polished porcelain cool to her skin. It was hers now.

Hers.

Sunday

Her face hurt.

Louise could hear him outside, in the cool predawn twilight, loading the pickup with fishing gear. He was whistling a tune she didn't recognize.

She knelt on the floor and continued picking up the pieces of broken plates, careful not to cut herself on the slivers of glass and china. Afterward she would have to go over the floor with a mop to catch all the bits and pieces of uneaten breakfast. It wouldn't do to miss something and have ants all over the place. Jack hated ants.

The screen door behind the kitchen rattled open, and Jack stepped inside. She didn't look at him, only continued to pick up the pieces. "I'm going," he said.

She nodded.

He stepped closer. "Let me see."

She stood and turned just enough for the light to fall on her cheek, where by now the bruise was purpling. She could feel the swelling pressing against the bottom of her eye, as though something were caught in the bottom lid. She tried not to blink too often. It made her eyes water. They were watering now.

"Ah, it's nothing," Jack said. "Don't make such a big deal about it. Such a little crybaby."

Louise looked away. "I'm sorry I burned the eggs."

"Well, it won't happen again, will it?" he said. "Now I've gotta get going. Those fish won't wait all day." She hesitated. "Come on, give me a kiss."

She lifted her face to his and kissed him, though it made her cheek hurt to do so. That done, he turned and headed for the door.

"When will you be back?" she called after him.

He stood in the doorway, shrugged. "When I get back. What am I supposed to do, punch a clock?" With a sound of disgust, he stepped outside, the screen door closing with a bang and a clatter. She could hear his boots crunching on the gravel driveway as he headed toward the pickup.

Pushing the hair out of her face, she went to the sink where she had deposited the bigger of the broken pieces. One plate had broken neatly in two, leading her to hope that perhaps it could be fixed. She tried to fit the two halves together, but they shifted in her hands, grinding grittily against each other. She pushed harder, as though she might force them to fit, but they kept slipping, more bits and pieces slivering off into the sink, and she was crying, and it wouldn't fit, and her face hurt, and nothing fit anymore, nothing worked anymore, and she was sobbing, great heaving sobs that wracked her lungs as she smashed the halves in the sink, picked up the new pieces and smashed them again, over and over until there was nothing left to smash and she knelt on the floor, her forehead against the cool tile of the sink.

She ran the back of her hand against her eyes, and when she opened them, the first thing she saw was the porcelain dog she had set on the kitchen counter when she'd come in to fix breakfast.

She hadn't remembered turning it so it faced the sink, and her. She reached for it and cradled it in her lap as she rocked back and forth on the floor.

"Damn him," she whispered, quietly, as though afraid to hear herself saying it, "*damn* him."

Outside, in the dark, the car refused to start.

Jack turned the key in the ignition. It caught, sputtered out, caught and sputtered out again.

What the hell? he thought.

Then, out of the corner of his eye: movement. Something black against black, at the edge of the woods behind the house. There and not there. He tried to find it, but there was only the dark.

He tried the engine again. It sputtered—

And suddenly the pickup rocked as the Doberman slammed into it. Big and black and half-mad, its lips curled back in fury, it bit and snapped at the air, at him, clawing at the glass window, howling and barking and rushing the door again and again, out of control. He shouted at it, yelled incomprehensible things at it, but it only launched itself at the door that much harder, eyes burning with anger, with hate and rage, trying to claw its way in, in where he was.

Jack hit the car horn, held it down. Somebody had to come. Somebody had to hear.

The porch light went on. He turned to where the door started to open.

"Louise!"

The night was suddenly silent.

She stood in the doorway, clutching her robe as she looked out at him. "What is it?"

He glanced around.

The dog was gone.

Cautious, in case it was still there, hiding somewhere in the dark, he popped the driver's door. "Jesus, did—did you *see* that thing?"

"What?"

"What do you mean, what? A dog. It was right here. Thought it was gonna tear right into the car."

"I don't see anything."

"Thing must've run off," he said, trying not to sound too relieved. "Probably scared off by the horn. Good thing, too. Man if I'd had my gun." He shook his head, stepped back into the cab. "You get back inside. First thing Monday you're calling the cops, the ASPCA, find out who's got a dog loose around here."

"All right," she said, and stood in the doorway, watching as he drove away. As he passed, he glanced back, and though he couldn't be sure, it looked as though she were cradling something in her hands.

"And it was just the most beautiful dress I've ever seen," Louise said. "I wish you could've been there, you would have loved it. The color was perfect."

Claire sipped at her coffee. "I'm sure it would go just right with the new color on your face."

Louise looked away, turning her attention to cutting out a piece of brownie. Claire was probably her best friend, had been for nearly three years. But some things were supposed to be off limits. Things that had remained unspoken for a long time, and would have remained so except for Claire's insistence on bringing it up again. "I don't want to talk about it."

"I know, I know—but you can't keep letting him *do* this to you."

"It's not his fault, not really. It's me. I do things wrong, I'm too slow. I try not to, but sometimes I just get him mad."

"That's garbage and you know it. There's no excuse for the things he does to you. And how about you? Don't you ever get mad? Don't you ever get angry at what he does?"

Louise stopped as she put the brownie down on the plate.

Don't you ever get mad?

She nodded. "Sometimes. Sometimes, like this morning, I get so mad at him—I could feel it burning inside me, like my whole body was about to explode in fire and smoke and I *hate* myself when I feel like that."

"So instead you bury it. For God's sake, Louise, let it out. It's okay."

Louise smiled. "That's not how my mother raised me," she said, and absently petted the porcelain dog on the counter, "or my sister. And though I don't know about her, there are times I'm afraid."

"Afraid of what? Him?"

"No," Louise said, and returned to the table. "Afraid of what all that anger might do if I ever let it out."

Tuesday

Louise put the finishing touches to the dining room table. Four place settings. The best china. Cloth napkins. A fresh floral arrangement in the middle of the table, just like the one she'd seen in a magazine. She was just lighting the candles when she heard the front door open and close again.

"I'm home."

"Back here," she called.

He stood in the doorway, still clutching his thermos. "What's with the extra place settings?"

"Phil and Claire are coming over for dinner. We set it up last week—remember?"

From the look on his face, he didn't. "Yeah, sure. How come all the fancy stuff?"

"Well, I just thought it would be—nice, I guess. Doesn't it look pretty? I found some of this stuff in the attic. We haven't used it in years. I just thought maybe you might like something nice. You work so hard. Maybe a nice dinner would help you relax a little."

The doorbell rang behind Jack. "That must be them now." With a final glance at the table, she moved past Jack into the living room. She could just see them through the window.

"Right on time," Louise said.

"As always," Claire said, holding a large salad bowl. "Where can I put this?"

"The kitchen's fine. Here, let me get some spoons for that."

Behind them, Jack closed the door behind Phil.

"How you doing, Jack?"

"Fine, fine—listen, can I see you in the garage a minute? Got something I want to show you."

"Sure."

"Don't be too long," Claire called to them as they headed toward the garage. "I think Louise has outdone herself here."

"Do you approve?" Louise said, nodding toward the table as she searched for the appropriate salad spoons.

"Very nice. Is this an Occasion?"

"No, I just thought from now on, maybe if I tried a little harder, Jack would—you know."

Claire nodded. She knew. She smiled, but it seemed to Louise a smile of resignation and care and dismay. She opened her arms and, to Louise's surprise, hugged her. "You're a sweet, forgiving fool, and he doesn't deserve you."

Louise turned away to continue the search for the spoons, embarrassed but somehow feeling very good about herself just now. One more check of the cutlery drawer revealed the spoons hiding behind the silverware tray. "Here you go," she said, and handed them to Claire.

"Thanks."

Louise checked her watch. "The roast's about ready. I'd better get Jack. You know how those two are once they get talking."

She headed down the hallway that connected to the garage, pausing just outside the door. She could hear them talking inside. Phil sounded upset about something, and for a moment, she hesitated, not sure she should interrupt.

"Look, Jack," she could hear Phil say, "what you do on your own time is your own business, but don't drag me into it, okay?"

"Will you give me a break? It's not like I'm asking something big here."

I shouldn't be doing this, she thought, but went ahead and pushed the door open just a crack. Phil was standing beneath the garage light as Jack absently put his power tools into their racks, talking all the while.

"All you have to do is say Frank called you Saturday to go fishing Sunday," Jack said, "and you couldn't make it because you had work or something, so I had to go with him. That's all."

"That's all. Just lie for you."

"Hell, Phil, it might not even come up. I just want us to be clear on this in case it does, okay?"

Phil shook his head in disbelief. "All right, all right. Jesus. How long do you think you can keep doing this? It's only a matter of time before she finds out."

"She won't find out anything. You got to realize she's not real bright, Phil. She believes what you tell her. You tell her the sun shines at night, and she'll go out at midnight with her sunglasses on. As a woman—hell, as a human being—she's not worth the powder to blow her up."

"And Denise is?"

Louise leaned against the wall, distantly aware of the fact that her hands were trembling. She let go of the doorknob, afraid the shaking might give her away.

Although she couldn't see his face, she could hear the smile in Jack's voice. "Phil, she's got legs up to here. And what's between 'em—oh, man, if you only knew."

The world kicked slantwise beneath her, and for a moment she thought she was going to be sick. As from a great distance, she heard her own thoughts. *Close the door, remember to close the door or they'll know you've been listening.* She did it, or thought she did, as if it mattered, as if anything mattered anymore, and walked numbly back down the hall toward the kitchen.

Oh, God, she thought. *Oh, God, oh, God, oh, God.*

She walked automatically to the sink, to the fresh carrots that needed slicing, the carrots she'd picked so carefully that afternoon at the grocery store, and she knew they were there for a reason, but she couldn't seem to remember what it was.

"Louise?" Claire appeared at her elbow. "Louise? You okay?"

Louise nodded. "I'm—I'm fine."

"You sure? You look—"

"*I said I'm fine, all right?*" She grabbed one of the carrots and began cutting, slicing it into neat, precise one-quarter-inch-thin slices, just like she'd been taught.

Phil came into the room behind her and said something to Claire. It might have been about Jack coming in, in a second, but she barely heard it, because she was busy slicing carrots, because that's what was important right now, nothing else, she couldn't think of anything else, didn't want to deal with anything else, just slice them the way she was supposed to because she always did what she was told, she took care of the house just the way she was told and she made the eggs just the way she was told.

Oh God Christ in heaven I hate him how could he do this to me he was hitting me and going to her putting his hands all over her the same hands he used to hit me and hit me and hit me and I hate him how could he

Inside the garage, Jack was hanging up the last of the power tools when he became aware of the sound. A deep, rumbling, low-pitched growl from somewhere behind him. He turned, slowly, knowing immediately that it was back.

The Doberman stood against the far wall, not moving, just watching him, chest vibrating with the growl that seemed to come from a place impossibly deep inside it. Watching him with a hatred that was terrible to see. Lips curled in fury.

It stepped forward.

Jack backpedaled along the worktable, not taking his eyes off it, fumbling for the rack he knew was there, the shotgun that was hanging on the wall, damn it, it had to be there somewhere.

Chopping. Chopping and carving and cutting and slicing.

A hand on her arm. "Louise?"

Chopping

The Doberman was halfway across the garage when his hand brushed the cartridges. He thought at any moment it would rush him. But it moved forward slowly, deliberately, one step at a time, never taking its eyes off him, slow and confident and inevitable.

He raised the shotgun to his shoulder.

and slicing and slashing and

"*Louise?*"

A hand took hers, more insistently this time. It took the knife out of her hands and turned her around. After a moment she managed to focus on Claire. "Are you okay? You're white as a sheet."

Only distantly aware of doing it, Louise nodded. Claire was looking at her *that way* again, with a mix of concern and pity—and in that moment the rage passed, and there was nothing left but a great, gaping numbness in the middle of her soul that chilled her to the marrow.

and *fired.*

Jack winced at the muzzle flash. He'd pulled both triggers and the kick had nearly knocked him over. He blinked to clear away the cordite in his eyes, and looked to where the Doberman had been, where it was supposed to be.

Except it wasn't there.

There was only a huge hole in the gun rack he'd started to build last summer. As he heard the others running down the hall toward the garage, calling his name, asking if he was okay, he broke the shotgun and pulled out the shells. There was no way it could've gotten past him that fast.

But it had been there. He *had* seen it, damn it.

The two policemen who came to the door a few minutes after the shotgun blast looked unconvinced. "I wish we could be of more help, Mr. Simonton, but we talked to your neighbors and they say they haven't seen a dog matching the description you gave us, and as far as we can determine, none of them owns a dog like that."

"Then it's from outside the neighborhood," Jack said, "maybe it got loose from some kennel, maybe it's got rabies, who knows? I'm just telling you I saw it twice already, and you people better do

105

something about it. That thing could kill somebody. I mean, what the hell am I paying taxes for?"

One of the policemen, the taller of the two, looked to Louise. "Ma'am? You're sure you didn't see it?"

Louise straightened in her chair. "No, I'm sorry, I didn't."

"Then I'm afraid there's really nothing we can do until it turns up again. We've put the word out. If you or anyone sees it, just let us know. Meanwhile, Mr. Simonton, I would remind you of the laws about the use of firearms within city limits. Next time you fire that thing, I suggest you be more certain what you're aiming at."

With that, they left. Claire and Phil made their good-byes a few minutes later. Nobody felt much like dinner now. Whether they sensed what Louise was feeling, she' didn't know and barely cared. With an uncharacteristic lack of interest, she watched them leave, cradling the porcelain dog in her lap.

Jack started up as soon as they were out the door.

"You were a fat lot of help," he said. "Why can't you back me up once in a while? Why can't you *do* something besides play with that damned piece of junk all the time?"

She left it in her lap. "I didn't see it, Jack. I can't lie, you know that."

"Great. One more thing you can't do."

He went across the room to switch on the television. She set the porcelain figurine down on the coffee table. "Jack?"

"Hmm?"

"How was the fishing Sunday? You never did tell me how it went."

He shrugged, didn't look back at her. "It was fine. You know Frank, talk, talk, talk. Scares away every fish in the county. Surprised he caught anything at all."

"And you didn't catch anything, all day."

"That's right," he said, swiveling around to face her. "What is this, the third degree or something?"

She said nothing.

He stood. "You know, I don't think I like the tone in your voice. Always suspicious, aren't you? So now you're saying I can't even go out fishing with a friend?"

"No, Jack, I was just—"

He moved toward her, his face darkening. She got to her feet quickly, backing up. "You said no, Louise. You know I don't like it when you say no. You got a problem?"

"Jack—"

"You got a problem? Huh? I'll give you a problem!"

Then she was shrieking at him, the voice hardly recognizable as her own. "*I heard you, Jack! I heard you with Phil! I heard you damn it!*"

He paused. For the first time, she'd given him pause. Then he started forward again.

And he was smiling.

"So what?"

"Jack—"

Advancing toward her. "So what're you gonna do about it?"

"No, Jack, please!"

And her head rang with the force of a slap that caught her across the face, and then another, and she held up her hands to fend off the blows but he was too strong, he was always too strong, and another slap knocked her head against the wall, and now she was screaming, "Stop it, Jack! *Stop it, stop it, STOP IT!*"

He stopped. Suddenly, abruptly, he stopped, and through her upraised arms she saw it.

A shimmering in the air between them. A twisting and a swirling and then the Doberman was there, just there, snarling and snapping, lips skinned back in feral rage. It lunged for his leg, teeth closing on air as Jack cried out and jumped backward, nearly falling over the coffee table in his hurry to get away.

It started toward him.

"Don't just stand there!" he yelled. "Do something!"

She didn't move. She stood with her back to the wall, hands pressed to her mouth. She knew she should cry out, or run, or call for help.

She did nothing.

The Doberman advanced.

Jack bolted for the door, threw it open.

The Doberman was outside, on the porch.

He slammed the door.

It was back inside. With him.

"Christ," he said, and ran for the kitchen, anywhere that was away from the Doberman.

She waited for it to run after him.

It didn't.

It paused, and turned, and looked at her.

She met its gaze. For only a moment.

But long enough for her to recognize the rage in its eyes.

"Oh my God," she whispered, and looked to the porcelain dog, the porcelain Doberman she had held and cradled and wept over. "Oh, God, no, it can't be."

The Doberman turned and ran into the kitchen, after Jack, howling and snarling, snapping at the air. "No!" she called, and snatched up the porcelain figure, running after it. "Stop! I don't want you to do it!"

Jack was already at the back door, throwing it open.

The Doberman was outside.

No way out.

He ran back into the living room, pulling her with him. "Come on! We've got to get out of here! Goddamn thing's not normal—some kind of *thing*, I don't know—"

She fought his grip. "No! Jack, I'm sorry, but I can't make it stop it just came out I didn't know and now I can't stop it I *can't stop it*!"

He grabbed her, shook her hard. "What are you talking about?"

"*It's me, damn it, it's me*! Don't you understand? It's here because I wanted you to stop hitting me and now it won't go away!"

He grabbed her by the shoulders.

A low, threatening growl came from behind him.

He spun around.

Too late.

It leapt, slamming into him. They fell to the floor, a tangle of limbs and teeth snapping at him, trying for wrists, face, throat, anything that was soft and vulnerable and Jack. He cried out, pushing it away, trying to get a grip on it, but it twisted in his hands, all teeth and fur and fury, and it was like trying to grab a handful of razors.

She wanted to stop it.

She didn't want to stop it.

God, it had hurt so much.

Blood appeared on his arms, through his shirt.

"No," she said, and she thought it sounded as though it were coming from someone else. "No."

The Doberman hesitated.

Jack lurched to his feet and stumbled down the hall, toward the garage.

She looked to where the Doberman was—but it wasn't.

She hurried to catch up with him.

"Where is it?" Jack was shrieking now. He looked at her in the doorway. "The shotgun!" The rack was empty beside him. "Where the hell's the shotgun?"

A growl behind him.

He turned, slowly, to face it.

The Doberman stood in the middle of the garage, straddling what remained of the shotgun.

He reached under the counter, came up with a crowbar and held it in front of him. "All right," he said,

"all *right*. You want a piece of me? You come and get it. Come on—COME ON!"

The Doberman launched itself at Jack, and they went down in a tumble, lashing out at each other, trying for the soft places.

The Doberman found it first.

Its teeth closed on his arm, and held on. He screamed and heaved his arm until the dog fell off, taking a piece of his flesh with it. It tumbled to the ground and came up snarling.

Jack held the crowbar in his good arm, no longer convinced of the good it would do.

The Doberman advanced.

"Louise," he said, "please, for God's sake—call it off! *Make it stop*!"

She held out the figurine, her hands trembling. "I can't, Jack! Don't you see? Maybe I could've, once. When I still loved you. But I—God help me, Jack, I don't love you anymore! And now—now there's nothing I can do! I can't stop it!"

Jack licked his lips, edging around as the dog came closer. "Look," he said, and she recognized the voice as the one he used when he was thinking fast, on his face a look of sudden realization, "just call it off and—and I promise it'll be different. Just give me a chance, okay? Just a—*chance*!"

And he lunged.

Not at the dog. At her.

At the figurine in her hands.

He caught it with the crowbar and knocked it clear across the garage. It struck with the crunch of shattering porcelain.

But the Doberman was still there, now positioned between him and the crowbar.

Louise didn't notice. She walked past him, toward the glittering debris at the far end of the garage.

The Doberman advanced.

He scuttled away from it, came up against the wall. "It didn't work," he said, his voice a mix of surprise and fear. "It didn't—Louise? Louise, get—get it AWAY from me!"

She stood over the shattered porcelain figure, and it was as though the man in the garage with her was a complete stranger.

The Doberman stopped. Waiting.

"You broke it," she said, crying. "You broke it and it was the only thing that was really mine and you *broke it* and I *hate you! I HATE YOU*! I wish you were *dead*!"

As though it had been only awaiting that final word, that last permission, the Doberman leapt at Jack in a killing frenzy, teeth snapping at his throat, its roar a nightmare sound, revealed finally in the totality of its madness and rage and pain, and she wanted it to hurt him, she wanted it to hurt him, she wanted—

She pressed her hands to her ears to shut out the sound of his screaming.

Snarling. Tearing. Just another second and it would all be over.

She closed her eyes.

"No," she said, her voice barely a whisper. "Stop it. Stop it! STOP IT!"

The garage vibrated with her scream.

The Doberman stopped, turned, looked at her.

Jack, crying out, but low, afraid to get its attention again, pushed back from it as far as he could.

Louise shook her head, sobbing. "I can't. I just—can't." She looked down at the broken porcelain figure, then at the Doberman. "I can't. But it's broken. I don't know where to send you, where to—"

She stopped.

She knew.

Though she had not wanted to admit it, she had always known.

She bent down on one knee and held out her arms to the Doberman. "Come," she said. "Come on. Come—home."

The Doberman padded softly toward her, and as it drew nearer, she thought it began to shimmer, to become less substantial. A foot away from her, she found she could just see through it to the far wall.

She reached out further. She wanted to touch it. Just once, before it disappeared, she wanted to touch it.

But it was gone.

When she came back the next morning to pick up her things, she had hoped not to find him there, hoped that he would be off somewhere with Diane or Debbie or whatever her name was.

And though he had not been there when she arrived, the sound of his pickup pulling into the driveway came as she was filling the last suitcase. He was getting out just as she crossed the driveway to the car she'd rented that morning. His face was bruised, and his arm hung painfully at his side where the doctor had bandaged it. Apparently he had had time to plan things out, because when she saw him, she recognized the look in his face.

She had had her pound of flesh. Now he would want his.

He came up alongside the car as she threw the suitcase into the trunk. "Where the hell do you think *you're* going?"

She slammed it shut. "Away, Jack. Away from you."

"That so? You think I'm just going to let you leave after what you did to me? You sent your little friend away, remember? And now I've got a score to settle with you, little lady."

She didn't answer, only kept on moving toward the driver's side door.

He put his hand on the door to block her way. "You leave, and I'll just have to come after you."

She met his gaze without flinching. "No. You. Won't."

And from inside the car...a growling.

Inside, the Doberman sat on the passenger seat, watching him warily with eyes like smoldering coals.

Jack took his hand off the car door and stood well out of the way as she got into the car, started the engine, and backed out of the driveway onto the main road, heading for any place that was not this place.

Never looking back.

SPECIAL SERVICE

The clock radio chimed at 8:30 A.M., then switched to the preset station. The usually pleasant disc jockey played the usual Vivaldi. John Selig stretched, then sat up in bed. Leslie was already up and fixing breakfast downstairs. The smell of bacon and coffee drifted up the stairs and into the bedroom.

Another day, another one hundred and twenty dollars and fifty cents, John thought, and staggered into the hall bathroom.

"One egg or two?" Leslie called upstairs.

"Two."

He'd risk the cholesterol. He was feeling particularly good this morning. His presentation was finished, the color copies had come out perfectly, the ad campaign was solid...everything inside told him that this was going to be a very good day.

As he began to shave, John noticed that the mirror was slightly askew. He frowned. He'd installed the mirror himself, as the one on the medicine cabinet wasn't quite the right height. He didn't like it when things he'd done himself started acting up. Somehow, it was easier if it was someone else's fault.

He nudged the mirror back into place, square with the floor and ceiling. It stayed for a moment, then slipped back. He nudged it up again, trying to get it to catch on the nail that was back there, he *knew* it was back there, he'd hammered it in himself.

It wouldn't catch. He tried to force it up again—and abruptly it slipped off its hanger and crashed to the floor. He jumped back, away from the spray of glass.

Concern over getting a shard of glass in his foot was, he would decide much later, the reason it took a full moment for the fact that there was a huge hole behind the mirror to register on his brain.

And another moment for him to recognize the object that was inside the hole behind the mirror: a television camera.

It was during that moment that a small red light suddenly began winking on and off, on and off, and he thought there was a curious buzzing noise coming from within the hole that wasn't there earlier.

"What the hell?" he said aloud, stepping closer to inspect it. Yes, it was definitely a television camera. And yes, that was definitely a worrisome red light. And yes, that was a most curious buzzing noise. He reached down and carefully picked up one of the pieces of the broken mirror. The mirrored side still reflected his face. But the other side of the glass was transparent. He could see right through it—as, obviously, the camera had also been able to do.

"What the hell?" he said again, deciding not to abandon a perfectly good question until it returned with an equally good answer.

From downstairs, he heard the front door open and slam shut again. "Les?" he called. "Leslie? C'mere!"

He could hear footsteps pounding up the stairs toward the bathroom. He turned, but it wasn't Leslie who stood breathlessly in the doorway. It was a repairman, dressed in overalls, carrying a toolbox, wearing a cap and a very businesslike expression.

"That's all right, sir," he said, brushing past John and heading for the mirror. "Don't you worry about a thing. Be fixed in a jiffy." He spoke with a pleasant English accent.

Moving quickly, he started to replace the broken mirror.

"Absolutely scandalous, just shoddy workmanship, pure and simple. Terribly sorry about all this, but that's just the way it is these days, isn't it? Always rush, rush, rush, nobody giving a fig for quality, not like the old days—"

The repairman hammered the new mirror into place. The entire job took only a few seconds. He was a very good repairman.

The only problem that was gradually dawning on John was that 1) he hadn't called a repairman and 2) no repairman could've gotten here that quickly even if he *had* called for one.

"Wait a minute," John said. "What do you think you're doing?"

"Fixing your mirror, what's it look like?"

"But there's a camera back there!"

The repairman looked around, seeming quite astonished by this bit of intelligence. "Where? I don't see a camera."

"*Of course not*! That's because you just covered it up!"

"Did I? Well, that's one job done, then. Good day."

113

With a tip of his hat, the repairman hustled out of the bathroom. John looked from the departing figure, to the mirror, and back again. "Hey!" he called. "*Hey!* Come back here!"

John took off down the stairs at a dead run, charging ahead of the repairman and barely managing to block the doorway in time. "Where the hell do you think you're going?"

"Back to work," the repairman said, "and I suggest you do the same. It's nearly nine o'clock, and you know how Mr. Fetheringall gets when—" He caught himself and shook his head. "Never mind. Ignore that bit. Never said a thing. Good-day."

He tried for the doorknob. John put himself in the way. "Oh, no, not until I—wait a minute! How do you know my boss's name?"

"I don't."

"Yes, you do! You just said it!"

"No, I didn't. Must have me mistaken for somebody else. Good-day."

He tried for the door. John refused to move.

"Look, are you going to stand there all day?" the repairman said.

"Yes! Look, I want to know what you were doing up there!"

"Up where?"

"UPSTAIRS! THE MIRROR! THE TV CAMERA! REMEMBER?"

The repairman looked vacantly at John for a moment, then nodded, quite calmly John thought, as though remembering at last where he'd left his keys. "Ah, yes. That. Nothing whatsoever. Just a little routine maintenance."

"That's a TV CAMERA! You've been spying on me!"

The repairman—John noticed the name tag on his shirt read *Archie*, written in script under the anonymous letters JSTV—looked greatly offended at this. "I have *not* been spying on you. It's just part of the job, that's all. You do your work, and I do mine, and now why don't you be a good fellow and let me get back to it?"

"No. I'm going to call the police."

"Oh, you wouldn't want to do that, no, I don't think so."

"Why not?"

"False complaint. Show me where fixing a camera is against the law."

John opened his mouth to reply, but nothing came out. He was quite right, actually, nothing illegal about fixing a camera—

What are you talking about? his brain screamed at him, and he came up out of his reverie just in time to block Archie's hand as he reached for the doorknob.

"That's not the point! I DIDN'T PUT THAT CAMERA THERE IN THE FIRST PLACE! IT'S NOT MY CAMERA! I DON'T EVEN KNOW HOW IT GOT THERE!"

Archie appraised him with a look of utter calm and sudden comprehension. "Ah, well then, you want Installation. Sorry, but that's not my department. Have a nice day."

He grabbed again at the doorknob, barely managing to get a piece of it before John slammed the door shut. "You know, you're really not as pleasant in person as you are on TV," Archie said.

"That's it. I'm calling the police."

He grabbed Archie by the arm and started marching him toward the phone. Archie twisted in his grip, but John wasn't about to let go.

"See here," Archie complained, "there's really no need for this, I—" He looked around nervously, then lowered his voice. "Listen, John—can I call you John?—I'd rather not we made a big scene over this, it makes everything so—complicated. I'd tell you, really I would, but—"

He looked around again, nervously. John wondered if this was a habit with him. "Look, all right, I'll tell you—but we have to stand right—in there."

John looked to where he was pointing.

He was pointing at the hall closet.

"You're mad," John said.

"That's the only place."

"In the *closet?* Why there?"

"It's outside camera range," Archie said, drawing him toward the closet.

"But the camera's in the bathroom."

"No, no, the *other* cameras."

John was still processing this when Archie jumped ahead and

stepped into the closet. "*What* other cameras?" No answer. "Get out of my closet!"

From inside: "No!"

"I'm not going in there."

"Then you'll never find out what this is all about."

John sighed. Waited a moment, then sighed again. Under the circumstances, it seemed the right thing to do. *I must be completely out of my mind*, he thought, and stepped into the closet, drawing the door closed after him.

It was dark inside. He reached for the string for the overhead light and pulled it. Nothing. He'd forgotten that the bulb had burned out last week. Fumbling around in the dark, narrow space, he tried to get hold of the flashlight.

He grabbed hold of something.

"That's not the flashlight," said the other voice in the darkness.

"Shut up," John said, and finally found the flashlight. He flicked it on. He thought that the light, beneath their faces, gave Archie a singularly sinister aspect. He hoped it did the same for him.

"You know, you really should have that bulb replaced," Archie said.

"Forget the bulb. Talk."

Archie hesitated. "I want you to know I'm risking my job just telling you this. You're not supposed to know, you see. I mean, it takes all the fun out of it, doesn't it?"

"Takes all the fun out of *what?*"

Archie sighed. "Look at my chest."

"Excuse me?"

He pointed to the name tag on his chest. "Here. See those letters? JSTV written in big, friendly letters?"

"Yeah, so? What about it?"

"Stands for John Selig Television. You're—well, you're on TV."

John blinked. "I am?"

"Yes. Twenty-four hours a day. You've got quite a following. Did you know you've got people who tune in, in the middle of the night just to watch you sleep? Extraordinary. Absolutely extraordinary."

John nodded, suddenly feeling as though his head had become somehow disconnected from the rest of his body and was frantically dialing directory information to get hold of it, only to find it had an unlisted number. "Who's—who's watching?"

"Oh, everyone! Well, everyone who subscribes, at least. It's a special cable channel, just started, oh, I guess five years ago. I hear the ratings are excellent, especially right here in this area. Only natural, I guess, you being a local and all."

"Everybody?" John said. "You mean—the neighbors—all the people I know—they—"

"They were quite helpful, yes. Helped us put cameras all over the place for maximum coverage. Your job, your car, the office, living room, den, bathroom—well, that one was less than perfect, wasn't it—bedroom—"

"My *bedroom?*"

Archie looked momentarily sheepish. "Well, it IS a cable service, adults only, that sort of thing. Well, now you know, so if you'll excuse me—"

With another tip of his hat, Archie plunged out of the closet and back into the hall.

"I don't believe you," John said, following him out. "How could something like this happen without someone telling me?"

"Shhhh!" Archie whispered, looking around. "That's the whole point! If you knew you were on TV, you'd act differently. It'd take all the fun out of it, like I said. So everyone on the service signs a contract specifying they won't spill the beans. Besides, it gives all the folks you know a chance to be on TV, and in my business I've learned that most people'll do *anything* to be on TV. They'll—"

He stopped as a beeper on his belt suddenly chirruped. He switched it off and took hold of the doorknob. "Sorry. Have to go. Be a good fellow and don't tell anyone I told you, all right?"

Then he was out the door and halfway to his van before John had sufficiently pulled himself together to even consider stopping him. He started out the door, but by that time the van was already backing up, Archie in it. The repairman waved as he turned around in the street and drove away.

As it disappeared, John noticed that the letters JSTV were painted in bright red colors on the rear of the van.

He stepped back inside, closing the door behind him.

I'm losing my mind, he thought, and walked down the hall toward the kitchen.

Leslie bustled toward him from the kitchen, dressed for work. "Breakfast's on the table, better eat it before it gets cold." She kissed him on the cheek, then drew back, smiling. "And you better finish shaving before you leave."

"Where have you been?" he asked.

"Fixing breakfast," she said, quite sensibly, he thought.

"But...didn't you see that man?"

"What man?"

"He came right into the bathroom. I just spent ten minutes with him in the closet."

She frowned, looked into his face more closely. "Did you sleep all right last night?"

"I slept fine. It's this morning I'm having a slight problem with."

She shook her head. "Sorry, but I have no idea what you're talking about. Then again, it's not the first time." She checked her watch, and her mouth formed a small O. "Oh, jeez, it's later than I thought. Got to go."

She hugged him. "You have a nice day, dear," she said.

Then, still holding him, she lowered her voice and whispered into his ear, *"Don't blow it for us! The ratings are terrific!"*

With a quick kiss on the cheek she hurried past him and out the door.

For a full thirty seconds, John Selig did not move, sure that at any moment the ground would open up and swallow him into some mad, shrieking void.

The ground did not open up.

He did not go mad.

He stepped numbly into the front room, and with wide eyes, began looking at everything as though seeing it for the first time.

No, no, Archie had said, *the* other *cameras.*

He stepped over to the wall and carefully lifted the painting to look behind it. Nothing. Trying to look casual, he wandered over to the sofa, lifted one of the cushions. Nothing.

Of course not, he thought. One really good fat person, and any camera would be history.

"Well," he said, suddenly aware of the sound of his own voice, and hoping he didn't sound too artificial, "let's see. Gee, I think I left my car keys around here somewhere. I think I'll look for them."

Which is more or less exactly what he began to do.

In every single room in the house.

By a little before noon, John finally decided to call the office and tell them he wouldn't be coming in today. He wasn't feeling well, he explained. Which wasn't exactly the truth, but it wasn't entirely a lie, either.

He racked the phone and looked at the huge pile of cameras he had collected from hiding places throughout the house. Big cameras, small cameras, cameras with microphones and cameras without (presumably providing coverage for other sound cameras in the room).

Cameras in the bedroom, behind the bureau mirror.

Cameras in the front room, in a corner of the bookcase.

Cameras in the garage, the workroom, the second bedroom, the bathroom, the *other* bathroom...minicameras in the dashboard of his car, the trunk, buried along the front sidewalk....

He picked up one of the smaller cameras. It was jet black and without markings as far as he could tell. He started to pry open the back panel, in search of a serial number, when the phone rang.

"Yes?"

A woman's voice came on the line. "This is to inform you that destruction of company property is to be avoided at all costs. Please inform maintenance and do not touch the equipment again. Thank you."

Click and disconnect.

He looked around. Apparently, he'd missed one. Or two.

"Try and stop me!" he said, and slammed down the phone.

He picked up the camera again and threw it against the wall. It shattered-with a particularly satisfying clatter of broken glass and crunched transistors.

The phone rang again.

He picked it up. "Hello?"

The same voice. "You were warned."

Click and disconnect.

John had no sooner racked the phone when the doorbell rang.

Now what? he thought, and opened the door.

Outside stood two very large men. John decided that they didn't look overly happy.

"Mr. Selig?" the first one said.

"Yes?"

"You're to come with us, sir."

They each took an arm and led him out of the house. The second large man closed the door behind them and locked it.

"Wait a minute! Let me go!" John started to struggle, but the look in their eyes said that it would not be a terribly wise thing to do. "Where are you taking me?"

They said nothing, only continued to march him toward a long stretch limousine parked at the curb. He could see the letters JSTV emblazoned on the side door.

"Look," John said, "I don't know who you are, but you can't do this to me!"

The two large men stopped beside the car and looked to one another with apparent surprise. "You should have told us sooner," the larger of the two said, and shoved him into the back of the limo.

Archie was already there, looking not at all pleased to be riding in the back of an otherwise splendid limousine. "Well, now you've gone and done it, haven't you?"

The engine roared to life, and the limo shot forward. "Done what? Where are we going?"

"Into quite a bit of trouble, I'd say. Yes, quite a bit of very serious trouble indeed." He pointed to the back of the front seat. "Smile for the birdy, Mr. Selig."

Naturally, there was a camera there.

The car finally came to a stop at a security gate outside a tall, glass-and-steel office building. As they pulled into the driveway, John noticed two things.

First, the truly extraordinary number of extremely attractive, nubile young women crowding the gate and mobbing the car as they drove through.

Second, the logo bannered in wrought iron over the security gate: JSTV.

The women elbowed one another aside, trying to get near enough to peer in the smoked-glass windows of the limo, pointing and shouting and generally carrying on. It was the sort of reaction he'd come to expect for rock groups and movie stars.

"Who're they?" John asked.

Archie seemed barely aware of them, staring glumly ahead at the office building with all the enthusiasm characteristic of a trip to the dentist for major gum surgery. "Fans," he said.

"I can see that. Whose fans?"

"Yours. Now that the secret's out, they can finally come out of the woodwork." He looked out at the pressing bodies, the tangle of hair and lipstick and polished nails, and shook his head. "All those hormones, repressed for five years—disgusting, isn't it? Probably rip the clothes right off you in a second. Just like that."

John glanced at the women. Part of him found the idea rather intriguing. "Do you really think so?"

Archie didn't answer, his sullen funk growing as they passed the crowd and entered the JSTV Studios main lot.

Just jealous, John thought, and waved back at the women as the car pulled away.

He was reasonably sure he saw one of them faint.

It was a *big* room.

Soft grey walls, maroon piping along the corners, a black granite desk with just one telephone on it and nothing else, and a reception-ist who smiled quite brightly at him as he and Archie stepped into the room.

Correction: as he was nudged from behind, and the door slammed shut behind him.

Accuracy was important in these things.

"Mr. Selig? Mr. Spence will be with you momentarily. Please, make yourself comfortable."

Archie took the first seat at hand, near a television set. John thought he was getting downright sullen.

"Thank you," John said, adding, "is there a rest-room around here?"

"Right in through there."

She indicated a door recessed into one wall. He smiled at her, and stepped through.

He was halfway across the bathroom floor when *it* occurred to him. He stopped in midstride, turned around, stepped back into the waiting room, and sat down next to Archie, who was fiddling with the remote control.

"What's wrong?" Archie said.

"Afraid there might be cameras in there, too."

"Ah."

It was then that John noticed what was on the television screen.

Himself. In the waiting room. Looking at the television. At himself.

Archie flicked through channels, and the same image was on every one. "Typical, isn't it?" Archie said. "All these channels, and nothing interesting on."

John was in the middle of deciding if it was worth his time to hit Archie when the receptionist's phone beeped at her. She lifted the receiver, listened quietly, said something he didn't catch, then hung up. She stood and smiled across at him. "If you please—right this way, Mr. Selig."

He followed her to the doorway at the other end of the office and let her open it for him, closing it again as he stepped inside.

The next room was just like the first—except that it was larger, the desk longer, and instead of a television, rows of books lined the walls. A slightly overweight, greying man sat behind the desk, dressed quite conservatively in a dark blue suit and what was probably an old school tie. Somehow, he reminded John of his grandfather.

Which was, he supposed, probably the intent.

"Sit down, Mr. Selig," he said. "Please, make yourself comfortable."

"Thank you." John sat in the nearest of the high-backed, leather chairs, sinking nearly an inch into the seat.

"Would you like a cigar?" Spence said. "Something to drink?"

"No. Thank you."

"Ah. Comfy, then?"

"Yes. Thank you."

"Good, good," Spence said, sitting back in his chair and staring up at the ceiling. "Now then, Mr. Selig...*what the hell are you trying to do to us?*"

The suddenness nearly knocked John out of his chair. He recovered quickly, however. "What do you *mean*, what am I trying to do to you? What are *you* doing to *me*?"

"To you? My dear Mr. Selig, look around. This is a multimillion dollar business. When we—when *you* first went on the air five years ago, we could barely get a hundred dollars for a thirty-second commercial. Now we're right up there getting a hundred thousand dollars for a thirty-second spot. We got here through long and careful work. We were just starting to break even, clear out our deficits—and now you pull this."

"So you're the one who decided to do all this?" John said.

"No. It wasn't me."

"Then who?"

Spence shrugged. "Who decided you have to pay taxes? Who decided you have to get up for work at eight instead of ten? Who decided what money you use, what fashions you wear?"

"I don't know."

Another shrug. "Same guy."

"This isn't the same thing," John said. "You can't just put my life on television! I have rights!"

"Yeah?" Spence reached into a desk drawer and pulled out a heavy book. "Here. The U.S. Constitution and the Bill of Rights. You show me where it says in here that we can't put you on TV."

"That's a technicality."

"Whole empires have been built on technicalities," Spence said. "Like this one." He took a long breath, let it out slowly. "Mr. Selig, I have no wish to argue with you, so let me come straight to the heart of the matter. Over the last five years you have become an institution in American television. People like you. I like you. Hell, I watch you every Friday night, playing bridge with the Clearsons.

Oh, and by the way—he cheats. We've got a better view of his hand than you do."

"I thought as much," John said, "he's always—"

What are you saying?

"Look, I just don't understand. Why put me on television? What could possibly be interesting about me?"

"You know Marilyn Carstairs," Spence said, "the woman on all those game shows, black hair, rhinestone glasses? What's the last thing she actually did that made her famous?"

John started to answer, realized he didn't have the slightest idea, and let his mouth close again.

"Can't come up with a thing, can you? Well, don't feel bad, neither can anyone else. But she's on TV. Some people are famous just for being famous. You put their faces on TV long enough, next thing you know, they're celebrities. We took the same chance on you. And it paid off. Things got slow once in a while, but you have to expect that. Like when you lost your job, two years ago. At first, the ratings went up. People were wondering what would happen next. You stayed out of work. The ratings went down. So we stepped in and arranged for that new job at InfoTech."

"*You* did that?"

"Of course. Mr. Selig," he said in a voice of infinite patience, "do you really think things happen by accident in this world? Haven't you ever noticed how sometimes things just—seem to go your way? Out of the blue, something'll happen, and you'll think, 'Well, isn't that strange? Isn't that lucky?'. That would be us, Mr. Selig. We have a whole department in charge of happy coincidences. How do you think you met Leslie?"

"My *wife*?"

"Hired by us, yes. We auditioned over a hundred women before we found someone right for the part. Though I suppose now we'll have to find her a new spot—if you persist in making a federal case out of all this."

Spence rose and went to the window, pointing to the parking lot below, at the people filing in and out of the building. "Thousands of jobs and millions of dollars of income are riding on you, Mr. Selig. Is your so-called privacy really worth more than that? Can't you just—forget it all happened? Go back, live out your life the way you did before?"

"No," John said, feeling, despite himself, a little less resolute than he had earlier. He hadn't realized that so much was involved, so many jobs dependent on him, so many—

Wait a minute.

"That's not fair," John said. "I didn't start this, and you've no right to make me feel guilty. I want my privacy back, and that's final."

Spence sighed. "As you wish, Mr. Selig. I'll have a car brought round to take you home."

He pushed a button on his desk and headed for the door, pausing just long enough to glance back at John and shake his head. "You could've been our biggest star, Mr. Selig."

Then he was gone.

Is that it? he thought. *That quick? That simple?* Somehow it felt anticlimactic. He'd expected a struggle,

tap, tap

a fight over who owned his life, a—

tap, tap

A tapping?

He looked to the source of the sound. A woman—a very *attractive* woman, part of his brain noted—stood on the window ledge. A considerable wind ruffled her hair, and she seemed quite adamant about getting inside.

Perhaps, John thought, it had something to do with the fact that they were six stories up.

He went to the window and opened it, helping her inside. As she turned to him, it occurred to John that she was one of the women he'd seen outside, as they'd driven onto the JSTV lot.

"It's you, isn't it?" she said. "Mr. Selig, oh, I'm your biggest fan, I watch you all the time, oh, I think you're just wonderful."

"Well, thank you very much, but I—"

She pulled a small book out of her purse. "Can I have your autograph?"

"No, I—" He stopped. Why not? "I suppose it couldn't hurt. It's all over now anyway."

As he signed his name, she leaned in closer to him. "I want to have your baby," she whispered.

"I beg your pardon?"

"Then a lock of your hair. A jacket."

"No!"

"Anything!"

"*No!*"

"Please!" She clutched at his arm, dragging him toward the floor. "Oh, Mr. Selig, I came all this way. PLEASE!"

He pushed her off him. "I said no. Now I'm sorry, but you're going to have to leave."

Taking her by the elbow and ignoring her protests, he led her to the door Spence had used a moment earlier, opened it—and there stood the rest of the women he'd seen downstairs.

"There he is!" they screamed as one, and lunged for the door.

John slammed it shut, locking it from inside. The door shook with the pounding on the other side.

Across the room, the other door banged open. John turned, relieved to see that it was only Archie.

"I'm supposed to take you home," Archie said.

The woman beside John pouted and pressed a sheet of paper into his hands. "Call me," she said, and headed for the window. "I'll let myself out."

She even blew him a kiss as she stepped back out onto the ledge.

"Amazing," John said. "Absolutely amazing."

Archie seemed not at all impressed. "Well, you'd best come along, now. I want you to know I've been sacked because of all this. Two weeks' notice, and out, cold as you please."

"I'm sorry," John said, truly meaning it. It seemed they'd been through so much together, and he'd only been doing his job. "I didn't mean to get you in trouble. I wish there was something I could do."

Archie glanced down at the sheet of paper with the phone number in John's hand and snatched it away, putting it in his own pocket and patting it through the cloth. "You just did."

The drive home in Archie's compact wasn't nearly as exciting.

Three days later, when the last of the repairmen had left, John took a quick tour of the house. All the damage done by his removal of the cameras had been seamlessly repaired, all paid for by JSTV.

He wandered back into the living room, to the sacks of mail that had been deposited there. He'd barely worked his way through a third of it, and more was coming everyday. He had plenty of time to read now that Leslie was gone (he'd gotten a telegram saying thanks for all the exposure, and inviting him to see her in summer stock in San Diego over the summer), and since Infotech had given him the week off (he wondered how much longer he'd have the job—apparently they'd gotten plenty of free advertising through him, and now that was gone).

He picked one of the letters at random. *Dear John*, it began, *I just wanted to say that I'm one of your biggest fans, and I think you're one of the nicest men I've ever seen, on or off television. I'm terribly depressed about your show, though. I'm sure it must be quite a blow.*

He was considering how to answer that one when the doorbell rang. He opened the door to find Archie standing on the porch.

"Oh, hi," John said. "Come on in. I was just going over the fan mail. I had no idea so much had been collected. And the gifts—offers of marriage—it's amazing."

"Hmm," Archie said, unimpressed. John wondered if he'd practiced that *hmm* until he'd gotten it exactly right. "I just came to drop this by. Finishing off old responsibilities before moving on, all that sort of stuff."

John took the offered envelope, began ripping it open.

"It's a check," Archie said. "Back pay for the last five years. Oh, yes, they always intended to pay you. They just kept it in a trust fund until you either found out or the show got canceled."

John looked at the figure in front of the decimals.

He'd never seen that many zeros in one place before. "This," he started, then worked his voice down into a slightly more natural register, "this is a *lot* of money."

"Hmm." There it was again. "Yes, I suppose it is."

He then went to the corner of the living room, where all the cameras had been stored for pickup, and began gathering them up.

"Um, what are you doing?" John asked, trying to sound casual.

"Company equipment. Not needed here anymore, now is it? Show's been canceled. Now that you know, it's not much fun anymore, now is it?"

"No, I suppose not," John said, unable to take his eyes off all those zeros. "But the money—the women—all this!"

"Sorry," Archie said. "Not my department."

"Then—it's really over? Just like that?"

Tucking the cables and equipment under one arm, Archie turned, looked at him. "You wanted your life back, just the way it was, right? Well, that's what you've got. And I hope you're satisfied."

With that, he started toward the door.

"I'm sorry about your job," John said. "Really, I am."

"Yeah, well, that's the way it goes. Thanks for the thought, though. Guess that makes two of us."

"Yeah, Funny thing is, I was—I was just getting used to it."

Archie nodded, balancing back and forth from foot to foot. "Well, nothing to be done about it, I suppose."

"No, I suppose not."

Archie glanced over at him and, perhaps reading the feelings John suspected were evident there, set down the cameras and walked past him into the living room. "Here. Come here."

"Where?"

"Into the closet."

John followed him inside, closing the door after them. He switched on the flashlight.

Archie indicated the bulb above them. "Still haven't got that fixed yet, eh?"

"I've been busy."

Archie nodded, then dropped his voice. "Look, you didn't hear it from me, but you know, I was thinking. If you were the guy in charge, and I were you, what would you do? Maybe you really *would* take me off the air, just like they said."

He leaned in closer, looking ghastly in the glow of the flashlight. "Or, on the other hand, maybe you'd just *tell* me I was off the air, so I'd think I was, but in reality I'm back on television again without knowing it. This way I'd go back to acting normal, which is what everyone wants in the first place, isn't it?"

With that, he clapped John on the shoulder and opened the closet door. "Good luck," he called back. "Break a leg."

Then he gathered up the cameras and stepped out of the house, closing the door behind him.

John stepped very slowly out of the closet.

And stood in the middle of the living room.

And looked around.

At *everything*.

It all looked just as it had before.

Perfectly normal.

As though there weren't any television cameras around him.

Which didn't mean there weren't.

Which didn't mean there were, either.

He could look, he supposed, but if there weren't any, he'd just feel silly.

And if there were—

He looked at the piles of fan mail, the check, the note from Leslie.

And cleared his throat.

"My," he said, his voice sounding unnaturally loud in the empty room, "but isn't it a wonderful day?"

Silence.

Didn't mean there was.

Didn't mean there wasn't, either.

The first rule of show business, John thought, *is never, ever bore your audience*...and segued, quite professionally, he thought, into an a cappella rendition of "Me and My Shadow."

And step *two, three, four*...

And *smile* for the birdy.

COLD TYPE

The fire-lit sign that sat alongside the Indiana freeway said WELCOME TO LAKESIDE. In truth, the nearest lake was thirty miles due east, in Jefferson County, but when the town was incorporated in 1873 the city fathers decided that Lakeside was a name more apt to attract settlers than Devil's Ladder, Indiana. But the false advertising didn't bother Jacob Hartley. He wasn't there for the lake, the scenery, the fishing or the historic sights.

The sight that mattered most to him was the one right in front of him.

Bits of blackened paper rose into the night sky, tinged by fire. They spiraled up into the darkness until they winked out and drifted back to earth again, like the Lord's fallen angels trying one last time to crawl back into heaven, only to find the door slammed shut for all time.

Men, women and children encircled the pyre, holding hands and singing "I Shall Not be Moved." Most of them were from Lakeside, others from neighboring towns as far away as Bierce and Fairfield. Their rapt faces shone in the red glow of the fire, its light dancing in their eyes, the smoke curling around them and rising skyward with their prayers. Jacob knew that not all of them were believers; some of them had just come for the show, or because they'd been dragged along by friends, or to meet someone of the opposite sex—social events that didn't involve bars were rare in Lakeside—but the Lord would attend to that in His own good time. Jacob's task was to bring them all together in His name; the rest would take care of itself.

Even the unbeliever with the hardest heart couldn't help but be moved by the gently rising voices, the carefully orchestrated symphony of prayers and speaking of tongues and warm embraces between strangers who shared nothing but their love of the Lord. It was performance art, as much a litany of the heart as a glorification of the Word, and that combination was unbeatable.

Another leaf of burning paper, too large to take wing into the night, tumbled and rolled toward his feet. He could see the fire eating away at the page, words disappearing letter by letter as the flames did their holy work. *Winston Smith loved Big Brother.*

Jacob idly wondered which book this had come from, then shrugged off the question. It didn't matter, really. The only books and CDs thrown on the pyre were the ones on the list, which had been carefully compiled by experts in satanism and the occult and pagan literature. If it was on fire, it was because it deserved the flame.

Winston Smith loved Big Br

As the last letters burned away, Jacob ground out the singed paper with the toe of a carefully polished shoe, and turned his attention back to the crowd, to his people, who had finished the last chorus of "I Shall Not Be Moved" and now stood silently awaiting his next words, the only sound the crackle of the pyre. Jacob Hartley smiled, and began to speak. He had no idea what he was going to say; he never planned these things out. He just let the words come on their own. He could feel the fire in his veins tonight, and he knew that whatever came, it would be good.

It was a fine night to be alive.

Shortly after eight o'clock the next morning, Jacob checked out of the roadside hotel, tossed his bags into the back of the 1987 Buick that had seen him safely through every state in the continental United States at least three times in the intervening years, and headed for the next big town. Once there, he'd set up his tent, distribute the pamphlets to churches and stores and barber shops and hair dressers, and start again. He'd done a good night's work, but the work would never be truly finished until the Rapture.

Jacob smiled, remembering again the incidents of the night before. His words had truly been inspired.

For our country is a nation under God, a great lady whose skirts have been smeared with a parade of filth and heresy that would make a Pharisee blush. These are evil times, dangerous times. We must be careful, ever so careful, and vigilant, ever so vigilant, and prepared to find those ideas which are an offense to man and God and purge them from the face of the earth, which has been entrusted to us as stewards of God's greatest creation.

Sixty miles short of Flinntown, his next stop, the rain started. It was typical of midwest storms; first nothing, then sheets that fell on the roads and fields as though first gathered in heaven's skirts and released all at once. He could barely see the road ahead of him, or the cars on either side of the road. The rain hammered harder, and the world was swallowed up in mist and water. He glimpsed cars pulling over to the side of the road, content to wait out the storm. *Nope, I've got places to go,* Jacob decided, and pressed on.

He continued on for another ten miles before deciding that discretion might in fact be the better part of valor. Besides, it was getting dark; he'd need to find someplace to sleep. He wanted to arrive fresh to begin his labors.

He caught the next off-ramp to a narrow country road, which wound through a stand of trees so thick on both sides that their branches met in the middle and momentarily cut off the downpour. Then he was out in the open again, and the rain slammed into the car like a frenzied animal, tearing at the hood. He couldn't read the signs on the side of the road, but knew it had to lead somewhere or else why would it have been built?

In another few minutes a light grew out of the darkness. A hotel. With a silent prayer of thankfulness for coming through dangerous places intact, Jacob pointed the car into an open parking spot and killed the engine. Steam rose from the hood, the hotel's VACANCY light reflecting off the water. Pulling his coat tighter around him, Jacob jumped out of the car, slammed the door, and trotted into the small, wood-paneled lobby. The warm air inside was a relief, and he approached the night clerk, already anticipating dry sheets and a good night's sleep.

The clerk was just like all the others he'd seen in twenty years of hotels and motels from Chula Vista, California to Roanoke, Virginia. A little more skittish than most when he pushed the door open and the wind slammed it shut, but Jacob attributed that to the weather and his assumption (from the full rack of room keys behind the desk) that they didn't do a lot of business. The town was well off the local maps; he had been lucky to find it.

Jacob signed the guest register, took his keys, and went upstairs to change into a pair of dark slacks, white shirt and a blue blazer that had seen better days. It didn't bother him. *The Lord doesn't care what you look like when you walk into paradise, just as long as you've got an invitation.*

There was only one restaurant in the hotel, small and private, looking more like a private dining room in someone's home than a proper restaurant. Logs burned in a brick-faced fireplace, and the table was covered with a lace cloth that looked to have been crocheted by hand. It reminded him of his mother's dining room, and he smiled at the memory.

As he walked around the lone table, wondering how he ordered here, or if he would even have any choice in tonight's fare, he felt more than heard someone enter behind him. He turned to find an older gentlemen in a wheelchair appraising him from the doorway. He was dressed in a carefully pressed white suit, with a string tie, and a southern plantation hat. Jacob put him at somewhere near seventy, but with bright blue eyes that looked as though they had been chiseled out of some much larger jewel. He found he was improbably reminded of Colonel Sanders... but Colonel Sanders had never been as kindly and sympathetic looking as the fellow who now sat gazing up at him.

Jacob liked him instantly.

The late arrival introduced himself as Aleister Hayes, and offered Jacob his hand. It was strong, firm, warm. "This your first time in Clearwater?" he asked.

So that's the name of this place, Jacob thought, not having seen it on the signs coming into town. He nodded. "Haven't seen much of it yet."

"Well, there's not much to see. Nobody here is much into urban redevelopment. We like our town just the way it is, nice and quiet." He gestured toward a chair. "Please, sit, or I'll have to stand, and I have a tendency to fall down whenever I try."

Jacob smiled and took the proffered seat.

"So what do you do?" Aleister asked.

"I'm a preacher," Jacob said. "Foursquare Baptist Church back in

Aberdeen, Oklahoma takes care of most of my expenses while I'm on the road, the rest I make up in contributions."

"Been on the road a long time?"

Jacob nodded. "A long time."

"Must be hard on your family."

"It was," Jacob said. Perhaps it was the warm room, or the familiar surroundings, or the fact that he still couldn't get Colonel Sanders out of his mind and was responding to thirty-plus years of conditioning, but he found it very easy to talk to Aleister. "My wife, Sarah, passed away six years ago. Our sons, Mark and John, work in the church back home. They understand; the traveling isn't a burden, it's a blessing.

"You see, Aleister, most folks go through life without a rudder or a compass, lost in indecision. In that sense, I'm very fortunate. I have a mission, a purpose."

Aleister nodded, as though already understanding, and Jacob continued.

"The world's a dangerous place, full of dangerous ideas. Problem is, nobody cares about anybody else these days, no one tries to protect anybody else. You look around, and you see crime, you see filth, it's not even safe to walk the streets at night. In my own way, I try to help. I tell people that we have to look out for each other, for the kinds of ideas we let near our children. We have to take responsibility for ourselves, and our fellows, our brothers and sisters in Christ."

Aleister nodded. "It's a powerful thing, responsibility. I think about that a lot." He smiled sheepishly. "You see, I'm not what you'd call an educated man. Not really. Most of what I've got is life-learning, not book learning."

Jacob waved a hand. "Doesn't matter, that's the best kind of learning you can have. I'd take that over all the books in the world."

"Maybe so," Aleister said, "but you... you've been around a lot, seen a lot of other places, been to college?"

"That I have," Jacob said. "Put myself through college at Oral Roberts University, where I got my degree in religious studies. It wasn't easy, with a young wife and a child to raise, and another on the way, but if you step out on faith, you find the Lord always provides."

Aleister regarded the fire for a moment before continuing. "I was born in this town," he said. "Born here, lived almost all my life here, and I'll likely die here."

"Married?"

Aleister shook his head. "Had some prospects once, but no, things never quite worked out. Because of these legs of mine, I don't get out much, and I don't get very far when I do, so that kind of limits my options a bit. Got crippled in an accident twelve years ago. Can't drive, none of the buses come this far off the main road, even the cab company in Shelby doesn't come out this far. Haven't been outside this town in years." Jacob looked to the clerk, who was setting out the table for dinner. "Can't you get anyone to drive you into town?"

Aleister shook his head.

"You see?" Jacob said, outraged. "That's exactly the sort of thing I was talking about. We don't care for one another anymore, don't do for people. I'm truly sorry, Aleister." He glared at the clerk, who didn't meet his gaze. "Folks around here ought to be ashamed."

"Yes, well, I've tried to induce some of them to help, but I've reconciled myself that it's just not going to happen. They do a little, help bring in my food, look after my place a little, but that's all. That's why I wanted to talk to you. When I saw you drive up, you being an educated man and all, a man of the cloth, I figured, maybe you could help me."

The clerk retreated into the other room as Jacob considered it. "I've got to be in Flinntown tomorrow night," he said, "I've got things to do, but... sure, if you need a ride somewhere—"

"No, not a ride," Aleister said. "I'm too old to go bumping around on some of the roads we've got around here. But there is something else. I guess... well, I guess I need your advice."

He rolled the wheelchair closer to Jacob and continued, his voice low. "What if you had the power, the real, honest to God power, to... change things? But what if you were afraid? What if you didn't think you were wise enough, or smart enough, to know what to do?"

"Well, I guess I'd try to find somebody who was wise enough. It's always been my experience that when you need somebody in particular, life has a way of sending just the right person to your door at just the right time."

"That's kind of what I thought," Aleister said.

The clerk came back into the dining room, carrying a tray of fresh-carved turkey pieces and gravy, mashed potatoes, carrots and cut corn. "I see your dinner's ready, so I'll let you eat in peace," Aleister said. "But if you have time, I'd appreciate it if you could come by the house in the morning. It's the big white house with blue trim at the end of the road, you can't miss it."

"All right," Jacob said. "I can't stay very long. As I said, I have to be in Flinntown by sundown, but—"

"I don't need much of your time," Aleister said as he rolled the wheelchair back out the dining room door. "Besides, once you hear what I have to say, you might just want to stay on for a while."

Calling a final goodnight, Aleister wheeled himself out the hotel's main door. Jacob caught a glimpse of him continuing down the street before disappearing around the corner. *A nice, kind old man,* Jacob decided. He definitely couldn't stay, no matter how pleasant the company, but he could at least make the effort to stop by after breakfast. He always believed in the importance of ministering to older folks, and did so whenever he could back home; surely he could spare an hour or two for someone in need.

The morning air was bright and clean, scrubbed by the hard rains which still guttered into storm drains in the lower parts of what passed for Main Street.

As advertised, Aleister's house was easy enough to find. He rang the doorbell, and a moment later was admitted into the front room, where Aleister was waiting. The room was filled with framed photographs, most of them chronicling the growth-years of his two sons, along with several wedding photos. Surrounded by familiar things, Aleister seemed more at ease here than he had at the hotel. There was coffee on the table, beside a tray of fresh fruit.

"I've learned to take care of myself ever since the accident," Aleister said. "That's why it's kind of hard for me to take anyone's advice, especially with something this important, but I guess after a while you realize you don't have much time or much choice, and you have to take your best shot. I'm not getting any younger, and if I'm going to do anything worth doing, I'd best do it now."

Aleister forced himself out of the wheelchair and into a recliner. For a moment he seemed to be deciding how best to say whatever it was he needed to say. Jacob waited for him; he had time.

"Like I said last night, I had an accident about twelve years ago. Cut off the nerves to my legs. Good part is they don't hurt, bad part is I could be on fire from the waist down and never know it until I smelled the smoke.

"I got pretty banged up. Hit my head and ended up in a coma for almost two weeks. Chemical fire seared the inside of my lungs pretty bad. Still can't breathe as well as I used to." He stopped, and smiled at Jacob. "Nothing more tedious than an old man going on about his illnesses, is there?"

Jacob smiled. "It's fine," he said. "Go on."

"Took me almost two years after the accident until I was more or less myself again. The other thing about the accident took me a while longer to figure out. The doctors couldn't figure it out either. They kept taking these pictures of my head, CAT scans and like that, and they said the way my brain wasn't working the way it had worked before, the way it was supposed to work. They talked a lot about brain waves and hormonal levels and pituitaries and that sort of thing, it's all way beyond me, but they seemed pretty exercised about the whole thing.

"Must've been, oh, eleven months, almost a year after the accident. I was sitting at home, reading a book I'd bought over at Edgar's Drug Store. It's the brick storefront on the edge of town, you passed it on your way in. Ever since my accident, I had plenty of time to sit and read. Now, I didn't know much about the book, only that the doctors back at the hospital kept saying it was a good one, but pretty soon I was horrified by what I was reading. It was all about fornication and drugs, sex and alcohol and this idea that man is nothing. A real sinkhole of a book. When I saw it for what it was, I got... well, I got mad, and I threw it into that fireplace, right over there. Burned it right up. Afterward I just sat there, upset, wishing I'd never read the damned thing in the first place.

"Next day, I went to the hospital to track down the doctor who'd recommended it to me and complain. But when I got to him, he said he didn't remember recommending it. Said he'd never even heard of it. Couple of other doctors said the same thing. I figured they didn't want to get in trouble for upsetting one of the patients. They said they were familiar with just about everything else this writer ever wrote, said they were big fans of his, but this one, all of a sudden they said they'd never heard of it. Well, you can say a lot about me, but I don't tolerate being played for a fool. I knew it was on the best seller list, everybody was talking about it while I was in the hospital, so I went back to the bookstore. Sure enough, it was gone."

"You mean it was sold out."

"No. I mean the book was gone."

"Aleister, you said yourself you burned it."

"No, you're still not..." Aleister sighed. "Best thing is to just let you see for yourself."

He pointed to the coffee table, where two identical books lay in a silver tray. Romance novels, Jacob concluded from the garish art on the covers that announced *Passion Island*, by Jennifer Grey. "I picked these up this morning, before you got here," he said, and frowned. "Don't know much about them. I hope this is okay. Hope nobody'll miss them."

He asked Jacob to hand him the book, but leave the other copy where it was.

Jacob complied. Aleister took the book and placed it in the roaring fireplace. Slowly, the book began to burn. "It's gone."

Jacob nodded. "Yes, it's a good start. But there are always others, and it takes time to —"

Aleister cut him off. "No. I don't mean that copy is gone. I mean that book is gone. Look over at the table."

Jacob looked.

The other copy of the book was gone.

"Where is it?" Jacob asked

"It isn't. It never was. The ideas, the words, graphic art, the print drums... all gone. As if it had never even existed.

"I don't know quite how it works," Aleister continued, "I only know that it does. Maybe it's a gift from God, maybe it's a talent I never knew I had, maybe it happened in the same accident that cost me the use of my legs. All I know is that it works. Whatever I burn, disappears. Only reason you still know about it is that I want you to.

"I believe I was given this talent for a reason. But what? How do I use it? Where do I use it? All my life, I've always tried try to do what's right. But this... it's beyond me. I don't know what to do with it. What if I disappeared the wrong book? Like I said, I don't get out much, I don't read like I used to, so I'm not qualified to decide which to go after, and which to leave. Sure, you could take out all the dirty books in Edgar's store—not that there are a whole lot of 'em there, Edgar's pretty conservative that way--but there's so many, taking out one or two here and there won't ever make a real difference.

"After a while I got to be like the mule stuck between two bales of hay, until finally I decided to leave well enough alone. If I didn't know what to do, then maybe I shouldn't do anything until I had a clearer idea where to use the power. Then you came into town. What you said about your mission makes a lot of sense. I don't know as much about these things as you do. I don't want to abuse this gift that I've got. But I also don't want to go hiding it under a bushel.

"So last night, I got to thinking about my garden. Thought about how every so often you have to go through and prune the trees, pull the weeds, and yank out the dandelions. Maybe that's what this gift of mine is for. Maybe I'm supposed to be a kind of gardener. You can't pull out every weed in the world, but you can yank the big ones, the ones that threaten the garden the most."

"And where do I come in?" Jacob asked.

"Like I said, you know more about these things than I do. Maybe, as you travel around, when you find one of these books and you decide it's just so evil and wrong and hurtful to people that it deserves special treatment, you can bring it to me. Tell me why it's bad. And I'll take it from there. Just once in a while. Like I said, I don't want to abuse this gift. But I feel like I can trust you."

Jacob sat back, nodding politely. He took a moment to compose his thoughts before going on, but before he could get any of them to form, Aleister sighed. "You think I'm crazy, don't you, Reverend?"

"Well, I'm not sure 'crazy' is the right word. But maybe you could talk to someone about this—"

"No," Aleister said firmly. He pulled himself into his wheelchair, and rolled toward the door. "You're the only one I've ever told about this. It's all true, every bit of it. You saw which book it was. You check it out once you leave here. See for yourself. Then, if you think I can help, just come on back. I'll be here."

Jacob took a last swallow of the coffee, and walked out of the house, letting the screen door clatter shut behind him. *Poor old man*, he thought. *It's this town. You leave someone alone like this, for this long, he's bound to start acting a little crazy. I would, too. That magic trick, making the book disappear when I turned my back... it's a cry for attention, sure as I'm standing here. The old man just needs someone to talk to, that's all.*

And yet... Aleister had been nowhere near the other copy of the book. Jacob had turned his back on it for only a moment and there was no one else in the room.

No, he decided, and pushed down the thought. The whole idea was ludicrous.

Then again, the first time anybody heard about Moses turning a wooden staff into a snake, they probably figured that was pretty ludicrous, too.

He walked across the gravel-paved street and headed toward the bookstore, figuring he had a few minutes yet before it closed. He decided it wouldn't hurt to have a copy of the local paper to help familiarize himself with the area.

While he was at it, he'd just look around a little, check out the inventory. Because he liked to stay current with the latest offenses rolling off the printing presses.

And because God sometimes worked in mysterious ways.

It was shortly after midnight when Jacob returned to Aleister's house, clutching a heavy bag and banging loudly on the door until a light went on inside. He knew the commotion might wake the neighbors, but he didn't care. Didn't care that he had run nearly all the way here. Didn't care that he was out of breath, dizzy with excitement.

Aleister opened the door, and Jacob rushed in, his words coming out in a torrent. "I know I didn't believe you, Aleister, and I'm sorry for that, I truly am, but it's not the sort of thing that... well, it's hard to accept... but the bookstore didn't have it, hadn't ever heard of it. So I checked the shelves, and it wasn't there, a best-seller and it wasn't there, so I checked the store next door, and they hadn't ever heard of it either, and then I got back to the hotel and I started calling...Aleister, I called every store on the west coast, the only ones that were still open, don't know how much it's going to cost me but I don't care. I figured sure, maybe you could've gotten to the folks around here, pulled them in on the gag, but not Brentano's in Los Angeles, not Book Soup in San Francisco, not...."

He finally stopped to take a breath. "Aleister, I called twenty bookstores. No one knew anything about that book. It doesn't exist. It never existed. It's gone, just like you said."

Tired, Aleister smiled. "So now you believe me."

"I think so, Aleister. Maybe I'm crazy, maybe this is the biggest gag in the history of the world, but I do indeed think so. I'd just like one more test."

He opened the bag containing some of the demonstration books he took on his travels, books he would hold up before the congregation as he explained why they should not be allowed shelf space alongside decent, clean works of fiction. He always carried several copies in case any of them got lost in transit. "I bought these with my own hands, and my own money," he said, pulling one out at random. "Let me see it happen just once more, and I'll believe you."

Aleister looked at the book in his hands. "Is that one of the books you were telling me about? An evil book? Because if it's not, I don't want to—"

"It's a story book, Aleister. All about how the devil can be your friend, how it's bad to be good, yes, it's an evil thing, Aleister. Now... show me."

Aleister took the book and rolled the wheelchair over to the fire-place. Hesitating only briefly, he gave the book over to the flames. When it was fully ablaze, Jacob opened the bag of books.

The other copies of the book were gone.

Jacob sat, hard, his knees giving out on him. "Aleister," he said, his voice barely a whisper, "do you understand... do you realize what you have here? You could change the world—"

Aleister shook his head. "I don't want to change the world, Rev-erend. God made it just fine. I wouldn't know what to make differ-ent. All I want is to clean it up a little, get rid of some of the things that might hurt people. Pornography, especially the stuff with kids in it. Books with bad ideas, books that tell kids how to make pipe bombs, encourage 'em to do drugs or blow up their schools or run away from home. But we've got to be careful not to go too far."

"Aleister—"

"And one more thing." He wheeled closer to Jacob, so he could look in the man's eyes. "This is probably no surprise to you, but I'm getting old. And I've been kind of sick lately. I don't think I've got a whole lot longer to live. Something inside me says that when the time is right, it might be I can transfer the power to the right person. Make you the guardian. Which is fine by me, I didn't ask for the power, and I never really wanted it, or the responsibility that goes with it. You can have it... if you'll take it."

"I would be honored and humbled to take on this awesome responsibility," Jacob said. "At the proper time, of course."

The next day Jacob canceled all his scheduled appearances and rallies. The gift that God had seen fit to drop into his lap made them superfluous. He could now do completely and in a matter of hours what he could never accomplish otherwise. He began calling local and area bookstores as soon as they opened for business. He went down the list of books, ordering them shipped to Aleister's house, then moved in himself, at Aleister's suggestion, to make sure he got to them first, so he could explain what made them insidious.

Over the next few days, as the packages arrived, they met each night to go over the latest arrivals. At times Jacob became irritated with how long it took to explain each of them to Aleister, to make him understand why they had to be dispensed with. The old man's caution was a sharp contrast to the crowds of enthusiastic believers he was used to dealing with, who happily tossed the proscribed books into the pyre without questioning. Nonetheless, he persisted, and by the end of the evening another handful of books were fed into the fire.

One at a time, the books began to vanish from the face of the earth. To help make Aleister comfortable with the arrangement and with Jacob's choices, he was careful to pick books that were clearly bad: pornography, books containing pictorials of extreme violence, pamphlets that urged the overthrow of the government, anything by Philip Roth... books that any reasonable person could point to and agree that they had no business being in print.

Once he had Aleister's trust, then he could proceed to the next level, bringing in books where the offense was not as immediately obvious but which were every bit as worthy of obliteration. That, Jacob knew, was the key: get the other person to support you at a commonsense level, where the target is clear and undefensible, then at a later point, when the issues became too complex for them to really understand, they would trust your decision because they trusted you before. The deeper you get, the more they invest in your guidance, the harder it is for them to turn around later.

On some level, Jacob understood that this was manipulation at its basest, but did the publishers and the writers of these books not engage in their own manipulation of the media? Did they not use television and sex and pictures to manipulate people to abandon God, to leave their families, to engage in behavior that was immortal at best and illegal at worst?

Jacob knew that sometimes the end really does justify the means, if the end was as clear-cut and lofty as this was.

Aleister could not always see the finer points that distinguished one book from another. But that was why God had sent Jacob, to ensure that this particular gift was used properly. If five minutes of manipulation saved two hours' worth of talk, and got three more bad books off the shelf, then it was worth it. Besides, weren't all good leaders manipulators, in their way?

But he didn't dwell overmuch on such thoughts. Like the pages that were the focus of his concern, they wavered and turned to smoke in each night's new fire.

It was less than a week after moving into Aleister's home that Jacob returned from the market, carrying bags of groceries, to find an ambulance parked in front of the house. He ran inside to find paramedics leaving, shaking their heads. Fearing the worst, he raced into the back bedroom, only to find Aleister in his bed, pale and trembling, but still very much alive.

Jacob sat beside the bed. "What happened?"

Aleister stirred, focused on him with some difficulty. "Damned ticker," he said. "I was getting out of the tub when it felt like someone hit me in the chest with a hammer. Dialed 911 and they got here as fast as they could."

"You should be in the hospital," Jacob said.

"No. With people watching, and me hooked up to a whole room full of monitors, we couldn't do... what we have to do."

"What do you mean?" Jacob asked, though already suspecting where this was going.

Aleister took his hand and squeezed hard. "I want you to make me a promise," he said. "Promise that you will use the power wisely, carefully, as we have so far. Prune away only what you have to, for the greater good. Be like a good gardener. Pull the weeds and the dandelions, but leave the roses."

"I will, Aleister," he said. "I promise."

Aleister studied his eyes for a moment, then squeezed harder, until Jacob thought the man's large hand would break his own. Then, abruptly, the grip relaxed. "That's all I can give you," he said, and let go of Jacob's hand. "Any more, and it might bring me to heaven a little faster than I had in mind."

"As long as it's enough to do the job," Jacob said.

"It should be." With that, Aleiser lay back on the pillow and closed his eyes. "I need to rest now," he said.

Jacob nodded, numb. *Is that it?* he thought. *Is that all it takes?* He didn't feel any different. Did he really have the power now? Could he do what Aleister had done?

He looked at the old man, who was already asleep. *Let him rest,* Jacob thought. *He's earned it, doing God's work.*

Now it's my turn to carry the burden.

Aleister wasn't sure what time it was when he awoke. The sky was grey outside his window. From the direction of the light he decided it was morning, before sunrise.

But what had awakened him?

Then he heard it again, the sound of movement from the back yard. *Jacob?* he thought. What was he doing back there at this time of day?

He pulled himself out of bed and into the wheelchair, then rolled down the long wood-paneled hall toward the screen door that looked onto the back porch. The door was open, and he could see Jacob moving around outside, piling up books in the middle of the yard.

Lots of books.

Aleister guessed there had to be hundreds of books in the pile. And Jacob was adding even more to the stack.

Jacob tossed the last books onto the pile and was reaching for the nearby can of gasoline when he saw Aleister in the doorway. "Good morning, Aleister. Sorry, I didn't mean to wake you."

"Jacob, what is all this? We agreed—"

"We agreed that I would use my discretion. I am, just on a slightly larger scale. Your problem, Aleister, is that you think too small. Don't you see the opportunities here?" he asked.

"If we burn the Koran, we get rid of all the Moslem fanatics. No Mideast wars, no terrorism, just like that! We can clear the way for Christianity across the globe by getting rid of the beliefs, while leaving the people available to hear the Word of God. No more Hindus, or Hare Krishnas, or Buddhists, no Jews, none of those beliefs will ever have existed. Here, look at this." He held out a slip of paper. "Cut this out of a law book downtown. Supreme Court decision on abortion. And these here—cut them out of the Constitution. Aleister, don't you see? We can make the world right. We can change it all."

Aleister struggled for words, appalled. "No—it's not supposed to go like that, you can't go changing everything!"

"Why not? We can get rid of rock music, and all the satanic influences the kids listen to every day. No more backward masking, no more hidden messages from the Devil, no more drum solos!"

"But for God's sake—where do you stop?"

"For God's sake, we don't stop until it's done," Jacob said, and held up his bible. "Right here is all writing the world needs. Now, I suggest you go back inside, Aleister. There'll be a lot of smoke here in a minute—and that's not good for you."

Aleister, weak and in pain, turned and wheeled his way back into the house, closing the door behind him.

Alone again, Jacob began dousing the books with lighter fluid, then turned back again at a rapping sound from inside the house.

Aleister sat in his wheelchair on the other side of the glass door. He was holding something in his hand. "You left your wallet in your room," Aleister said.

Jacob held up a hand to block the sunlight, so he could see what Aleister was holding in his hand: Jacob's driver's license.

And a match.

"Good thing I held back a little of the power," Aleister said, "just in case."

"What're you—"

"I'm sorry, Jacob. It was my mistake. I never should have put such a burden on anyone else. It's my cross to bear, I suppose you could say. Unfortunately, I don't know how to undo what I've done, by giving it to you."

He lit the match.

"All I *can* undo... is you."

"No!" Jacob shouted, and ran for the door as the fire touched his driver's license.

"I'm sorry, Jacob. I'm real sorry."

Jacob leapt up onto the back porch as the door before him seemed suddenly to grow brighter, glowing with a terrible intensity.

Soon the white was everything, and Jacob felt his thoughts slipping away into the white, into the void.

In the beginning was the Word, he thought.

And then thought no more.

Aleister unlocked the door and wheeled himself out onto the back porch. There was no sign of Jacob Mayhew, no indication that he had ever existed.

Except....

There on the edge of the porch was Jacob's bible. He strained to reach down and pick it up. It opened to the front, where the name of its owner would have been inscribed, but that was gone as well. There was just the book.

All this trouble, over just one book, Aleister thought.

And he paused.

And considered, looking from the fireplace to the Bible and back again.

I wonder what would happen....

Slowly, his joints stiff and tired, Aleister turned and wheeled his way back into the house, the Bible still in his lap.

He had hoped for guidance in using his ability, had hoped that Jacob would be the one to give it to him.

And as the door clattered shut behind him, Aleister wondered if perhaps Jacob had done just that after all.

THE WALL

T he corridor smelled strongly of wet paint, motor oil, burned rubber, and freshly poured concrete. There were no windows. At two hundred feet beneath the surface, there was no day, no night, no season, no movement of stars or sun to track. The only sounds were his own muffled footsteps, and those of the guards on either side of him. They looked straight ahead, their uniforms crisp and starched. They had said nothing more than "This way, sir," since he'd shown them his identification. *Major Alexander McKay, AF117B59, Clearance Level Blue-5, Date of Issue: 7/17/92, Date of Expiration: 7/17/93.*

At every corner, they passed another checkpoint and went through the same routine (ID card, retina scan, phone check with the office upstairs) before continuing. Conversation was kept to a dead minimum. He'd seen tight security before, but rarely anything like this.

Something was up.

They reached the final checkpoint, set before a massive steel door that reminded him of a bank vault. The guards, once again, put him through the routine. He watched the reflectorized scanner as his face was probed for retinal and profile verification. It was a face no longer as young as he still saw it in his dreams, showing lines from sun and space. The red light of the sensors brought out the flecks of white in his hair. There were more of them every day, it seemed.

The scanner beeped once and glowed green. One of the guards removed a magnetic disk on a chain from beneath his shirt and slipped it into a slot in the vault door. With the sigh of pneumatics and escaping air, the door opened and the guards who had accompanied him this far preceded him into a room filled with computers, monitors, and whole banks of equipment he didn't recognize and couldn't begin to put a name to. They hummed and clicked and beeped at him from three sides, a constant undercurrent of the sort of noise machines make when they think. Cables and power cords ribboned away in every direction, the equipment looking hastily installed.

The fourth wall, dead ahead, was the only one not lined with equipment. It was either very thick glass or some kind of heavy-gauge polymer, at least three inches thick. Just on the other side of the glass, also running the length of the room, was a solid steel wall. There were still holes in the walls on either side, places where the brickwork had been crudely sawed away to make room for the glass-and-steel barrier. *This was all done very quickly*, Alex thought. *They must've had to move fast. But why?*

It took him a moment to notice Gregory Phillips, seated at one of the consoles. It was only when Greg got up and started toward him that the movement caught his eye. His first impression was that Gregory hadn't been sleeping well, or much, lately. His eyes were red and tired, his grey hair matted in the back from where he'd probably been resting when Alex had entered. He extended a hand with a look of weariness and relief at the sight of a friendly face. "Alex."

"General."

Gregory looked pained, as he always did when reminded of the difference between the two of them. Though Gregory was the older of the two, they'd come up through the ranks of the Air Force together, before taking separate roads to where they wanted to go. "Ranks later, all right?"

Alex nodded, and as he released the handshake, he noticed Gregory's face fall slightly, as though it had required great effort to maintain even this much of a sense of normalcy, and having done so, now returned to its worried, distracted expression.

"So what's the job?" Alex said. "With all the secrecy around here you'd think we were back in the Manhattan Project."

Gregory started to answer, then gestured to the two guards still inside the door. They saluted smartly and headed out into the corridor. The vault door sighed shut behind them.

Gregory stuck a cigarette in his mouth and lit it. As he spoke, he paced the room, indicating the equipment surrounding them. "Two months ago, this was a research lab. Government contract, particle physics, that sort of thing. Nothing special about it. Then something happened. Either something very right, or something very, very wrong."

He paused in front of the glass wall, gazing at the steel on the other side and, Alex thought, actually *through* it, to whatever was on the other side. "But I'm getting ahead of myself," he continued. "Just before everything happened, the research team was running a new experiment on wormholes, theoretical subspace corridors, like black holes, that let you go anywhere in the galaxy in a second. Somewhere along the line, things got—out of hand, shall we say. There was an explosion. And when they cleared the rubble, they found what's on the other side of this wall."

He stepped away from it and picked two pairs of dark goggles off the nearest console, handing one to Alex. They were heavy, the smoked glass unusually thick. "Better put these on," he said. "They'll help, a little. But don't look directly into it."

When the goggles were secured, Gregory toggled a switch. With a sudden sharp *clang* and the sound of gears grinding under a tremendous load, the steel panel behind the glass began to rise up, receding into a troth in the ceiling.

The room was instantly filled with a brilliant white light that bled through the widening gap between the steel wall and the floor. Even through the goggles, it was painful to look at. It was a terrible, bone-white light that bleached everything it touched but, curiously, seemed cool where it struck his skin. With the additional barrier down, he also became aware of the sound—a relentless roar and rush of wind that buffeted the glass wall like a winter storm. A whirl of smoke and fog curled in the room beyond the glass, and as his eyes slowly, painfully adjusted to the brilliant light, he could distinguish its source.

The room extended another ten feet beyond the barrier, ending at a brick wall at the far side.

The light and sound and wind were pouring in through a seven-foot-wide hole in the far wall. All of which would have been unusual enough on its own—Alex had never seen a light like that before, not from any natural source—except....

Except that the wall, like the rest of the lab, was at least two hundred feet beneath the ground.

So where was that light and that wind coming from?

"My God," Alex said.

Gregory nodded. "My reaction precisely. Once we saw it, we brought in scientists from all over the place. Cornell, NASA, JPL, they've poked, prodded, scanned—the high-IQ types from CalTech said terminology is irrelevant. Something about phenomenology exceeding the limits of language. I called it a gate. They didn't argue."

"Where does it go?"

"We don't know. The data from the experiment was wiped out in the explosion. All we know for sure is that, somehow, the equipment here is generating it. We might be able to figure it out in time, but until then we haven't the vaguest idea how it's doing it. It's as if we've unlocked a door, but we can't remember the combination, so if we close it, we may not be able to open it again."

He shook his head, crushed out the cigarette. "We *have* to know what's on the other side, Alex. That's why we called you. The brass wants you—to go *in there*."

Alex rubbed at his eyes. Even though the wall had been lowered back into position, when he closed his eyes he could still see the hole, and the terrible light that streamed through it. "How," he started, his mouth dry, "how can you be sure it's a gate?"

"We weren't sure," Gregory said. "Not at first. Then we found there was a wind coming through from the other side. That's why we put up the wall. No telling what kind of bacteria might be coming across. Then, after a while we—well, we started sending things through."

"*What?*"

Gregory stepped across the room to a file cabinet and pulled out a thick folder. He dropped it on the table in front of Alex. "Background's all in there. We started off with just a rock. One point three ounces. Tossed it into the heart of—that. It disappeared instantly."

"Vaporized?"

"We thought about that. So we sent through a homing beacon, about a foot around. We maintained contact with the beacon for just under a minute. Then it went silent. Same for a video camera on a motorized dolly. Maybe it was destroyed once it reached the other side, or couldn't find its way back. Maybe the signals can't reach back, we don't know. But without question there is *something* there, on the other side. And we have to know what it is."

Alex nodded. "So why me?"

Gregory flipped open the folder. Inside, clipped to sheets of computer readouts and transcripts and memos marked CONFIDEN-TIAL were five photographs. "You weren't the first name on our list, Alex," Gregory said, flipping through them. "They went before you. Colonel Jeff Massie, Second Lieutenant Emilio Perez, two sergeants—Ed Marks and Len Sinclair—and a captain. Henry Kincaid. They all volunteered. They all took with them the best equipment we could give them. And then they all went *in there*. None of them have come back."

"No contact at all?"

By way of reply, Gregory walked over to a tape recorder built into one of the consoles, and hit PLAY. At once the room was filled with static, coming from concealed speakers. Then, faintly, a voice: *I'm through, do you read me, Com-Con? It's—there's something here—can't quite—my, God—can you see it? Can—*

Then the voice was swallowed by static. Gregory let the white noise rush over the room for a moment before shutting it off. "That was Kincaid. Maximum contact time: ten seconds. Then—static. Five men, Alex. Five good men. State Department wants to close us down, pull the plug and make it all go away, just forget it ever happened. Pentagon's pushing on grounds of national security. They wanted one more chance. As for me, if there's any way to rescue those five men, assuming they're still alive—"

Alex nodded. "Understood."

Gregory studied him for a moment, his lips thin. "It's only fair to tell you that I didn't want you for this, Alex. You've paid your dues, and then some. But the brass decided we needed someone with your experience. Even so, you don't have to go. Just say the word."

Alex stood and wandered over toward the glass wall. He could see Gregory's reflection in its surface. "Don't know if they told you," he said, "but I got the word last week—seems I'm getting a little too old to be a rocket jockey. They're putting me behind a desk, Greg. I can't live with that. Given the choice..." He glanced over his shoulder at Gregory. "Be a hell of a way to go out, wouldn't it?"

"You'll come back. If anyone can, you can. You're a good soldier, Alex."

Alex looked back at the wall. "Yeah. That's what Sarah said the day she left me. Good soldier, always ready to follow orders, do his duty."

If Gregory heard, he said nothing. Only waited.

Finally, Alex turned, smiled. "So, where do I suit up?"

2

Twenty-four hours later, as a phalanx of technicians escorted Alex down the corridor to the lab, he was reminded of the scenes of crewmembers boarding the space shuttle. Video cameras winked at him from both sides, recording every moment as he maneuvered through the narrow doorway. "A complete record is kept of every attempt," the technician had explained as they were sealing him up into his pressure suit.

"Let's hope this'll be the last one," Alex had said. The technician had smiled back at him, but hadn't looked convinced.

The outfit they'd stuck him in was only a little slimmer than a full space suit, with digital readouts and telemetry that would be relayed back to the lab constantly—or for as long as he was in contact, at any rate.

Ten seconds, he thought. *The record so far is ten seconds.*

A lot can happen in ten seconds.

The lab, previously empty, was now a hive of activity. A dozen technicians manned consoles, tested telemetry, ran checks and counted backwards to zero. He caught snatches of conversation, little of it making much sense.

Gregory hovered over it all, looking nervous. He found Alex and moved toward him, stepping around cables and wires. The others began to take note of Alex's presence, and he could see them looking at him nervously before turning their attention back to their consoles. It was a look he'd learned to recognize the first time he took off in a jet that needed testing, a jet that nobody was sure could do what it was supposed to do.

It was a look that said, *He's not coming back.*

It disturbed him less than he had thought it might, after all this time, to finally see the same expression on Gregory's face, too. "Almost time," Gregory said, glancing back at the wall. The steel barrier was still locked down. "Just in case—I mean, *just* in case—is there anyone you want me to—"

Alex shook his head, saving Gregory the pain of finishing the sentence. He held out his hand. Gregory took it. His grip was firm, even through the thick glove.

"See you soon," Alex said.

He stepped toward the only access to the other side of the room—a pair of thick glass doors that served as an air lock. He bent low to allow one of the technicians to slip the helmet over his head, then fasten it tight. There was a *click* from somewhere at his back, and a flow of cool oxygen began whispering into the helmet.

Gregory's voice came into his ears, filtered and tinny sounding. "You receiving, Alex?"

"Loud and clear."

"Proceed."

Alex stepped into the air lock, and a moment later the door closed behind him. In an instant, all sounds from the lab were lost. He felt, for a moment, as though he were underwater. Then the door on the opposite side hissed open, and the silence was gone, replaced by a roar of wind. He staggered momentarily as the wind buffeted him, then leaned into it as he moved into the other half of the room. Behind him, the steel wall rose into the ceiling, and he could see the technicians watching him.

Closer now, he could make out details of the earlier *incident* that had opened the hole. Consoles showed scoring and black marks where an explosion had melted circuits and blown out controls, merging everything into a new and thus far unknown configuration. There was blood on one of the computers.

And always, in the middle of it all, that terrible brilliance. It cut through even the helmet's filtered visor.

He pulled out the tie-line that fed out through the side of the suit and looped it onto a hook on the floor, then stood and gave Gregory a thumbs-up.

Gregory nodded, then looked around to the rest of the technicians. "Are we recording?"

A technician nodded, said something the microphone in the other room didn't pick up.

"All right, Alex," Gregory said. "We're clear to proceed. Remember—no heroics. Strictly threat analysis. Get in, take a fast look around, and get out of there. Do you copy?"

"Affirmative, General. Entering the gate—now."

He moved toward the pulsating center of light. Curiously, the closer he came, the less resistance there was from the winds. He seemed almost to be pulled toward it. *Gravity effect?* he wondered.

Then it had him.

It was like being grabbed in a giant's fist and slammed against a wall. The wind was knocked out of him, the light blurred, and the only sound audible over the sudden roar was a voice, already broken up by static, that filtered into his helmet. Gregory's voice.

"God go with you, Alex," he said.

Light. Wind. *Sound.*

Alex tried to force words out. *Come on, damn it, talk!* He was disoriented. He felt he was falling, but wasn't sure if he was falling up or down. The force of movement pressed him against the back of his suit. (*Acceleration?*)

"... moving, moving fast," Alex managed, his teeth rattling so that he thought they might fall out of his mouth, "feels like it's—like it's shaking me apart. Acceleration. Tremendous. Can't see anything—just white—just—"

White.

And the sudden blackness that appeared behind his eyes.

Fight it, damn you! Don't black out on me! Don't black out! Don't—

The last thing he heard, or thought he heard, was Gregory, calling his name, over and over, from someplace that sounded impossibly far away.

And then the white went away.

And so did Alex.

3

My nose itches.

His arms felt strangely heavy as, eyes closed, he tried to scratch his nose. But for some reason he couldn't get to it.

He opened his eyes. There was glass between his face and his hand.

Helmet.

Then he focused past his hand, to a vaguely purple sky that pinwheeled above his head.

Damn, he thought, and sat up, *damn, damn, damn!*

He toggled the SEND switch. "McKay to Com-Con. Do you read, Com-Con? I repeat: This is McKay. Do you copy, Com-Con?"

Silence.

How long was I out?

Fighting the heavy suit, he levered himself to his feet. He was on a grassy clearing. Leaves, green shot through with delicate white veins, clung to his suit. He brushed them away. Trees lined the clearing on all sides. If he didn't look too closely, they could be the same as trees he'd seen all his life. But even from here he could see the white, pulsing veins that ran through the thick trunks, the unnaturally straight branches reaching toward a foreign sky.

He gained his footing and caught himself before falling over in the opposite direction. *Gravity difference,* he decided. He felt more than a few pounds lighter than he had moments earlier. He felt behind him for the tie-line and found it had been severed cleanly. The end looked almost cauterized.

He looked around again, and it was then that he saw the glove lying on the ground a few feet in front of him. He picked it up, careful not to let the top-heavy suit throw him over again, and checked it against his own glove.

They matched.

He toggled the SEND button again. He could feel the tiny recorder in his chest console begin to whirr, preserving it all for posterity. If he could find one. "Don't know if you're getting this or not, Com-Con, but I'm going to keep recording anyway. If someone else finds this record, maybe they can get it back. I've found evidence of one of the pressure suits. Your men made it, General, at least one of them. Looks like it might have been abandoned. Don't see any sign of a struggle."

He twisted around to read the atmosphere sensor. It showed a slightly higher oxygen mix than Earth-normal, and a few trace elements the sensor couldn't identify. "Atmosphere and environment appear similar to our own. I'm going to try it. If it's livable, I'll switch to that. If not—well, I've got about half-an-hour's worth of air left in the suit."

Gingerly, he popped the helmet. Air rushed out past his face. He held his breath a moment, then sniffed at the new air that filled his helmet. It was good, clean air, full of the smell of leaves and pollen. "Oxygen atmosphere, all right," he said for the benefit of the recorder. "Sweet, cool, crisp air."

He looked around. There was nothing out of the ordinary in his surroundings. "Don't see any sign of the gate on this side. Perhaps it's not in the visible spectrum here...."

Or he had rolled or fallen from his original location.

Or he had been moved.

And wasn't *that* a comforting thought?

"Moving on. Will continue log entries at five-minute intervals."

4

It was fully half an hour later when Alex topped the last rise and stood looking down at the village.

You're dreaming, he thought.

It was like something out of a Brueghel painting.

Even from here, there was a feeling of serenity about the place.

Men and women—also Earth-normal, as far as he could tell—carried earthen jars and gathered grain. Children were playing with sticks, rolling a rounded stone ahead of them and laughing as they fought to determine which way it would go. Animals grazed near a series of thatched huts ringing a communal building of sorts—

"Welcome, Major," a voice behind him said.

Alex spun around, hand instinctively reaching for the gun that rode his belt.

A woman stood ten feet from him, wearing a long peasant skirt, her face all but hidden beneath a wide-brimmed hat. But the voice had not come from her; it had come from the man beside her. The uniform he wore was standard Air Force issue, identical to the one that Alex wore beneath his pressure suit. The man's face was equally familiar, and it took Alex only a moment before realizing that he had seen it in the folder Gregory had given him to study.

"Kincaid? Captain Henry Kincaid?"

He saluted smartly, smiling broadly. "Present and accounted for. We've been waiting for you. Well, not you in particular, but someone like you. Have to say that I'm happy with the selection, though. I can't think of a better choice, for their needs—and ours."

Alex wasn't quite ready to drop the gun yet. "Excuse me?"

This time the woman answered. She lifted her head a little, so that he could see her. Her face was plain, but not unattractive. At first glance, she looked a few years older than Alex, and when she smiled, Alex thought that it was the purest, least self-conscious smile he had ever seen. "Everything will be explained in time, Major," she said, her voice soft and vaguely lilting. "In the meantime, please, if you will come with us."

They started off down the hill toward the village.

Alex didn't move.

"Come with you where? What is this place?"

Kincaid glanced back over his shoulder at Alex and laughed. "Call it—heaven," he said, and continued toward the largest of the huts.

Alex hesitated, then followed them down. At a discreet distance.

For the moment, at least, there was nowhere else to go.

5

"Still no communication, General."

Gregory paced the lab, looking at his watch. It had been five hours since they'd lost contact with Alex. "Boost the signal."

"We've tried. We're still not getting anything."

"*Then boost it some more!*"

He walked to the glass wall, peering through slitted eyes at the too-white hole in the wall. Had it eaten him, too, like the others? He touched his palm to the glass. It vibrated under his touch.

"C'mon, Alex," he whispered. "Where the hell are you? Talk to me!"

6

"Please try and calm yourself, Major," Berenn said. That, he'd learned, was the name of the woman who'd met him alongside Kincaid.

"I will," Alex said, "just as soon as somebody gives me a straight answer to a simple question. Where are we? What is this place?"

He looked, one at a time, to the faces surrounding him at the table. They were all here—Massie, Perez, Marks, Sinclair, and, of course, Kincaid. They sat at the big table in the middle of the communal building. There was straw on the floor, and bowls of strangely textured fruits on the hand-hewn table.

Glances were exchanged at his question, and Perez sat forward. "Lieutenant Perez here, sir. Navigational specialist. I've been here for about a week, and the stars—well, Major, the stars are all wrong. I don't know where we are, but it's not Earth. Frankly, I don't think we're even in the same neighborhood anymore."

"Why haven't you tried to get back?"

This time Kincaid spoke up. The others seemed willing to defer to him. "Stone-cold truth is, we can't go back. We've surveyed the area, and as far as we can tell, the gate doesn't exist on this side. It only works one way, from there to here. Like it or not, we're stuck here, Major. Permanently."

Alex felt as though a cold fist had seized hold of his stomach and given it a sharp twist. He looked to the rest, but they avoided his glance, possibly not wanting to replay their own feelings at the discovery, perhaps—

Don't get paranoid, there's no cause—so far.

"Is it such a terrible fate, Major?" Berenn asked.

He turned in his seat to look at her. She sat on the outer perimeter of the circle they had formed, watching them as a teacher might watch a particularly interesting class.

"That's not the point," Alex said. "A lot of this still doesn't track, in my opinion. Like you. This place. How can you know my language?"

"Funny as it may sound," Kincaid said, "it's a matter of economics. Seems each of the communities around here has its own language or dialect. Since they operate on a barter economy, they select the one with the greatest facility for language to be in charge."

"Then why not let her speak for herself?" Alex said.

"It is as you have been told," Berenn said. "Ours is a simple existence. What we do not need we trade in exchange for that which is required. Which is very little. We are quite self-sufficient here. But we believe in maintaining the peace, and there is no peace without communication. That is my task."

"She's good at it, too," Sinclair piped in. "She was speaking pretty fluent English within a week. She only had to hear a word once to memorize it and know how to use it properly. The rest are a little slower, but most of them are picking up on it now."

"As for the similarity to Earth-normal," Massie said, "we're as much in the dark as you. If I had to make a guess, I'd say that maybe the experiment they were running had some correlation to a search for livable planets. If that part of the program was in memory when everything blew, then that may have had something to do with it. Otherwise—chalk it up to blind, dumb luck, the way a drunk manages somehow to drive home without wrapping himself around a tree."

Alex looked back at Berenn. She returned his gaze calmly and with, he thought, a hint of amusement at his instinctive distrust of the situation. "And you just welcome everybody. Just like that."

"It is my prerogative, as leader of this community. We are a peaceful people, not suspicious. Of supplies we have plenty, more than enough to share. If we have become an unintentional prison for you, please be assured that we will exert every effort to make it a pleasant one. There is much we have to offer."

She studied his face for a moment, and her expression became more serious. "They have told me about the world you come from. A place of such *hate*, that at first I could not believe it existed. A terrible, dark place where more and more struggle for less and less. Here, Major, we have no wars. What would we fight over? No one lacks for food, or shelter, or company. We have no possessions to steal; no religion save for the sanctity of life; no law but one: be kind to one another. That's why we were pleased to see it was you who was sent. They say you are a man of honor. There will always be a place among us for such as you."

"It's the kind of place we've all dreamed about, Major," Massie said.

"I think I'll reserve judgment on that until I've checked things out for myself," Alex said. "Meanwhile, I hope you won't mind if I poke around and see for myself whether or not there's a way home."

"Not at all," Berenn said. "We encourage you to explore. We will give you all the help we can, as we did for the others. Let me show you our world, Major. In time, I think you will come to like it."

And again, that look, as though she were hoping that if she studied him just so, at just the right angle, she might be able to see right into him. "I sense in you a man who has searched for peace a long time, without finding it. Here, in this place, you will."

She said it so earnestly, that for the barest flicker of a moment, he almost believed her. But he knew it would pass.

It always did.

7

The lab was empty. Dark. The hole, with its swirling white madness, was safely tucked behind the steel retainer. Gregory could almost pretend that it wasn't there at all, wasn't still thrashing around in some kind of electronic storm, wasn't still holding his friend in a place he couldn't reach, an unknown place of infinite white.

I never should have listened to them, he thought. *Anyone but*

Alex, I should have told them. He's too old. Let him retire while he can still walk away from the last one.

Then: *Get on with it.*

He clicked the dictating machine back on. The cassette whirred softly in its casing. "It has now been three days twelve hours since Alexander McKay entered the gate. In another twenty-four hours, we will consider him lost in action."

He leaned across the desk to pick up a file folder. One more folder. One more name. "I've recommended we shut down operations, and send no more men through the gate without a more detailed analysis. The brass wants to try a few more times. 'We lose more men in training exercises,' they told me. They've already picked the next volunteer. He comes highly recommended."

He flipped open the folder and gazed at the photo inside. A serious, thoughtful face. Someone's son. Someone's lover. "I don't know him. Thank God for small favors."

He switched off the recorder and left the room, turning off the lights behind him.

8

The sun, despite being smaller and whiter than the one he was used to, shone down warmly on Alex's face. A dozen yards away, just down the hill from where he was sitting, children were playing. Their laughter had the same curious lilt he had come to associate with all those who lived here, and the words they called out to one another were foreign but needed no translation. He smiled as he watched them, and he was surprised at how easily the smile came.

He felt relaxed. More relaxed than he had felt in a long time. Perhaps it was the lighter gravity, the richer oxygen mix.

Or perhaps it was just that for the first time, he didn't have to report anywhere, didn't have to do anything but sit here in the sun.

His attitude surprised him, but it was something he'd come to accept over the last five days.

He'd accepted a lot of things in that time.

But he still wore his pistol.

But he also accepted that, in time, that too would probably change.

"Good morning, Major."

He looked across to where Berenn came out of one of the huts and, waving to him, climbed up the modest slope to where he sat. He never ceased noticing the grace with which she moved, her total and complete ease with him and everyone around him.

She glanced over her shoulder at the children chasing a hoop in the clearing. "You do not play, Major." It was less a question than a statement.

He shrugged, pulling at the high grass in front of him. "Too old, I guess."

"That will change. You're not quite as old as you think." She smiled and joined him in watching the children for a moment before looking back at him. "Have you had any luck trying to find the way back?"

"None. You were right. From dawn to dusk we've searched every square inch of the area I came through. Nothing. Funny thing is, the more time I spend here, the less I begin to worry about it."

"Really." It, too, was less question than statement.

He nodded. "See, I've been a soldier all my life. And my father, and his father before him. They always said you have to fight for what you believe—but they never told me what to believe. They told me you have to follow orders—but they never told me why. If you stay busy enough, though, I guess you don't have time to think about it. Maybe that's what I've been doing all these years."

He laughed. "Friend of mine calls that *water skiing*. I didn't know what the hell he was talking about. He said it's when you keep moving as fast as you can, never slowing down, because you know that what you're standing on isn't enough to support you if you stop moving."

"The others said you were a—a test pilot?" She said the word as though she were trying it on for the first time, and seeing if it fit. She nodded to herself, deciding that it did. "Is that dangerous?"

"I suppose. That's pretty much what I was getting at. When you're in the cockpit, there's no time for questions. You're caught between the blue and the black, with death always just over your shoulder.

163

It made me feel alive—and disappointed, when I landed. I sometimes thought about how I'd like to go, in a blaze of fire and glory, doing what nobody else could ever do, just once. But it never happened, and now I'm wondering if maybe all this time I've been trying to find something worth dying for without having anything worth living for."

She sat quietly for a moment, then asked, "Do you have a family?"

He looked away. It wasn't something he liked to talk about a lot. "Not really. My wife walked out a year ago. Said she didn't believe in bigamy. Took me a while to realize it, but she was right. How do you compete with honor, and duty, and orders, and all the rest of it? It's just—"

He tried to find the words, but found that he had run out of steam. The pain wasn't there anymore. Just a sadness, at all the words he had never said, the words he *had* said, and now regretted. He felt tired, but it was the kind of tired that comes after finally dropping a great weight, and realizing at last that he was no longer burdened by it all.

He glanced up to find her studying his face with great gentleness. She put her hand on his and tightened it. "I'm glad you're here with us, Alex. Very glad."

He smiled. It was the first time she'd called him Alex.

9

It was well after dusk when Alex returned to the center of the village. Earlier, he'd walked nearly a mile into the woods before stopping, when he was sure he would be alone. He needed to sit, and to think—about this place, about home, about their inability to find the gate from this side.

Kincaid had been right. This was heaven, of a sort, and if there indeed wasn't any way back, as now seemed to be the case, then perhaps he should begin thinking about his other options.

He wanted to find Berenn.

They would have much to discuss if he were to try and make a place for himself here until help came.

If it came.

And if he wanted it to come.

He entered the communal building, passing Perez, who was on his way out.

"'Evening, Major," he said.

Alex clapped him on the shoulder. "I think Alex will do for now. Have you seen Berenn around?"

"I saw her go out a little while ago with Kincaid to draw some water. She'll probably be back in a few minutes."

Alex nodded and continued into the large hall. It was empty, everyone else having either retired to their own huts or enjoying the night air. He wandered over to the corner where they had let him store his equipment with the others' gear. When he'd been told that they didn't have locks, he'd been concerned about having his equipment stolen. But it remained just as he'd left it five days ago.

He looked at the pressure suit in the smoky light cast by the oil lamps that hung from the walls. It seemed to him now a foreign thing, a curious artifact that had nothing to do with him or this place.

Some of the other suits were nearby. The name tag on the closest read KINCAID. In a niche on the chestplate was a tape recorder, similar to his own. He picked it up. It felt unusually light.

Alex popped the EJECT button. Nothing came out. The cassette had already been removed.

He checked another recorder, on the suit marked MASSIE.

The cassette on that one was gone as well.

A quick check showed all five cassettes missing.

He frowned. *Who would have removed them? And why?*

He rummaged through the corner, pushing aside the piles and tangles of gear. As long as they were here somewhere, perhaps put away quickly, without anticipating a thorough search, he should be able to find them eventually.

He did.

10

There were footsteps approaching the communal hut. Footsteps, and the sound of laughter. It was loud, against the night, but not loud enough to drown out Kincaid's voice on the recorder.

...this place is Paradise. We can't go back. We know that now. We've told Berenn of our decision and asked her to keep the children away from the area of the gate at night, to make sure none of them accidentally wanders in. They say they'll set up a watch, keep an eye out for anyone else who might come through...

It was much the same as the information on the other four cassettes.

The door opened, and Berenn stepped inside, Kincaid following her.

"There you are!" Berenn said as she drew near. "I was wondering where you'd gotten off to. We were just—"

They stopped at the sound of the recording.

Alex switched off the speaker and held up the other four cassettes. "You lied to me."

Berenn paled. "Alex, please, we can explain—"

He threw the cassettes to the dirt floor and they clattered away. "No! You *lied* to me! You told me there was no way back! But there is! The gate's there, all right. But because of the refraction, the way the light bends and gets sucked into it, you can only see it at night."

He glared at Kincaid. "That's why you would only take me there during the day. You knew I wouldn't find anything. 'Stone-cold truth is we can't go back.' No, Captain. The stone-cold truth is that you *decided* to stay here—and make sure no one else went back."

"We told you the truth," Kincaid said, "the best way we could. Look, Major, if we went back and reported what we found, pretty soon this place would be swarming with troops and experts and God knows what else. They'd ruin it."

"That's garbage."

"Is it? You know how the military thinks. What do *you* think would happen if they got hold of it?"

Alex paused at this for a moment, then shook his head. "You could have left out some of the facts."

Kincaid snorted. "Wouldn't work. They'd just keep asking more and more questions, and eventually they'd find out all of it. There are ways of making any of us talk. Truth serum, you name it.

"We didn't want to lie to you. Given a choice, we wouldn't have. And eventually we would have told you the truth. But until then, we couldn't let you go back—not until you'd discovered for yourself what this world was like. Perfection is a fragile thing, Major. It doesn't survive the microscope. So once we saw what kind of place this was, we took a vote. The decision was unanimous. We're not going back. We're happy here, for the first time in our lives. This is Eden, Major. Would you want to be the one to bring the snake into the garden?"

"You're forgetting something," Alex said. "I didn't vote. Now, you're young, so maybe you can forget your duty, and your responsibilities, but I can't. And I'm going back."

He moved for the door. Kincaid stepped in his way.

"I'm afraid we can't allow that, Major."

"I don't recall giving you a choice, *Captain.*"

For the first time since he'd arrived, Alex's gun was off his belt and in his hand. It was ironic—he'd come tonight to turn the gun over to Berenn as a gesture of his trust. Now he was glad he hadn't.

Kincaid gazed down at the gun without moving out of Alex's way. "You see how easy it is, Major? The first solution of the angry man. How many other guns do you want to turn loose here?"

"I don't want to hurt you, Kincaid. But I'm ordering you to get out of my way."

"Then you'll have to kill me, Alex."

Alex studied his face. He had no doubt that Kincaid meant exactly what he was saying.

He lowered the gun—then brought it up quickly, cracking Kincaid under the chin. He went down hard, and Alex ran past him toward the door.

"Alex!" Berenn cried out. "No!"

He hit the ground running, heading across the clearing toward the path he had searched so many times before, always by daylight. He knew it well enough now to follow it even in the dark. Behind him he could hear Berenn calling after him, calling to the others.

"Help! Please, someone stop him!"

She was running after him, and a quick glance behind showed others coming out of their huts, running into the woods after him.

He ran.

(*to what?*)

Lungs pounding, not daring again to look behind him, he ran

(*where?*)

toward where he knew it was waiting, where he knew he had to go, no matter what.

(*why?*)

Because I've got orders, damn you!

Down the next hill, over the rocks, and finally he saw it—a five-foot-wide rectangle suspended in the night air just above the ground. It glowed dully, and he noticed as he worked his way toward it that it was visible only from the front.

He hurried toward the gate, hearing them behind him. Almost there—

"Alex! Wait! Please!"

He stopped, just a foot short of the gate. Even from here he could feel the force pulling at him. He risked a glance to where Berenn came up the path toward him.

"Please," she said, "don't go!"

"I'm sorry—but I have to."

"*Why*? You told me yourself, there's nothing back there for you."

(*why?*)

"Because I'm a Good Soldier," he said, hearing the bitterness in his own voice. "It's all I've ever been. Maybe it's all I'll ever be. If you take that away, then what's left? You said I was a man of honor. Please, leave me that. It's—it's all I have.

"Good-bye, Berenn."

And then, even as she reached for him, he dived into the gate.

And the white took him.

11

"So you're convinced they're a totally agrarian society?"

Alex nodded. "Judging from everything I saw—yes."

The others exchanged glances. As soon as he'd come back through the gate, to the sound of alarms and Gregory's surprised, pleased face, calls had been put through to a half-dozen government agencies. The rest would be showing up soon. He didn't know the names of the men talking to him across the table, and he knew he wouldn't be told even if he inquired.

They asked. He answered. That was the game, and he knew it by heart. They had been at it now for over two hours.

"What's your estimation of any potential threat they might pose to national security?"

"Nil. They have no offensive capability whatsoever."

"No weapons? No technology?"

"Not that I saw, no, sir."

"What about their defenses?"

"Same thing."

They exchanged a look, and Alex thought he didn't much like what he saw in their eyes. "Thank you, Major. If you'll just give us a moment."

Alex stood, saluted, and moved to the other end of the lab. Gregory was there, chain-smoking but pleased. He knew that the men at the table were from about as high up as you could go without hitting the Oval Office, and that their presence signaled a massive escalation in the importance of the operation. There was no telling how big things would get, but Gregory intended to be a part of it all the way.

"Comments?" said one of the men at the table, and the rest huddled into conference with him. Their voices were low, but still carried in the small lab.

"I think we're in a perfect position," one of them said. "The press isn't aware of the situation—it's a whole new frontier."

"What about trade? We could set up a barter situation. Technology, advisors, maybe even weapons to support their system of government—whatever it is."

There was a short laugh from one of the others. "I think we'll keep the guns in our own hands—for the time being. I kind of like the symmetry of that."

Gregory gestured for Alex to come closer, then clapped him on the shoulder. "Good job, Alex."

He shook his head. "I stink."

"No. Sure, it was hard. But you did what you had to. You followed orders."

"Yeah," Alex said, without enthusiasm. "Yeah, I did that, didn't I?" He looked behind them, to where the advisors were locked in discussion. "Tell me, Greg—would you have let the snake into the Garden of Eden?"

Gregory shrugged, lit another cigarette. "Fortunately for me, it wasn't a decision I had to make."

From across the room, one of the advisors signaled to Gregory. "Be right back," he said, and went to join them.

There was a whispered exchange between Gregory and the top advisor, while the others continued their analysis.

"I think you're overlooking the strategic value of all this," the first one continued. "What if we can open more gates from that world to anyplace on earth? We could use it as a transfer point for troops and materiel."

"Agreed. The first-strike potential is enormous! There's nowhere on Earth we couldn't hit with troops or tactical nukes in a hot second. Hell, we could store the stuff up there and the Russians would never be able to take it out with a first strike."

Alex reached up and carefully removed the major's cluster from his epaulet and placed it on the console in front of him.

No one noticed.

"Except what happens if the Russians get their hands on the same technology?"

He stepped back across the room, past the MP, to stand in front of the air lock that led into the other side of the room. He brushed his fingers along the cool metal.

No one noticed.

"It's a chance we'll have to take. Which is why we have to get in now, so we can call the shots. The Pentagon—"

He was through before they could stop him.

Red lights flashed, and he could hear alarms shrieking all around him. He yanked a metal pipe out of the damaged wall and jammed it into the air lock, ignoring the pounding from the other side.

Don't stop, he thought. *Don't stop or you'll never go through with it.*

Water skiing.

He was through the second door, into the main chamber, as the steel barrier started to rise into the ceiling. Behind it, through the glass, he could see all of them. Some were pointing at him, some cursing, one was shouting into a phone. *Probably calling security.* He could hear none of it through the soundproof glass.

He found another damaged pipe loosely hanging from the wall and yanked it out as Gregory finally found the intercom switch.

"...the hell do you think you're doing?"

Another MP was coming at the glass wall, a fire ax in hand.

It would take them at least a minute to break through all that glass.

Time enough.

Alex toggled the intercom switch on his side of the room. "Listen! General! I have a message for you! Tell the brass—tell them that perfection is a fragile thing! Tell them that I did my job! And tell them...*tell them I retire!*"

And with that, Alex brought the heavy lead pipe down on the nearest console. It struck with a flash of sparks and the clatter of shattering gauges and instruments. He slammed it down again and again, no longer hearing the protests from the other side, keeping one eye on the gate, watching, watching—

—as it flickered, then suddenly looked tenuous, like a bulb, about to burn out.

Now! he thought, and with a final blow to the console, he leapt into the gate.

As the white took him, he could hear, but not see, the explosion that ripped the last of the consoles apart.

He hoped only that the gate would finish carrying him to his destination before finally winking out of existence.

12

They stopped beside one of the trees that reached toward the sky with too-straight limbs. Far below, they could just barely see the village. They had walked all morning to get here. The view was every bit as glorious as she had promised.

After a moment, Berenn gazed over at him. Even before she spoke, he knew what she would ask; knew that she had waited until enough time had passed without further arrivals that they could be certain that the gate had truly been destroyed. "Are you sure they won't be able to build another one?"

He nodded. "It was a freak combination in the first place. If the gate were still there for them to study, maybe they could duplicate it in time. But it's gone. Permanently."

She smiled and took his hand. "So what do you do now?"

"For the moment," he said, gazing out at the fresh world that stretched before him, "absolutely nothing."

THE MIND OF SIMON FOSTER

There wasn't much left to sell.

Simon sat on the narrow bed that had been shoved into one corner of the dark, one-room flat. Clothes were piled on the dresser, and the curtains hung at an angle that stopped just short of the windowsill. He couldn't remember the last time he'd bothered to clean up the place. Not that it mattered. Nobody came by anymore. Not in person.

He cast a glance toward the vid. He supposed they didn't want to soil their hands by actually coming and talking to him face-to-face. No, anything but that.

He continued packing.

Shaver, cassettes, the few old coins he still possessed, a handful of books...and the watch. That was the hardest one of all. It was his father's watch, bought on impulse back when the old man had won a couple thousand dollars on one of the lotteries. It had been expensive, far too expensive even then, in better times. But he'd never once regretted the decision. When things had started to get bad, and he'd lost nearly everything else, the watch was his father's one remaining luxury, his last source of dignity in a world that had stripped away most the others.

On his deathbed, he had given the watch to Simon—and oh, in that moment, hadn't he been proud, though sad and shrunken and weathered? Hadn't he been so proud to have kept hold of it all those years. until he could pass it on, a real, honest-to-God legacy from the old man?

"No matter what they take away from you," his father had said, "as long as you've got this, they can never take it all away." Then he closed his eyes, and went away, and the state claimed its long overdue account.

He looked at the watch one last time before putting it into the box and closing the lid.

Don't think about it. Just do it.

He sat there for a long moment, running his hand over the rough corners of the cardboard box, when the vid rang. He let the answering machine catch the message. He knew what news it would be bringing.

"Yes, hello, Mr. Foster, this is Jennie Maloshevsky from the unemployment office returning your call." There was the sound of papers being shuffled. "I'm sorry, Mr. Foster, but as we discussed earlier, your benefits for the period two-seventeen-ninety-nine have expired as of this past week. If you wish to discuss this further, you can reach me at the usual number, but as I explained to you before, I'm afraid there's really nothing I can do."

The message cut off with a CLICK, and the screen filled with a moment of static before going black.

Simon Foster picked up the box and, careful as always to lock the door, stepped outside into the harsh sunlight. He made his way along the catwalk to the narrow stairs that led down the side of the housing complex. He wondered sometimes if during the night, little men didn't emerge from some unseen corner of the building to add more steps to the staircase. The journey down seemed to get longer with every passing day.

The pawnshop bell rang softly as Simon stepped inside. No one was behind the counter. He looked around the shop as he waited for someone to come out. He'd never been in this one before—he rarely ranged this far downtown—but it was like all the others. Row upon row, and aisle upon aisle of brass and silver and mortgaged moments.

He started at the sound of a door closing behind the counter. "Mister Quint?" That had been the name engraved on the store window. QUINT'S PAWNSHOP—BEST PRICES IN TOWN.

He was a large man, with a square face and eyes that looked at Simon with only marginal interest. "Yes, sir? Something I can help you with?"

"Well, I'm—afraid I'm not buying."

Quint's shoulders sagged slightly. "Ah. Selling, then."

"Yes."

"Bring it here, let's see what you've got."

Simon put the box up on the counter and stepped back as Quint rummaged through it. He tried to look interested in the racks of musical instruments, tried not to notice which items were received with silence, and which elicited an occasional *hmm* or a shrug of disinterest.

He wandered back to the counter, despite his best intentions. "It's all in good condition," he said, trying to make conversation. "It's not much, I know, but I sold off most of the rest. Rent to make and everything, you know how it is. Been having some hard times, lots of—well, lots of things going wrong, you know? But I guess you hear that a lot in this business, don't you?"

"Yes, I do." Simon could see him adding up the figures in his head. "Fifty dollars."

"Fifty! The watch alone is worth at least that!".

Quint looked back inside the box, frowned. "Sixty, then. But that's as high as I'll go."

Anguished, Simon gathered up the box and started toward the door.

"You can take it somewhere else, but you won't get any more," Quint called after him. "And when you come back, the offer will be fifty. Flat."

Simon slowed, then stopped. He glanced inside the box. The watch dully reflected the overhead lights. *I'm sorry, Dad, God, I'm so sorry.*

He stepped back to the counter and set down the box. "At least—could you at least make it sixty-five?"

Quint frowned, then nodded. "Done."

He went to the cash register, rang up NO SALE, and slowly counted out the sixty-five dollars, not looking up as he said, "You're sure you've nothing else to sell, then?"

"No, nothing else."

"You weren't sent? Referred?"

"No, I—look, if I *had* anything else to sell, it'd be in that box. I've got nothing left. Just a gut full of pain. Why? You want to make me an offer? Go ahead, Mr. Pawnshop Man, tell me—what's the going price for pain these days?"

Mr. Quint said nothing.

Simon took the money and started toward the door, his hand almost on the handle as he heard Quint's voice.

"Perhaps there is something *else* we can negotiate over."

Simon hesitated, looked back at him. Mr. Quint unlocked the other door behind the counter. "Come," he said, and stepped through into another room.

Simon hesitated, then followed him in.

What the hell, he thought. I got nowhere special to go.

The room within was black, windowless, its contents all but invisible until Quint switched on the single bulb that hung suspended overhead. A computer console ran along one wall, bleeding off into an unsettling number of plugs hanging from a minimum of outlets. A chair squatted in the middle of the room, covered by a black sheet. He could make out bits and pieces of electronic apparatus protruding out of the cover, tenting it in places. It looked quite uncomfortable.

Quint stepped toward the chair, circling it slowly. "You are familiar, I trust, with memory dipping?"

"Only what I read in the papers. Supposed to be the big trend these days, renting people's memories."

"Yes, it's become very popular among those able to afford it." He pulled off the black sheet to reveal the chair in its entirety—the drouds, the scanning equipment, the displays, something that looked like a laser-probe, and a lot of equipment Simon didn't recognize. A series of digital relays led across the room to the bank of machines on the other side.

"The usual practice is to scan a subject's memories and copy them onto a computer chip," Quint said. "The process is very selective. You can take a skier, copy his memory of his best jump, and by plugging into that, you can experience what he felt. His thoughts, his feelings, the way the snow felt when his skis hit it, the roar of the crowd—you feel it all, as if it were you. A fascinating concept, is it not, Mr.—" He smiled a too-friendly smile.

"Foster. Simon Foster."

"Mr. Foster. As I was saying, a very trendy item. Unfortunately, *dubbed* memories aren't as vivid as some might like. It's like seeing a video that's been copied too many times: the color is washed out, the experience less than one hundred percent real. And that's the point of electronic entertainment, isn't it? To give you the feeling of actually *being there*?"

"Go on."

"So a market has developed for connoisseurs looking to sample a far more intense experience. For that, they require not dubbing, but *direct transference*." He circled the chair, his hands passing gently over the equipment. "For that, we go in electronically and slice away memories. A minute, an hour, a year, ten years...we can remove those specific memories and store them for use by others." He glanced at Simon, and catching the expression there, quickly added, "The process is quite painless, of course."

"And illegal."

"Eminently. And the wonder of it all is, the product is not a distortion of reality, it is reality *distilled*. For those who buy, the risk is quite worthwhile. Love, sex, hate, the everyday experiences we take for granted, the facility to peek into someone else's life, they get it all. And for those who sell, the rewards are quite reasonable."

"I've never really done anything special—"

"Unnecessary," Quint said. "Look at the soap operas, Mr. Foster. No alien invasions, no vast sagas. But they know the value of voyeurism. And so do I."

Simon glanced at the chair and felt his mouth go dry. It was just one more piece of furniture, but being in the same room with it made him feel somehow—dirty.

Sixty-five dollars. You got sixty-five dollars for damn near everything you had left in the world. What's the difference?

"I don't know," Simon said. "I mean, how much would I get?"

"That depends upon what we find. Memory is like an old penny, Mr. Foster. You may think it's quite worthless, and to you, it may be. But to a collector, ah, that's something else again." He switched off the overhead light, and instantly the room was plunged back into darkness. Finding Simon's elbow, Quint led him out into the front room. The light from outside stung his eyes as he emerged.

"Every day we forget a little more of the past," Quint continued. "It does us no good to wallow in it; We've been there, after all. So why not let someone else enjoy it? Me, if I had to choose between remembering something that happened fifteen years ago, and eating a good meal at a fine restaurant today, well—"

Simon edged toward the door. "I'll have to think about it."

"Of course, of course," Quint said. "Wouldn't have it any other way. Do think about it. And while you're thinking about it, think on this: What have your memories done for you, lately, Mr. Foster?"

Simon looked back once, as the door closed, then moved away down the street, pulling his jacket closer about him.

Simon carried the small bag of groceries up the stairs toward his flat. The bag was depressingly light. It was amazing how little fifteen dollars bought these days. He was nearly to the top of the stairs when he heard the sound he had hoped to avoid: the door on the first floor opening. The door to the manager's apartment.

"Hey, you. Foster!"

Simon stopped. "Yes, Mr. Ferelli?"

The thin, wiry man in the jogging suit came to the bottom of the stairs. "In case you haven't heard, the rent's due first of every month. Today is the sixth. Either I get the rent from you by tomorrow, or I'm throwing you out of here right on your ass."

Simon nodded and continued up the stairs.

"Hey, you listening to me?"

Simon closed the door to his flat and leaned against it. He had heard just fine.

The nights were getting colder. The smell of chowder coming from the hot plate smelled good, even if the date on the can was a little old.

As the soup reached full boil, he shut it off and poured it into a small bowl, letting it cool as he went to the closet and pulled out a sweater. He buttoned it as he stepped back into the kitchen.

Something was floating in his bowl of chowder.

He nudged it with the spoon. It rolled over to reveal legs.

Cockroach.

Must've fallen into the soup while he was getting his sweater, he decided, the thought coming to him from somewhere far away.

Cockroach.

The can had cost him two dollars.

178

"Damn it!" He slammed his fist into the table so hard that for a moment he thought it would splinter. It rocked badly, but held. *"Damn it!"*

With a kind of manic desperation, he carried the bowl over to the sink and spooned out the roach, careful not to move it around, as if by keeping it to one place he might somehow confine the germs to what he could spoon out.

He rummaged in the drawer for another spoon, then went back to the table. He closed his eyes and tried to see the chowder the way it had been earlier—warm and fragrant and inviting. He picked up the spoon, dipped it, brought the chowder toward him—

And stopped, the spoon an inch from his lips.

"It's not fair," he whispered. "It's not fair, it's just not fair...."

He stood and threw the bowl into the sink. It struck with the crash of breaking glass. "It was the last can I had—it was the LAST CAN I HAD AND IT'S NOT FAIR! IT'S JUST NOT FAIR!"

Not one bit.

Simon stood nervously in the pawnshop doorway. As usual, no one was about. He pulled the door closed loudly, and a moment later Quint appeared behind the counter.

"It's not fair, you know," Simon said.

"Very little in life is, Mr. Foster."

He opened the drop leaf and ushered Simon behind the counter. Feeling numb, Simon allowed himself to be led through the curtains into the dark room just beyond.

"I've just had a very good offer from a fellow who collects high school graduations," Quint said, and closed the door behind them.

...a swirl of colors and faces, twisting and bending, a sense of violation as they were seized and sucked and whirled away somewhere up there, into the darkness, all of them, Ben and Mrs. Massie, his mother and father...sitting on the bleachers, so proud, the sun hot but hanging in desolate emptiness, and the voices, overlapping one another like small waves...class of '66...proud to have been a part...the highest grade-point average in...like to welcome our valedictorian...Richard Fleming, Michael Flores, Karen Ford, Simon Foster...

"Mr. Foster? Mr. Foster?"

Quint's face slowly emerged from the surrounding darkness, inches from Simon's own. He was slapping Simon on the face, not hard, but firmly. Simon blinked hard, then tried to sit up, when the nausea hit him like a tidal wave. He slumped back into the chair.

"You are all right, Mister Foster?"

Simon licked his lips. They were dry, and seemed too sensitive to his tongue. "Yeah, I—I suppose so."

"The first time is always rough." He handed Simon a paper cup filled with water and helped him close his hand around it. "Drink this. For whatever reason, the process tends to dehydrate a little."

Simon drank the water in slow, grateful sips as Quint went to the bank of equipment along the far wall. ...*for whatever reason*, Simon thought, the realization slowly coalescing in his numbed brain. *Of course he doesn't know how it works. Why should he?*

Quint flipped a row of switches, then squinted into the monitor. Colors played across his face. Simon wondered what he was seeing, wondered in what digitized, three-dimensional, full-stereophonic form the memory of his high school graduation now existed.

Existed without him, separate from him.

He probed at his thoughts, tried without success to summon up a single image from that day. It was gone, like a phone number that just slips away, never to return.

"A perfect transfer," Quint said, switching off the monitor. "How do you feel?"

"All right. I don't feel any different, except—"

"Except that there is now just a tiny gap in your memory, just so." He held thumb and forefinger a quarter-inch apart. "Everything between eight o'clock in the morning and eight o'clock in the evening, on the day in question. Twelve hours, poof, gone. And are you any the less for it? No. In fact, I would dare say, you are quite the richer for it."

As Quint said it, he handed across an envelope. Simon didn't need to open it to know it contained his fee. It felt sufficiently thick—not overwhelmingly so, but enough.

Quint helped him to his feet. Simon balanced and waved him away. "I think I can manage it from here."

"Excellent. Well, good doing business with you, Mr. Foster, Next time, when you—"

"No," Simon said, "there's not going to be a next time. I just needed enough to get ahead a little. That's all. I thank you for your—your *help*, but I think once is more than enough."

Quint shrugged. "As you say. But *if* you should ever change your mind, you know where to find me. I'm sure I can get you a very good price."

Quint helped him to the door, then stood aside as Simon walked off, heading in no particular direction, the envelope in his shirt pocket warm against his chest.

Twelve hours. Twelve hours he would never miss in exchange for a few weeks free of worrying about where his next meal was coming from. As deals went, it wasn't the worst he'd ever made.

So why, then, did he feel so unclean?

Simon peeled three hundred and twenty-five dollars off the roll and handed it to the manager, who accepted the money with a look that reminded Simon of a dead fish he'd once seen on the beach. It had been lying there for at least a week.

He started away when the manager put a hand out in front of him. "Plus the money for next month, too. New policy. Got a lot of transients coming through here—owner says we have to have an extra month's deposit." He paused for effect. "Helps discourage the deadbeats."

"Look, you can't do that—"

"Yeah?" he said, feigning amazement. "Look, I'll tell you what, why don't you run off to the housing commission and tell them all about it—and maybe when you get back you'll find your apartment rented. One of those clerical errors you hear so much about."

Bastard, Simon thought, but cut it off before the thought escaped...and began counting out more bills into the manager's open hand.

Simon paced nervously, not wanting to sit. He'd pulled his best suit out of the closet for the interview, had it cleaned and pressed. He didn't want to wrinkle it. Across the room, on top of the bureau, sat the remainder of his money, a little over thirty dollars. The rest had carried him this far, and now surely something would break. Something *had* to break.

When the vid finally rang he caught it on the first ring, and the unreadable face of his employment counselor appeared on the screen.

"Hi," Simon said, a little too cheerfully, he thought.

The counselor nodded. "You requested an interview," she said. "How may I help you?"

Simon's mouth worked. This wasn't what he'd expected to hear. "It's—well, it's time for my six-week review."

She blinked, and checked the forms in front of her. "Yes, so it is." She glanced them over briefly. "I'm sorry, Mr. Foster, but there are still no openings in your area. You'll just have to wait until something opens up."

"But I resubmitted my application two weeks ago! You told me then that something was in the works."

"Things have a habit of changing, Mr. Foster. I'm sorry, but you'll just have to wait your turn. When we're notified of a vacancy in your field, you will be notified at that time. That's all I can tell you. Good-bye."

Click and disconnect.

He walked over, switched off the vid. On his way back, he passed the bureau and glanced down at the remaining money.

Thirty dollars. Enough for another two days, and then—

You're not going to do it. You did it once only because you absolutely had to. Not again.

Five dollars.

Simon sat on the bed, near the window, angling the high school yearbook perched in his lap so that it caught the fading daylight. He paged through it, smiling at the passing faces, the pictures of pep clubs and school plays, rallies and footraces.

Five dollars.

He recognized the names, and the faces—most of them, anyway—and nodded at the familiar buildings captured in grainy photographs. Then he turned the page, to the two-page foldout he knew would be there, a panoramic photo of his high school graduation, everyone lined up on the bleachers, clad in caps and gowns, smiling for the camera. He managed to find himself in the photo. He ran his finger over the image, as though hoping to feel the memory vibrating somewhere just beneath its surface.

Nothing. The photo could have belonged to another place, another school, another Simon Foster whose similarity to him ended at the name.

"...gone," he said, and the silent room embraced the word.

'Five dollars.'

Five dollars left.

He slammed shut the yearbook and walked out of the room.

As Simon stepped into the pawnshop, the improbable thought occurred to him that Quint had actually been waiting for him all this time, in the very spot he'd last seen him, there behind the counter.

"You're in luck," Quint said, picking up the conversation as though it had never been abandoned. "We just had a call from someone interested in buying birthdays."

Simon shut the door behind him. It closed with a too-loud *click*.

He sat in the chair.

Make a wish...how did you know?...It's from Aunt Sara—I bet it's socks...is it okay if I stay out late?

He sat in the chair.

Oh, look, darling! He's taking his first step! Look!

He sat in the chair.

And they took his college graduation. And his first year of college.

"—It's for the daughter of a client of mine. She's going to college. But who wants to study when all that information is locked away in your head? It's only a semester, six months—"

He sat in the chair.

And they took away his day at the circus, age ten. And his second year of college. And his first date.

—wanted to say it's been—you're a great dancer. Thank you. It—was very nice. But I have to go inside now. I'll never forget this, though...not ever.

He sat in the chair.

And they took it away.

And they paid him for it.

Simon awoke as the alarm buzzed annoyingly in his ear. He forced himself to sit up, rub the sleep from his eyes. He had an hour before the counselor would call. They were punctual. They were always punctual. He staggered into the bathroom and splashed cold water on his face. He had to be alert, had to be sharp. It had taken another six weeks to get the interview. He had a real shot at this one, he could feel it.

An hour later he sat before the vid, straightening his tie and checking himself in the mirror one last time as the vid beeped at him. He flicked it on, and the face of the counselor filled the screen. He smiled at it. The face sent back the barest flicker of a smile.

"Right on time, Mr. Foster. Very good."

"Thank you."

"As we indicated in our letter, we have a job in the repair field for which you might be qualified. We just have to ask you a few questions. What high school did you say you graduated?"

Graduated? I—no, wait. That's right.

"Clifford—ah, Cliffordville High, in—Madison."

"With two years of junior college."

"That's right."

"What was your major?"

Simon hesitated. "I think—I think it was—"

"Your resume lists engineering."

"Yes. Look, if you could just give me a minute, I think I have the records around here somewhere—"

"I'm sorry, but we're pressed for time, Mr. Foster. If you're not ready for this interview, you should have notified us."

Simon straightened. He couldn't afford to lose this one. "No, no, I'm—ready. Sorry. Go on."

She looked at the forms in front of her. "Please describe your training in that field during your college experience."

Simon fought to remember, but his thoughts kept slipping over the gap like a tongue worrying the space where a tooth had been removed. "Well, I—we worked very hard, covering a lot of different areas, it's difficult to describe."

"I require specifics, Mr. Foster."

He opened his mouth to respond, but nothing came out. He searched desperately, trying to find some fragment to throw up in front of him as a defense, but it was gone, all gone. "I—"

The face on the vid lifted and stared into his own. "I'm sorry, Mr. Foster, but if you're not going to cooperate, there's nothing I can do for you."

"I want to cooperate. It's just—it's difficult sometimes—"

"It's difficult for us all, Mr. Foster. The unemployment rate is thirty-two percent as of this Monday, and there are many applicants who are looking for this kind of job."

"Look, if you could just—it's coming back to me, really it is, you have to understand it's been a long time—if you could just give me a chance."

"I'm afraid you've used up your allotted time, Mr. Foster. If you will resubmit your application—"

Simon stood, stepped toward the vid. "No, wait a minute, please, you can't do this to me—I need this job!"

"Perhaps you will think of that prior to your next interview."

"Don't you *understand*?" He was shouting now, hardly aware that he was doing it. "I'm nearly broke! I can't go on like this! You've got to listen to me, it's not my fault!"

"If you wish to appeal the interview, that is your option, and it will be taken up at the proper time. Meanwhile, please resubmit your application to central processing. Good day, Mr. Foster."

Then the vid flickered, and she was gone. He clawed at the screen, as though by an act of will he could reach through to wherever she was, where the jobs were, and pull her back. "I can't go on like this," he cried. "Don't you see, you've got to listen to me! Come back here! Come back—damn you!"

After a while, he went back to his chair and sat down, rocking slowly in the filtered light from outside. He wouldn't get another appointment for six weeks. Six weeks.

Next time he would do better.

He would have to do better.

Simon stepped back into the pawnshop, the tiny bell overhead announcing his presence. By now he had developed an almost Pavlovian hatred for the bell.

No one stood behind the counter. "Mr. Quint?" He stepped slowly toward the counter, going over his planned statement for the third time. *I'm sorry, Mr. Quint, but I can't sell you anything more that might affect my hiring. If you want to buy something else, we'll discuss it.*

They would definitely discuss it. He had put off coming back for a long time, and now he was down to his last few dollars. But no matter how desperate he was, he wouldn't swerve from his decision. He couldn't afford to.

After a moment, the door behind the counter opened, and Mr. Quint emerged. Beside him was a young woman, about Simon's own age. She looked pale, drawn, almost feral. She clutched an empty paper cup in her hands, and when he looked at her, she avoided his gaze.

Ashamed.

Oh, God, Simon thought. No.

Quint opened the cash register, pulled out an envelope stuffed with bills, and handed it to her. She accepted them without a word and made quickly for the door. As she brushed past Simon, she glanced up. There were tears in her eyes. For a moment, he thought she was going to say something. But she quickly turned away and ran out the door, slamming it behind her.

The bell jingled softly to mark her departure.

"Good to see you, Mr. Foster," Quint said, as though nothing had happened.

Simon turned away from the door and focused on him. "My God," he said, "my *God*, how many? How many others?"

"You mean her?" Quint shrugged. "I run a business, Mr. Foster. Like any good business it depends on volume—and diversity. One must be responsive to fluctuations and changing demands in the market. Surely you didn't think you were the only one."

Simon started toward the door, toward fresh air, toward any place that was not this place.

"Save me your grand gestures," Quint said. "You're not going anywhere. And even if you leave, you'll be back. Your kind always comes back."

Simon turned, and he could feel his face burning. "Yeah, we come back," he said. "Because bread is three dollars a loaf and meat you can't even buy except on the black market. Matter of fact, I look around and the only person I see eating—is you."

"I pay you a fair price for what you have to sell."

"*Well it's not enough*! Who are you to say this minute is worth a nickel, an hour—maybe a dollar? Five, if something interesting's going on? What gives you the right to put a price tag on my life?"

"I didn't," Quint said, and walked away, toward the counter. "You did."

Simon stepped back as though slapped. He tried to find some biting response, but suddenly it didn't seem to make any difference. He was right. Damn him, he was right.

Simon looked away, nodded. "Yeah," he said at last, more softly now. "Yeah, I did, didn't I?" He crossed the room to where Quint stood. "So what'll it be today, Mr. Quint? A trip to the zoo? A ride on a roller coaster? Why don't you take my first marriage and save us both some grief?"

"Not interested," Quint said. "Market for birthdays and conventional stuff is down. It's only temporary, though, I'm assured by my people. Academics are also down, since school's out for the summer, which I'm sure you'll find of some relief. No, Mr. Foster, I'm only buying one thing today. We need a companion piece to the young lady who just left here.

"We want to buy the first time you made love to a woman."

Simon's knees went soft beneath him. He shook his head, slowly. "No...."

"I'm prepared to make you a very good offer."

"No, I can't. There's got to be something else—"

"Sorry. Take it or leave it, but that's all I'm buying at the moment. Walk away and who knows if I'll buy anything else. I need a reliable supply of material. Either you're here to do business, or you're not—and if not, then get out."

With that, Quint stepped back through the door behind the counter, leaving it open just a crack.

Her name was Carolyn. Carolyn of the auburn hair, the green eyes, the ruddy Basque complexion, the dancer's legs, and the small, delicate breasts. They'd argued the night before, and he'd brought her roses the next day to apologize. She cried when she saw them. No one had ever brought her roses before. "Make love to me," she'd said, her voice small, her face still moist from tears. He'd been about to enter her when she held his face in her hands.

Tell me you love me.... Don't be silly, I—It's not silly. Just tell me you love me. I don't even care if it's true or not.... I love you...For always. Forever and ever...For always. Forever and ever and ever and ever and ever and

"That will be all."

Simon flinched, his gaze fixed at a no-place point beyond the wall, but he didn't move as Quint removed the drouds. He tried to summon Carolyn's face to mind, tried to find some trace of that evening, but it had all turned to mist behind his eyes.

Gone. All gone.

"I said that will be all, Mr. Foster. You can go now. Your payment is on the counter."

Simon took the paper cup beside the chair and knocked the water back in one swallow, his throat burning. The process did not get much easier with time. He pulled himself out of the chair and started for the door—then hesitated. He looked at the bank of equipment along the wall, then slowly made his way toward the row of scanners and readouts and digital displays.

He peered into the monitor, but all he could see was row after row of numbers, swimming in front of his eyes. "She's in there, isn't she?"

"Please stay away from the equipment," Quint said from the door, "you might damage something."

"Somebody told me once," Simon said, "that you always remember the first, you always remember the last, but nobody remembers the second. Guess now I'm the exception to the rule, aren't I?"

"Well spoken, Mr. Foster. Now if you will please step away from the equipment—"

Simon turned, faced him. "I want her back. I've changed my mind."

"Sorry. No refunds. Take your money and get out."

Simon advanced on him, backing him toward the door. "I said I want her back. I want her back in my head, where she belongs. I want my life back." He grabbed Quint before he could bolt from the room. "You've got my life. I want it back. *Give me my life back!*"

"Get away from me!" Quint said, struggling in his grip. "Let—me—go!"

Quint pushed away, ripping his shirt, and bolted from the room. Simon ran after him, found him reaching under the counter—

Gun!

He tackled Quint, and they went to the floor, struggling for the gun. Simon closed his hand over Quint's, finally managed to rip the gun out of Quint's hands. He rolled away fast and came up with the gun clenched in both hands. Quint scrambled to his feet, and Simon caught him in the crosshairs.

"I want my life back! Damn you!"

"I haven't got it! I sold it! Don't you understand? It's not here anymore!"

"Then get it!"

"I can't!"

Simon cocked the hammer. He didn't need to see his own face to know there was the light of madness in it. "Then I suggest you try," Simon said, "because right now, I haven't got much of anything to lose. I want a life. I want to be whole again. Now."

"All right!" Quint licked his lips nervously. "There—there is a way. But it's not perfect."

"Like you said, Mr. Quint—what in life is?"

Simon Foster waited in his room, sitting in his usual place in front of the vid, dressed in his best clothes. He awaited with quiet calm the beep that would announce the incoming call from the job placement bureau. When it came, he toggled the vid and smiled at the face that shimmered into view. He felt good. He felt confident. He felt whole.

The counselor returned the smile, though it looked false and without conviction. "Punctual again, I see."

"As always."

"We've received your new application, Mr. Foster. Very professionally typed. Did you have it done by a service?

"No, ma'am. I typed it myself."

"Did you?" She glanced back down at the form. "Yes, I see you've added clerk/typist to your job goals. And a number of other occupations. Where, exactly, did you learn to type?"

"I took three years of typing at Sorworth College. It's all on the resume."

The counselor looked up at him and frowned. "But Sorworth was a women-only college at that time."

Simon nodded. "And I graduated on June twelfth, on the year shown. And then I graduated again, on July first of the following year. I attended and graduated from Lennox High School. Also Chula Vista High School. Did I mention Matawan Regional High School?"

"Mr. Foster," the counselor said, trying to interrupt. She looked concerned. But Simon kept on going. He knew that everything was going to be all right now.

"That was shortly after I returned from London. Did I tell you I have two children? I remember when they were born. It was such a moving time for me, being an only child. I remember when I turned five, my brother and my sister helped make the decorations—"

"Mr. Foster...?"

"But of course the credentials are what's at issue here. I should mention that my German is quite fluent. I spent much of last year in Vienna—or was that Spain—yes, it was, and I worked as a translator, and a bus driver, and a secretary, and I interned for two years at the Institute de Neurologica...."

Simon smiled as he spoke.

Everything was going to be just fine.

WE KILLED THEM IN THE RATINGS

Carl Sarotkin was getting desperate. He tried to hide it from everyone else at the station, carried on with a Business As Usual smile stamped firmly on his face, but he could feel the stress building every day. He was losing weight, his thinning hair was looking even greyer than before, and his eyes felt pinched behind his wide-frame glasses.

StreetScene was slipping in the ratings.

It had started out as a terrific idea. Competition between the Los Angeles independent stations had kicked into high gear, and the general manager was leaning on everyone to develop something snazzy to bring up the seven-thirty to eight P.M. time-slot, before the network feed at eight. Scuttlebutt said the station managers and owners wanted to sell it to one of the new mini-networks, but they needed to boost the ratings first. This would increase the ad revenues and therefore the going price of the station. The other local affiliates filled the 7:30 slot with syndicated "infotainment" strips, talk shows or magazine format shows covering local stories, elections, whatever made the front pages of the Metro or Style sections in either of the local daily papers. It was good business, low-cost, and gave the news anchors another venue for getting their face out in front of the public, which in turn kept them from jumping stations.

That's what it all came down to, after all. Business.

Just business.

That was all Carl had in mind when he created *StreetScene*.

StreetScene: a mobile minicam unit dispatched to a different neighborhood every day, from the high-priced enclaves of the rich, to the theater district, Chinatown and (during sweeps) the high-crime, hooker-infested tenderloin areas, combining interviews with hidden camera shots taped through the mobile unit's rear window. The idea was to show the contrasts of Los Angeles, portray it as a vibrant city in transition, showing the highs and the lows and the in-betweens, the glamour and the gutter, the pimps and the powerful (when you could tell them apart, which was becoming increasingly difficult.) As icing on the cake, the show would be broadcast live, adding an element of immediacy to the show.

Given his background producing other live shows for the station, Carl took the helm of *StreetScene*. It was his idea, after all, and he wanted to see what was happening out there for himself. *Thou shalt know thy audience.* It was the second rule of television.

The first rule being, *Thou shalt make a profit.*

When it came time to present the concept to the news department, he pitched it as The Man On The Street meets *Our Town*. To the advertising department he pitched it on its local angle, and to the program director he pitched it as sleazy and sexy and timely, with a slightly illicit edge (but never going over the line) that would appeal to concerned citizens and busybodies and voyeurs; the same people who had turned *Cops* into a license to print money.

That had sold it immediately. That, and the fact that it would be cheap to produce. They almost always had a spare minicam left out on the streets after the local news, no sets were required, and the only on-screen talent they needed was the local citizenry... and they were always camera ready.

The first three weeks of *StreetScene* did solid numbers. Not spec-tacular—it would have to grow, find its audience, and the PR department would have to get off its butt and actually promote something for a change—but there was real potential. Viewers were curious: which neighborhood would show up next? It seemed to Carl that people had an endless capacity for fascination when it came to watching ordinary people doing ordinary things that sud-denly became not so ordinary because they were being done on television. That was one of the things that fascinated Carl about television: its ability to elevate the mundane simply by pointing a camera at it and hitting the ON switch in a TV news control room.

A few years before, Carl had been invited to speak before a class of telecommunications students at San Diego State University. Because the proceedings were being taped for the campus library, monitors were positioned at strategic locations throughout the hall, allowing those who were further back to see what was going on at the front of the room.

After a few minutes, he noticed again what he'd seen a hundred times before: even the students close enough for a good view of him and the stage preferred to watch the monitors, to watch the phosphor-dot image rather than the person, even though he was right there. At accident and murder locations, when the TV cameras arrived and lit up red at broadcast, onlookers watched the stand-up reporter's TV monitor of the scene rather than looking at the crime scene itself, only five or ten feet away. Same ground, same yellow tape, same dead body covered by the same rubber coroner's sheet, but the crowd looked at the monitor rather than the real thing.

Because it was on television.

Carl had been willing to take a chance that the rule would obtain with *StreetScene*. His gamble paid off: ratings for the seven-thirty to eight time-slot continued to improve. He was able to move into a better office, with a view of the hillside behind the station. His phone calls were returned more quickly. There were even rumors that the show was being watched closely by the network, which was thinking of adapting the format and putting it on nationally, if it continued to prove itself locally.

He would, of course, become the producer for that show as well. It was, after all, his idea.

And it was clear he knew what the people wanted.

The only nagging question, the one he couldn't answer, was how long would they want it?

The ratings began to slip just as the station was gearing up for sweeps. Focus groups confirmed what Carl had dreaded: the immediacy was wearing thin, local curiosity was turning into apathy. Seen one hooker hanging her butt out of the passenger window of a too-small Toyota at midnight, seen 'em all. They had gone from a twenty share, to a seventeen share, to a twelve share. People stopped returning his calls. A new station executive brought in from out of town was sizing up Carl's office every time he walked past.

Carl couldn't deny it any longer. *StreetScene* was fading fast, and taking him with it. He sat in his office, looking out at the hillside that was rapidly turning brown, and closed his eyes, hoping it would all just go away.

He started forward again at a knock at the door. "Yes?"

The door opened slightly, and Margie stuck her head inside. "Andrea says there's a call for you, but said you told her you didn't want to be disturbed. I told her I'd check and see if you really meant it."

Carl nodded. "I did, and I do." As his personal assistant and associate producer, Margie was the only one he allowed into his office when he was in a Blue Funk. She had also been much more. But that was history. Six months' worth of history.

Breaking off their affair had been hard, but he knew that if he didn't, his wife would find out about it sooner or later. Better to cut it short than extend the error and eventually find the affair exposed to gossip, his wife, and her attorneys. Margie had understood, or seemed to. Either way, for six months she had continued to work as efficiently as ever, though now that work consisted mainly of bailing water out of *StreetScene*'s sinking ship.

"What's the call?"

Margie shrugged. "He wouldn't say. But he insisted on speaking only to you. Said it was important."

"I've heard that before." He reached for the phone that, as always, was lit with calls. "Which line?"

"Six." She turned and stepped back into the other office, closing the door behind her.

He pushed the blinking button and sat back. "Carl Sarotkin speaking."

The voice at the other end of the line was quiet, soft-spoken. Carl had to strain a bit to hear the words. "Is this the man in charge of *StreetScene*?"

"You got him. What can I do for you?"

"Monica Fairburn's eyelids were nicked. Two small vertical slashes and a line across."

The sentence took a moment to register. Then Carl's chest tightened and the room suddenly seemed to tilt. Monica Fairburn's body had been found three nights ago, the third victim of the Angel killer. That was the name signed to several postcards sent to the police. The stations had agreed to cooperate with the District Attorney's office and not release some of the physical details, to avoid compromising the investigation. The nicks were one of the things they had not released.

"You still there?"

Carl cleared his throat. "Yeah," he said, "I'm still here." He gripped the receiver tightly, wishing he'd left the door open so he could signal Margie. If they could somehow flag the call and trace it....

"I won't be on very long," the caller said, as if anticipating his thoughts. "So you better get this right the first time. Do you have a pencil?"

"Yeah, sure." Carl grabbed a pencil and notepad. "Shoot."

"Never. A knife is so much more elegant, don't you think?"

Angel laughed. Carl's stomach tightened but he said nothing. Somehow he hadn't thought serial killers could have a sense of humor. Granted, it wasn't that terrific a joke, but being a serial killer means never having to listen to someone tell you your jokes aren't funny.

"Seven-fifty tonight," Angel said. "Corner of Aberdeen and Fourteenth. You got that? Read it back."

Carl read back the time and address. As if from a great distance he noticed that his hand was shaking. "Is that your address? I mean, if you're going to surrender we can have—"

There was a snort of disgust from the other end. "Not on your life, asshole. Think about it."

He looked at the time. Seven-fifty. If he wasn't going to surrender at that time, then what—

Suddenly, he understood. "Oh, shit...."

"Then you understand," Angel said, and Carl heard a smile in his voice. "That's good. But get this straight: no one comes near me, no one tries to talk to me, no one does anything. You tell your people to stay in their van and do their job or there'll be four more people meeting the Angel tonight."

"Why are you doing this?" Carl asked.

"People have to understand. They have to listen to the message of the Angel. Seeing is understanding. Seeing is believing. They must believe. In time, they'll understand what I'm doing. Once that happens, I'll stop. You're doing them a favor. So think it over. But don't take too long."

Click and disconnect.

Carl racked the phone and for two minutes did absolutely nothing, allowing himself two minute of panic as he decided what to do.

His first impulse was to call the police. But his hand didn't reach for the Rolodex, where the pager number for the lead detective investigating the Angel murders was two cards down, just past Domino's Pizza. He was a producer of a news/ information show, not a cop. Catching murderers wasn't his job.

The relationship between police and reporters was a delicate and constantly changing one. TV stations were frequently subpoenaed for tapes to be used as evidence in trials. Those subpoenas had been successfully fought, but always with great difficulty. At the Atlanta Olympic pipe bombing, camera crews had recorded the blast, the panic, the crush of people falling over one another in a blind rush for the open streets, the wounded bleeding onto the cobblestones, but hadn't moved to help, to bind up, to resuscitate, to hold hands or staunch bleeding.

Because that wasn't their job.

Reporters weren't supposed to take sides, they were to be uninvolved observers. The reporters who'd covered Vietnam weren't there to fight for their country, they were there to report the news. Reporters traveling with Central American guerrilla troops fighting American-backed government forces had to refrain from passing back intelligence to "our" side, always for the same reason: to report, not make, the news.

Reporters in the Midwest had even stood by, tape rolling, as a man immolated himself on the lawn of City Hall. It had been a terrible thing. But the report made national news, got constant airplay, and the networks paid good money for the rebroadcast rights. Carl was reasonably certain that, whatever moral concerns had been running through the mind of that cameraman, he did his job, and had been rewarded for it with a big new office...maybe even one overlooking a hillside.

Terrorists, hostage takers, snipers, bombers, kidnappers, they had all realized the McLuhanesque dream of brief fame on television courtesy of the all-seeing Eye that does not blink, does not judge, and does not turn away.

Was this really any different?

If he notified the police, they'd send out a SWAT team and probably spook the Angel into going underground. Then when he emerged, he'd be even more dangerous than before. And somewhere on the list of victims-to-come, Carl suspected, would be his own name. If the Angel were telling the truth, they'd lose their chance to help people understand why he was doing this, which in the final analysis was all the guy wanted, and then he'd go away. They'd lose a chance to save lives.

Besides, if a minicam crew just happened to be at the scene of the crime moments before it became the scene of the crime, they might be able to get the first pictures of the Angel... pictures that could be critical in bringing him to justice.

There was one more factor to be considered: no one else knew that the call had come. He could choose to keep this to himself for now, and send out the *StreetScene* crew the same way he sent it out every weeknight. No one else needed to know. Afterward, if there were any questions or suspicions, Carl could plead coincidence. Like the man who got a photograph of a falling PSA Airline jet that was so clear that you could almost see the faces through the windows, or the Rodney King case, or the amateur photographer who shot ten minutes of tornado on his home video camera, it would simply be a case of synchronicity. The right camera in the right place at the right time.

"Margie!"

The door swung open a second later. "Yeah, boss?"

"Which location are we slated for tonight? The street faire or the Boy's Club Olympics?"

"Street faire. News division found out the Mayor's going to make a surprise visit, so we scrubbed the boy's club. They were pretty mad. I didn't think they allowed that kind of language in the boy's club."

Carl nodded, wondering if the Angel had planned it this way. Strike when the mayor would be across town, taking with him a substantial number of cops and tying them up with the need for crowd control and Hizzoner's personal protection.

Carl chewed his lip, hesitating.

"Something up, Carl?"

He nodded. "Scrub the street faire. Reroute the van to the corner of Aberdeen and Fourteenth. Then get hold of research, see if they have any interesting historical stuff on the neighborhood: colorful residents, crime rate, has anybody big come from there, anything and everything. Just give us something for voice-over, okay?"

"Yeah, I guess." Margie's face was unreadable, a mask. "It's a grungy neighborhood; I doubt research will find much. You sure you want to do this?"

"Nope. But let's do it anyway."

Margie threw up her hands and headed out into her office. "Okay," she said doubtfully, "it's your neck."

As the door closed, Carl added, "Not necessarily."

Seven-thirty P.M.

They were on the air.

It was the longest twenty minutes Carl Sarotkin had ever known. Research had done their usual good job, and had come up with a few useful facts with seconds to spare before they hit broadcast. The neighborhood featured some of the oldest homes in the city, and many of them were faced with demolition, barring an effort by the Historical Society to stop the redevelopment, or at least relocate the structures to another location. Covering that part took them to the first commercial break.

Carl ran through it in his head. The audience would still be with him to this point. They wouldn't start channel surfing until they got closer to the top of the hour. And people always go for the little-guy vs. the big bad developers story. But it wouldn't hold for a full half-hour.

Not unless something happened.

After the commercial break came the man-on-the-street segment. One of the news crew stood outside the van, soliciting comments. The first few passersby declined to be interviewed, which was standard for this sort of thing. Others were content to stop and answer a few questions about the upcoming mayoral election, and the gun-control initiative on the ballot this year. In the background, a handful of kids waved at the camera, while a few adults further back studiously avoided the camera's glare. Carl guessed they were drug dealers, but studied them closely, wondering if any of them might be him.

They were running out of story.

"This is gonna kill us," Margie said from behind him. The control room was just big enough for the director, himself and Margie. It was always tense, but now the frustration in the air was almost palpable. "A ten share tops, mark my word. Shit." She sat back, lit up another cigarette.

Carl glanced up at the clock as the sweep-second hand passed 7:48. Just how punctual was this guy, anyway? On the monitor, he could see the number of people on the street starting to thin out. They always happened once they pulled the cameras back inside the van for the next segment, a taped background piece they'd put together earlier. A few people walked by, but most were inside the two-story walkups on either side of the street, eating dinner, or—most likely, he thought with some discomfort—watching the other channel.

Carl had to admit that by now he'd have switched channels himself. If they could hold on just a minute longer....

Then a scream came through the monitor.

Even filtered through the van's wall speakers it sounded horrible, barely human. The director sat up at his console, all attention now, shouting instructions. "What the hell's going on out there?" He listened for the frantic response from the van on the closed-circuit audio feed. Carl could hear the shouting from the director's headset even several seats down. "Get the camera around! Two, go two! God damn it, get it around!"

The image on the screen cut to a shot of the street from camera two, positioned at the van's side window.

There. A flash of movement in an alley barely lit by a street lamp. A man. Long coat. Hat. His face concealed behind something dark, maybe cloth. He had her up against the alley wall, forearm against her neck, pinning her back, hard, and forcing her face up. Her eyes glittered in the lamplight.

He's playing to the camera, Carl thought, distantly. *He wants us to see her face.*

"Oh, my God," Margie said. "Oh, God, look!"

It happened in an instant. Another flash. Something bright glittered in his hand, then disappeared in the gap between them. She screamed again. Briefly. Then slumped to the ground. He stood over her, his back to the van.

The director shouted over his shoulder. "Camera crew's asking to go outside. They want to—"

"No! Tell them to stay put!" Carl was almost frantic now. "Margie, get the police, fast!" Not that it was necessary; by now there were probably half a dozen squad cars en route to the scene. But it would help keep them off the track.

Keep them from finding out what Carl knew.

He looked up at the monitor again. The killer was still there. Taking his time. The dark figure bent over the smaller one, and did something the camera couldn't pick up. Probably nicking the eyes, Carl thought, surprised at his ability to look at this objectively. Then the Angel ran off down the alley, never turning back, never allowing the camera a clear shot of him. He made it out of sight around a corner, the sound of his footfalls replaced a moment later by the roar of a car racing away into the gathering dark.

The Angel's newest victim did not move.

The police arrived within minutes, too late to do anything but cordon off the area, and expel the camera crew and van after questioning them thoroughly and getting statements.

No one even thought to question Carl. Everyone assumed that it was coincidence, nothing more. If anything, the police seemed grateful, though they'd never admit it. For the first time they had something to go on, could at least add the basics of height and weight and build to the Angel APBs. They compared relative heights to points in the alley, examined the position of the van and its angle relative to the assault, and worked out a whole series of measurements.

They would not be the only important measurements made that night.

The overnight ratings said that the last ten minutes of *StreetScene* shot up to a thirty share, the highest rating anybody could remember for a long time. Carl knew it would drop a little over the next few weeks, but they could keep it at a good level by holding the exclusive rights to the segment and rebroadcasting it on a twice-weekly basis, ostensibly to help capture the Angel. But it was simply good business... provided he could keep the station manager from selling the footage to competing stations in order to make a few short-term dollars.

The program director had been sickened by what he saw that night, horrified when he reran the raw footage, but eminently satisfied with the numbers. It was at least as good as the SLA shootout and the Reagan near-assassination combined, and when the footage went out on their proprietary feed, NBC jumped in fast, picking up the details for overnight and national news the next day. Even Ted Koppel mentioned it, though he couldn't show any of it. Wrong network.

With that kind of exposure, viewers who had left the show came back out of curiosity, and those who had never previously watched *StreetScene* tuned in to see the segment that had made history, when the crew happened to be in the right place at exactly the right time. Suddenly the station was looking even better to both the mini-nets and the big boys at the three-letter networks.

Carl was determined to hold onto that audience. He sent minicam units back into the neighborhood for follow-up reports: interviews with neighbors and those who saw the attack, statements from police officials and Neighborhood Watch advocates. Were there sightseers at the scene of the murder? Did local tourism go up, or down? What was the impact of the murder, and what was the impact of their coverage of the murder? Carl loved it when a story lent itself to them doing a story on themselves. What was the responsibility of journalists in a situation like this? How did it affect the news team? Would the coverage have effects on the community? There was a parade of consultants, psychologists, councilmen, attorneys and ministers. It was a TeeVee Mobius loop, feeding from viewer to reporter and back again, and because he was in control of it, he could play out one aspect after another.

And, of course, they ran the tape of the attack endlessly. For the public good. Strictly to help find the Angel killer. But as rich a gold mine as he'd struck, he knew he could only mine it for so long. Sooner or later, they'd have to go back to their normal programming.

The question then was, what next? How do you top something like this?

Having built up momentum for the series, he had to find ways to keep that momentum going when the sensationalism died down. Over the following weeks, he tried out several of them. He tried changing the thrust of *StreetScene*, so it would no longer focus on street faires, festivals, tanning salons for rich, or the all-too-frequent hundredth birthday of some local citizen who—just to piss off the doctors who had poked and prodded and prescribed foul-tasting medications for a full century—would ascribe that longevity to four cigars and a glass of gin every day.

StreetScene dedicated itself to examining the underbelly of the city it served. They began with a series of stories about the city's growing porn industry, setting up shop in front of a motel known for renting out rooms to producers of x-rated videos, leaving only when threatened by a lawsuit by the manager, citing interference with his trade. Which was true and not-true. The minicam didn't violate the letter of the law, which required that they present a physical obstacle to those wishing to enter the motel. But who wanted their face broadcast all over the city as they went inside to star in the Hi-Eight production of "Twins In Love"?

They got a few good pieces of film out of that one. Audiences loved sidewalk spats and people driving off with coats over their heads to hide from the media. But the ratings still dropped two points.

So they moved the minicam into progressively seedier parts of town. They broadcast drug deals going down, followed hookers as they plied their trade along dark streets. Mid-week they caught a break and managed to spot a mugging in-progress, the story going out live and continuing as police—alerted by the broadcast—sped to the scene in time to apprehend the muggers. Ratings jumped back four points that night, and stayed there through Friday, bolstered by the realization that the police were watching this show, too, and might respond if things got hot. That would increase the potential for action.

At this point, Carl decided to go to tape-delay. The feed would come in to the station, be processed, and go out to the viewers five minutes later. As far as the audience ever knew, it was a live broadcast. And technically, it was. They just fudged a bit, to make sure the police didn't arrive on the scene too early.

After all, they had half an hour to fill.

"Carl?"

Carl rolled over, half asleep, and pulled the covers up over his head. Why did Grace always wait until he was ready for sleep before she would bring up Matters Of Importance? He could tell that this was going to be one of those. She had that sound in her voice. "Hmph?" he said.

"When are you going back to the old format?"

"I dunno. Soon, maybe."

A moment passed. "I just don't like it. The way you've got it now."

"I've noticed."

"It's so, I don't know—so *seedy.* I always feel like I need a bath afterward."

"We're performing a public service."

She shook her head. "You're going for the numbers."

"Same thing."

Another silence. "How's the show doing?"

"Okay. But I'm not. I need some sleep, okay?"

He closed his eyes, knowing sleep would be denied him now that the wheels had started turning again, now that The Problem had flagged down his attention.

The ratings were slipping again.

Carl's intercom buzzed as he was going over the schedule for the coming week. Andrea's voice came through a moment later. "Line five, Carl."

Carl didn't look up from his schedule. "Who is it?"

"He wouldn't say. Just said to tell you it was an old friend."

Carl reached for the phone, his gut tightening. Even before he heard the voice on the other end, he suspected—no, *knew*—it would be him.

"You did real well," the voice said, a voice like dry leaves rustling down a sidewalk.

"I did my job, that's all."

"Yeah, right. We all got our jobs to do, don't we? You got yours, and I got mine. We're both in the education business. We just have different ways of going about it."

"Look, what's this—"

The voice cut him off. "Pencil and paper."

Carl rubbed at his face. "I don't know...."

"Paper and pencil or I hang up."

Lips thin, Carl reached for a pen. *If I don't take it, he'll just call some other station.* "Go ahead."

The voice on the other end supplied a time, and a place.

Carl recognized the address as a slightly better district than the Angel had previously hit. It wouldn't be difficult to divert the min-icam team there, wouldn't seem too much a break in format.

Carl stopped short. Was he really going to do this? Give the Angel another broadcast? Send his crew into a possibly dangerous situation? What was he thinking of?

"They must be there," the voice said, anticipating him again. "They must carry my message."

"We can't give you air-time for a statement. No way."

"No statement. The mission is the message." He hung up.

Carl cradled the phone. "Margie!"

She appeared in the doorway a moment later. "Yeah?"

"I've got a change for tonight. Here's the address. Have research—"

"I'll get them," Margie said. She took the slip of paper, looked at it, lingered longer than she had to. Then she reached behind her and shut the door, lingering inside.

"First a phone call comes. Then you turn several shades of pale, and now this. Same as the last time you changed the schedule on me. The night we ran into the Angel."

Carl said nothing. He never could hide anything from women. Not her. Not Grace. Which was why there was only Grace now and not her in his bed.

"You've got a pipeline to this guy, don't you?" she said.

"That's pure speculation."

"Which whenever a politician says it, always means yes. Relax. Nobody'll know but us. Nobody'll even suspect. Things are so disorganized around here that I don't give anyone the schedule for the evening shoot until a couple of hours before they leave anyway."

"I don't know what you're talking about."

"Okay, then let me try this on you for size." She held up the sheet of paper. "If—just if—anyone should ask me when you gave me the address for tonight's shoot, I'll tell them that we arrived at this by mutual consensus as early as last week. Do you have a problem with that?"

Carl looked away, said quietly, "No."

Margie nodded, turned back toward the door, then hesitated. "What's he... I mean, what does he sound like?"

"Like death," Carl said, looking at her hard. "What the hell did you expect?"

The Angel's next attack was almost a carbon copy of the one before. Except this time the victim was a man, a harmless looking little fellow wearing a Dodgers baseball cap who was yanked into an alley as he passed it on his way home. The camera caught it all. The cry of surprise, then the bludgeon—a claw hammer, the police would later determine—coming down, once, twice, again and again. Then the speedy retreat, pausing only to nick the victim's eyes.

The ratings skyrocketed.

This time, though, there were questions to be answered. The police noted the coincidence, but went in the wrong direction. They assumed the Angel was following the mobile unit around in hopes of finding the right moment to get on television. This possibility did little to comfort the minicam team, who were far from mollified by the offer of police protection for the next week or so, just until it could be determined if the van was, indeed, being followed.

After they left, Margie stepped back into the office and closed the door behind her again. "We've got the standard offer from the networks for the piece, although they want this one edited down a little better than the last one. Seems some folks out in DuBuque got a bit nauseous last time."

Carl nodded numbly. It would be a difficult editing job. There had been blood everywhere....

"Did you hear the latest?" She waited until he shook his head. "Rumor from upstairs has it that the NBC owned-and-operateds are willing to commit to a weekly national series if we can keep an average rating of a twenty share for the rest of the month. They'll make some changes, broaden the appeal a little, but that's to be expected. They buy you for what makes you different, then take away whatever made you different and interesting so you'll fit their format. That means you lose the whole point of the show and, over time, the viewers. But what the hell, by then we're in at a network and we can write our own ticket."

She came over, sat on the edge of his desk. "Who knows? Maybe we'll turn it into The Crime of the Week. Make it into a game show. Thieves! Robbers! Rapists! C'mon down! Show us your stuff! Call early for reservations, and don't forget the home game version. What do you think?"

"Charming."

She nodded. "Yeah, it does have a certain *je ne sais quoi*, doesn't it?" Smiling down at him, she brushed his hair back from his forehead, letting her hand linger for a moment. "We're going places together, aren't we? I always said we made quite a team."

"You're forgetting someone, aren't you?" he asked, tapping his ring finger with his thumb.

"Not one bit," she said, and leaned over. She kissed him gently, and to his surprise Carl found himself returning it. She sat back, nodded as if satisfied with something he'd said—or, more precisely, hadn't said—and swept out of the room, looking quietly pleased with herself.

As she walked out, Carl remembered reading somewhere that the Chinese ideogram for trouble was a symbol showing two women under one roof.

"Trouble," Carl muttered, "on top of trouble."

Two weeks later Carl was coming back from a lunch that went later than he had planned. The ratings were still fairly solid. They generally petered out a little in the last quarter hour, once it became apparent that nothing major was going to happen, but they were sticking around long enough to give the sponsors the overall half-hour rating they needed. As he headed past Andrea at the front desk, the mannequin-pretty receptionist flagged him down and handed him a number of pink sheets. "Your messages."

"Thanks," he said, pressing on.

"Oh, and while you were out, your friend called again."

Carl turned back toward the desk. "What friend?"

"I don't know, I'm just repeating what he said. He told me he had some information for you, but he wouldn't say what it was. He was very upset that you weren't here, and said he'd try to get hold of you at home."

Carl felt the blood rushing in his ears. "He had my home number?"

"Yes," she said, but he was already past her and heading for his office. *Grace,* he thought. *Oh, shit.*

He slammed through the office door and was dialing before he even sat down. One ring. Three. Seven.

He held the receiver to his ear, panic squeezing his heart.

A knock, and Margie popped in. "Oh, good, you're back," she said

"We've got to do something, he knows my—"

She pressed a finger to her lips, and nodded toward the waiting room. "Your wife's here, and she doesn't look happy. You don't think she's found out about us now, after all this time, do you?"

Carl racked the phone, relief flooding in. "That's the least of my worries right now. Send her in."

Margie stepped out. A moment later the door reopened, and Grace entered, shutting the door behind her.

"Doesn't look happy" doesn't begin to describe her, he thought.

"Carl," she said, "I want you to tell me what's going on. I want you to talk to me."

"About what?"

"Don't lie to me, Carl. This isn't the time, and I'm not in the mood. I got a call at the house an hour ago from a man who said he was a friend of yours. He wouldn't give his name. He kept trying to give me an address, but when I asked him what this was about, he got... strange, angry. And his voice...." Her own voice tapered off. Carl knew all too well what she must have heard.

"I asked him how he knew you. He said he'd only spoken to you over the phone, and you'd never met in person. Then he asked if I'd seen the broadcasts on the days those two people were killed. I said how could I not see them, they were all over the place. Then he asked me what I'd learned from watching them."

"What did you say?"

"That it proved there are a lot of sick people out there who ought to be locked up for the rest of their lives. That's when he got really angry, that kind of angry that comes out cold and hard and quiet. He said to never mind, and he'd call you here, later."

Carl nodded, said nothing. He felt the trap closing around him.

"For the last time, Carl, what have you gotten yourself into? How did this man get our phone number?"

"Grace, I'll explain it all later. Honest. But right now, I just can't."

Grace's jaw worked, the cheeks tightened. "It's him, isn't it? That... that monster. I felt something was wrong, something inside you. I just didn't know what it was. But as soon as I picked up the phone, as soon as I heard him, I got a chill. I was afraid. I just want you to look me in the face and tell me that it isn't him."

He looked up at her, knowing that the truth was in his eyes, and knowing that she would see it, as she always did. "And if it is?"

"Then I want you to cancel the show. I want it over! I won't tell anyone about this if it stops now, because it could ruin both of us. But if it happens again, I'm going to the police. I love you, but I won't let you get involved in this madness. For your own sake."

She stepped closer to him, but stopped halfway across the room, hesitant to touch him. "If there's no killing tonight, maybe I'll believe you, that it isn't him. But if there is, I'll know, and one of us will have to do something about it."

With that, she turned and, without looking back, stepped quickly out of the office.

The click-clack of Grace's heels was no sooner gone than Margie stepped into the office. "Boy, it's a good thing you have me here to save your ass."

Carl groaned quietly, wishing the ground would open up and swallow him. "Too late."

"No, it's not," she said, and for the first time he noticed the slip of paper in her hands. "He called while you were talking to Grace. Lucky for you I was here to take the call. Your friend is getting loonier every day."

"He's not my friend."

"I know. But he sure takes rejection personally. He gave me the time and place, said if the team's not there, he'll go on a real rampage, double the killings. Of course, we'll say we were planning to be there all along, as soon as we—"

"Forget it." He stood, taking the sheaf of papers with the week's schedule and dumping them into a drawer. "Grace knows. She threatened to go to the police if there's another killing."

"Well, that's too bad, because we don't have any control over what he does. We can't even get hold of him."

"No, we can't," Carl admitted, "but we can at least not put it on the air. That'll count for something."

She made a sound of disgust. "What a waste."

"Yeah, and it happens every day. Remember, there was a time when every casual murder didn't show up in your front room in living color."

Margie shook her head. "You're really going to do it, aren't you? You're knuckling under." Her tone verged on amazement. "Unbelievable. This is the best chance we've ever had to get out of here, go network, and you're pissing it away because you don't want wifey getting all shook up. This has been good for us, damn it!"

"Swell choice of words."

"All we need is one last good show, one more good ratings night and we're out of here anyway. The Nielsen people think we can hit a forty share or better, Carl. Forty. Christ, we haven't had a forty since the networks were blown off the air during the fires five years ago. You want to drop it then, walk away, fine. We'll be on our way and away from all this anyway. Wifey'll get her wish. You'll be free and clear. Everybody gets what they want."

"And if Grace doesn't see it that way, and goes to the police?"

"She won't. She's not the type. She only wants you out of this. She doesn't really care about what's going on out there. She can't relate to it. As long as you're not involved, as far as she's concerned, that's the end of it. And that'll happen after tonight."

"You don't know her like I do. At the very least she'll leave me."

"So? You once told me that wouldn't be such a bad thing."

"Different circumstances." He sat back heavily. "I'm sorry, Margie, I don't see any way around it. We're going back to our old format, starting tonight. If he calls after that, we'll figure out some way to put him off. Tell him the station manager overrode us, that we had technical difficulties, anything. If he gets abusive we'll just stop taking his calls."

"And then what?"

"I don't know, but we'll figure out something. Now I suggest you get hold of the crew and give them their schedule. Pick anything, I don't care." He thought for a moment. "Isn't there a block party going on in Little Italy tonight?"

Margie winced, nodded. "Yeah."

"Then that's it," Carl said. "We'll go with that. As of now, it's over. Clear?"

She shrugged and headed out. "Whatever you say, boss."

There was a tone in her voice he didn't like, but then, he could understand her feelings. This was their chance, and he was cutting them off at the knees on the last lap of the race. But he couldn't risk losing Grace, or going to jail, or both.

It was the right thing. She'd see that in time.

Stu, the director, glanced up as Carl entered the control room. "You're late." The clock read 7:26.

Carl ignored him, found Margie, asked if she'd told the station manager they were changing tonight's format. She nodded.

"What'd he say?" Carl asked.

" 'Whatever it is, just make it good.' " She shrugged. "Well, we'll try, but the way things are right now, I have my doubts."

Carl nodded, looked back at the clock. 7:29. There was nothing on the console. "Shouldn't we be receiving the feed by now?" he asked. The time delay was usually five minutes, sometimes seven.

"No point to it now," Margie said. "There's nothing to delay. Just endless shots of pasta and pizza and overweight grandfathers dancing with little girls standing on the tops of their shoes."

There was a knock at the door, and Andrea stuck her head in. "Call for you on seven, Carl."

"I don't think you should take it," Margie said quietly, giving him that look that said trouble might be at the other end. He knew exactly what kind of trouble she meant.

"Tell whoever it is that we're about to go on the air and I can't be disturbed, all right? Just that and no more."

Andrea shrugged, looked as if she had a question, but chose not to voice it. She said only "Okay," and stepped back out of the control room.

Stu glanced over at both of them. "Is there something going on here I should know about?"

"No comment," Carl said, smiling as winningly as he could.

Stu shrugged resignedly, then turned back to the control board, fingers hovering over the rows upon rows of switches, faders, levers and illuminated buttons with easy familiarity.

The sweep second hand on the wall clock hit 7:30 exactly. The station ID flashed on the on-air monitor.

"It's showtime," Stu said, and his fingers flew over the board. "Cue open," he said.

The monitor went from the ID to true black. Held for a beat. Then two. Then the music, low but building. Under the music, the sounds of conversations, laughter, snatches of street-talk; car horns, heels clicking on sidewalks, trucks rumbling down streets, each sound cross-fading over the next, an audio montage designed to suggest a busy, active, vibrant street life. Then, on the black screen, jagged white lines began to appear, slicing down the screen, forming letters that became words that became *StreetScene*.

"Hi, baby," Carl whispered to the monitor. "Bye, baby."

Margie said nothing, only sat and smoked in stony silence, watching the credits flicker by.

PRODUCED BY CARL SAROTKIN

WE KILLED THEM IN THE RATINGS

Associate Producer Margaret Whitmore

Then: a fade to black, dissolving into scenes shot by the van as it traveled to its latest destination. This was the only pre-taped part of the show. The voice-over provided background on what land-marks they were passing, what the neighborhoods were like....

Carl barely heard it. "We might get a thirty share for a block party," he said, trying to be positive. "We have a large Italian pop-ulation here. And there might be enough of an audience hanging on from the last broadcast to carry us through."

Margie's eyes reflected the same sure doubt he held in his own mind. "Only if it's one hell of a block party. Or if all of them are Nielsen or Arbitron families, or if they get abducted by aliens...."

"Skip it," Carl said, and sat back to watch his baby go down in flames.

"Okay, ready two," Stu said into the closed-circuit mike that kept him in touch with the van. He paused, then: "Go two." The image on the monitor shifted, stabilized. The camera crew had arrived at their destination and were cruising slowly through the streets, shooting out through the window.

"Give me a follow shot," Stu said quietly as the van passed a few kids playing on a corner, and another few further down who were trying without much success to open a fire hydrant. A couple of cars passed the van going in the opposite direction.

Odd, Carl thought. When they have a block party they usually cut off the street to thru-traffic. "Must be a smaller party than we thought," he said.

He swiveled at the sound of the door opening. Andrea stood in the doorway again. "That was your wife on the phone again, Carl. She said to tell you she understands, she accepts your offer, and she's waiting. Oh, and she wants to know why you picked such a crummy neighborhood for dinner." Andrea stepped back out to the sound of the switchboard ringing in the other room.

"Go one," Stu said. A long, darkened street appeared on the monitor. The street lamps had come on nearly half an hour ago, but they didn't seem to do much good.

Carl swiveled back, looked at Margie. "What the hell was that all about?"

Margie hesitated before answering, appearing inordinately inter-ested in the burning tip of her cigarette. "I just thought I'd call her and let her know your decision. She seemed very relieved." She kept glancing furtively at the clock.

"Zoom in," the director said. On the screen: deserted shops, a few still open, bars on their windows. A liquor store. "Pan along."

"But dinner—"

"It just seemed like a good idea, get the rapprochement off on the right foot," she said. Then she looked at him... and something in her expression froze him to the spot.

She said I picked a crummy neighborhood....

He glanced at the monitor. "Where did you tell her to meet me, Marge?"

Silence.

"God damn it Marge, where did you—"

"Go two."

"Jesus Christ, Margie!" But she was looking at the monitor.

Not looking at him. At the monitor. Where a lone woman stood waiting outside a questionable looking restaurant. She checked her watch, visibly impatient. He couldn't see her face, but he didn't need to.

In a second, Carl was on his feet, grabbing for the control room phone.

"What're you doing?" Stu asked, then glanced up sharply. "Oh, shit!"

Carl spun about.

He was there.

He glided out of the shadows with practiced ease. The camera had found him, but Grace hadn't. She stood with her back to the darkness. *Look around, God, please look around!*

He was on her in a second. Fast. Christ, how fast! The flash of a steel blade, almost too quick to see. They fell to the ground.

"Oh God oh God oh God...." Carl's knees went out from under him. He fell into the chair, horror squeezing at his heart. He couldn't breathe.

Suddenly a spotlight pierced the night from above. The blue-white light illuminated what he hadn't seen until now, had hoped he wouldn't see, knew he would never stop seeing whenever he closed his eyes.

There was so much blood, an impossible amount.

"Pull back!" Stu shouted. He was frantic, trying to follow the action, unmindful of what was going on behind him. "There!"

Three squad cars screeched up at both ends of the street. Police jumped out, guns drawn. The spotlight danced crazily, lancing down from the helicopter hovering above.

"Freeze!" someone shouted. "Drop the knife!"

The Angel turned from the still body, and in the fierce light Carl could see every detail of his face; the madness, the anger, the determination. The eyes so wide, so full of hate and frustration.

He ran forward, reaching into his long coat as he screamed something so garbled and throaty that Carl couldn't catch it, could only make out: *have to understand!*

They opened fire.

A spray of bullets, more than Carl had ever seen, splattered the wall behind the Angel, wave after wave of them, splintering brick, shattering wood, opening flesh, exploding bones into shards.

For a moment the Angel stood under the onslaught, body suspended by the force of the bullets driving into him, holding him up against the wall by sheer momentum. Then he fell. Everything right there. On the monitor.

Now there were two bodies on the sidewalk.

The firing stopped.

"Go in! Go in!" Stu was screaming now, ordering the crew out of the van, to take the hand-held cameras, get on-the-spot interviews. Reactions.

Close-ups.

"We got it!" Stu cried. "Jesus, we got it! The cops must've been watching, went in as soon as they saw it go down. Thank God we weren't on tape delay." Then he was back on line with the minicam crew.

The camera moved in for a better view of the bodies. In a second, Stu and everyone else would know that the wife of the producer of *StreetScene* had become the last victim of the Angel, that fate had closed the case with a final, cruel irony.

Margie stubbed out her cigarette, exhaled slowly, and nodded to herself.

"A forty share, at least," she said.